Judge Harrison was furious.

He'd reread the Devereaux case three times to make sure there wasn't something he'd missed. There wasn't. That trial ten years ago had been a classic example of railroading. Someone had been manipulating the law to fit his own ends. Thirteen-year-old Deanna Deveraux hadn't had a snowball's chance in hell. He stared at her—she was a woman now, and a pretty one. Clearing his throat, he flicked his gaze over her handsome young attorney.

"Deanna Deveraux, it is the finding of this court that the murder case and verdict brought against you was a miscarriage of justice. There was insufficient evidence to prove without a doubt that you took the life of your grandmother.

"It is therefore the decision of this court that you are hereby cleared of all charges against you and are free to go."

The sound of the wood gavel was like the opening of locked gates.

She was free—but so was the killer.

D0651084

ABOUT THE AUTHOR

Evelyn A. Crowe worked for twelve years as a media director in an advertising company before turning her hand to writing in 1983. Her decision to change careers was certainly a stroke of good fortune for Harlequin readers, as Evelyn's bestselling books are favorites with readers around the world.

An avid nature-lover, Evelyn makes her home in Houston, Texas.

Evelyn A. Crowe

Legacy of Fear

Harlequin Books

TORONTO • NEW YORK • LONDON
AMSTERDAM • PARIS • SYDNEY • HAMBURG
STOCKHOLM • ATHENS • TOKYO • MILAN
MADRID • WARSAW • BUDAPEST • AUCKLAND

ISBN 0-373-70646-4

LEGACY OF FEAR

Legacy of Fear

PROLOGUE

THE NIGHT WAS MOONLESS, starless, silent but for the whisper of snow cascading down. The patio and pool lights illuminated the drifting snow and turned the flakes to golden fluff. The ground was colder now and the snow was taking longer to melt as it kissed the earth.

Deanna sighed deeply and shifted her shoulder to a more comfortable position against the window frame. Rubbing her cold hands up and down on the dark velvet sleeves of her dress, she continued to stare hypnotically at the falling snow.

Christmas Eve in Houston. Who'd have thought the weather would have taken such an uncharacteristic turn? She was used to spending the winter holidays in seventy-to eighty-degree weather, wearing shorts, the air conditioner going full force. Oh, she could remember a few severe winters in her forty-two years, but snow on Christmas Eve—never.

Weather forecasters were gleefully predicting a white Christmas for the city, but Houstonians were not prepared. Overpasses were closed. Car accidents were too numerous to count, taxing the police and wrecker services to their limits. Traffic reporters urgently warned people to stay inside and off the roads.

Deanna only half listened to the television reports. She knew that her father, while supervising the tree trimming from his wheelchair, would keep an ear tuned to the weather advisories. All she could think about was her daughters out on those dangerous roads. Sixteen just wasn't old enough to be driving in such treacherous conditions.

She sighed again, louder this time, and let her gaze shift from the falling snow to her reflection in the big window. Her husband told her repeatedly that she still looked twenty-five. Deanna snorted with amusement as she watched his movements reflected in the glass. He stood high on the ladder, one long arm suspended in midair, a sparkling ornament dangling from his fingers as he fulfilled his traditional job of stringing the lights and adding decorations to the topmost branches of the twelve-foot tree.

Deanna sighed a third time, louder and more soulfully. Why should she worry herself into a headache alone. Let her husband share some of her anxiety. She bit back a satisfied grin when she heard the deep rumble of male voices attempting to whisper. She watched as her tall beautiful son, so like his father, turned his head, nodded in her direction and took the bright shining ornament from his father's hand.

Deanna closed her eyes and waited, then smiled when she felt her husband's strong arms wrap around her waist. "You worry too much," he whispered in her ear as his hands slid down over the small mound of her stomach.

"Feeling okay?"

"For a pregnant middle-aged woman, you mean?"

"No, love—"

She didn't let him finish. "The girls didn't take the news very well, did they?"

He chuckled. "No. But they'll accept it. They have to. There's not a damn thing they can do about it."

"Maybe we should have waited until morning to tell them. Sam said we deliberately ruined her night." His arms tightened around her and she leaned back into the familiar warmth and comfort of his embrace. How she loved this man, a love that had grown stronger and deeper over the years.

"Samantha's spoiled and hot tempered," he growled, the displeasure he'd felt at his daughter's comments still lingering like a dose of bitter medicine.

"Sam's just like you, you mean."

"But that didn't give her the right to say those things to you. Victoria wasn't much help, either." He sighed, his breath tickling her ear. "She just looked at me with those soulful eyes. Made me feel like a criminal." He caressed his wife's stomach. "You know what the problem is? Why they're so shocked and upset?"

"Because they're sixteen years old and they're going to have to face all their friends' teasing when I waddle by with a huge belly."

"No, it's that they've been confronted with the undeniable fact that their parents actually have sex. That we do all the things they're learning about."

Deanna laughed, her warm breath making a foggy circle on the glass and bringing back the worries of the night. "They should have been home by now. Maybe you ought to go look for them." Her emotions were running as rampant as her hormones, and tears quickly filled her eyes. "We should never have let them take the car, not to their first formal party. Not on Christmas Eve and not in this weather. What if—"

"Stop it, love. The party is only three blocks away."

"Three very long, twisting, slippery blocks. And what if Bob and Mary can't get here? It'll be the first year since we were married that they haven't been here for Christmas Eve and..." She pressed her lips tightly together and a hot tear splashed down her cheek.

"You know very well that Mary would make Bob drive to hell if that's what it took to get here," her husband reassured her, easing his arms away and pushing down his sweater sleeves. "As for the girls, if it'll make you stop worrying and feel better, I'll go pick them up."

Deanna turned and, smiling, kissed him on the cheek. "Good. I'll make us all some hot chocolate." She caught her son's knowing glance and gave him a big wink.

The quiet was suddenly shattered by the sound of the front door slamming. The ornaments on the tree shivered, the crystal chandelier overhead tinkled like a thousand bells.

"Seems like our darling little angels have arrived safe and sound."

Deanna frowned at the sound of high-pitched voices in hot debate—they were arguing, as usual. But they were safe, and she felt the weight of her worry melt away. Her family was home now. She could relax.

Two small-boned, budding beauties with long blond hair, cheeks red from the cold, whirled into the room, dropping coats in a swirl of motion, only to stop simultaneously and fix their identical blue gazes like laser beams on their mother.

It was Samantha's shrill voice that sliced through the air. "Jane Harmon's mother told her, and Jane told us, that when you were our age you were in a loony-bin—a place where they lock up crazy people. It's not true, is it?"

A startled silence settled over the room, as if everyone had suddenly had the breath knocked out of them. Deanna could swear her heart was pounding so loud they could all hear. Then she took a couple of deep breaths and sat down rather heavily on the couch.

"Well, Mother. Why would she say something like that? You weren't really in a place like that, were you?"

Deanna squeezed her eyes shut for a heartbeat, and in that space of time all the pain, sorrow and fear of the past came rushing back, threatening to overwhelm her. This day had always been there, in the back of her mind, lurking like a monster ready to leap. Over the years she'd planned a thousand times what she would say. But now as she looked at her daughters, seeing the hope that their friend had lied lingering in their gazes, all her well-rehearsed plans vanished. God, how she'd dreaded this day. She patted the couch beside her for the girls to sit down.

The twins glanced at each other. Victoria sat with the grace of a ballerina, then grabbed her mother's icy hand. Samantha stomped to her sister's side but stood rooted to the floor, her hands on her hips. "Mother, answer me. Was Jane right? *Were* you in a nuthouse?"

"No, Samantha." Deanna stared for a long moment, first at Victoria—sweet, easygoing Vicky. So careful not to hurt others' feelings. Then she looked up at Sam, so like her father—quick to lash out when she was hurt. She could see the relief in their fixed gaze and knew that if she didn't handle this properly, she could shatter their young innocent world.

"I was not in a 'nuthouse,' as you call it, Sammy. I was in a private sanitarium." Deanna shook her head at her husband and smiled. "It's time, isn't it?"

"I'm afraid so, love," he said, and sat on the arm of the couch where he could put his arm around her shoulders and give her comfort. "Do you want me—"

"No, it's for me to tell." Deanna glanced at each member of her family, wondering how, or if, they were going to change once she told them her story. Her son, now nineteen, was strong, but would he look at her differently? She let her gaze shift to her father—the man who'd started it all. He sat hunched in his wheelchair, his lap covered with a blanket to hide his useless legs. He looked at her and she saw the glimmer of tears in his eyes. Immediately she felt guilty for the rush of old anger that had swept through her.

"Why, Mother?" Samantha hovered beside her sister, then her legs seemed to give way and she dropped like a stone to the floor, heedless of the damage to her first evening gown. "Why were you there?"

There was no easy way around this, Deanna thought, but the cold hard truth. "I'm going to tell you the reason I was in a sanitarium for ten years." She struggled to ignore her daughter's strangled gasp. "It's a long story, some of which was told to me later, some in bits and pieces. But I'll tell it all together and in order so you'll understand." Deanna knew she could never tell her children of the feelings she had for their father or the intimate nature of their relationship. She glanced up at him and smiled a secret smile. Even after twenty years she wouldn't be able to put the emotions into words for others, but she could relive them herself, remember every wonderful detail. She caught the wicked sparkle in his eyes and knew he was going to enjoy remembering, too.

"Mother, please," Samantha whispered, her voice hoarse with fear. "Why were you in such a frightful place? What did you do?"

Deanna reached out and smoothed back her daughter's hair. "They said I stabbed my grandmother to death."

At her children's wide-eyed, openmouthed shock, she again wondered how to start. Where to begin. She looked up at her husband, gave him a brave, if rather weak, smile. To clear her head, she inhaled deeply, breathing in the pungent scent of the Christmas pine.

She knew where to start.

CHAPTER ONE

Summer 1976

THE SCENT OF PINE filled her nostrils, not the sweet pine of the outdoors, but the strong smell of an industrial cleaner. Deanna Deveraux shuddered at the mixed odors of damp mops and soap. She wanted to leave the cramped confines of the janitor's closet, leave the nauseating smells of disinfectants, but she couldn't move. Her head felt as if someone was standing over her, hitting her with a hammer. With every heartbeat, the hammer slammed down with debilitating force and she would flinch and squeeze her eyes shut.

She remembered—everything.

After ten years with no memory of her past, of who she was or why and how she'd been committed to this sanitarium, she knew. All the mixed-up memories came like a wave of pain, unhappiness and torment crashing in on her in bright flashes, pictures so real they left her shaken and weak.

With a trembling hand she swiped the thick blond hair back from the sides of her damp face, glancing down at the broom handle she had wedged between the door and the jamb. Along with the shaft of light that entered through the crack came the soft, monotonous tones of the phantom voice.

"J'ai lu un bouquin sensa. I read a fabulous book. Now repeat the phrase—*J'ai lu un bouquin sensa."*

It was the French that had triggered the headache, that had made her remember. Just minutes before she had been so happy she'd thought she'd burst if she didn't tell someone what had happened. She'd left her cabin, snuck across the grounds to the main building and slipped up the stairs to the third floor. Patricia Nelson, head night nurse and a friend, was on duty. Deanna just had to talk to her, to find out if Pat knew that now, after ten years, she was going to be released. But as she approached the nursing station, something stopped her eager steps as if she'd walked into a glass wall. Pat was going to France on vacation, everyone knew that, but Deanna didn't know her friend was taking French lessons. It was the soft, androgynous voice of the instructor that had shocked her, flooding her mind with memories of her past. In panic she had fled, seeking the dark confines of the closet, her body curled into a tight ball, until the terror subsided.

Deanna shook her head violently in an effort to slow the memories. For ten years she'd been a blank sheet of paper. Oh, they'd told her who she was—her name, her past and what she'd done to be sent to Twelve Oaks Valley Sanitarium. Dr. Ernest Gresham had told her everything, repeatedly. He'd filled in all the empty spaces on the pages of her mind.

As hard as it was to believe, she had accepted what he'd told her because that was easier—on her, the doctors and the staff. She'd learned one hard lesson here, she thought as she gazed at that small crack of light, hearing the French lessons drone on. She'd learned to lie.

Deanna squeezed her eyes shut so tightly the tears trickled down her cheeks. She didn't want to remember, but abruptly, without warning, she was a child again, sick, dizzy, confused, wanting only comfort, a warm arm around her.

"Please, God," she whispered, "I don't want to remember." But as the voice of the French instructor filled the small space around her, she could hear another voice, one she hadn't heard in ten years but knew immediately—the heavily accented speech of her grandmother. She was angry, arguing with a man. They were yelling at each other, but she couldn't make out what was being said. She was a little girl again and her head hurt. She felt sick, forced to sit down on the stair landing. Suddenly she heard something in her grandmother's voice she'd never heard before—fear.

Deanna huddled now against the wall of the closet, her hands over her ears to stop the voices of the past, but they wouldn't stop, nor would the kaleidoscope of pictures flashing in her head.

Her grandmother had been so angry with her that day. She could see the long-forgotten child she had been, standing there holding her stinging cheek, her eyes hot with tears as she stared up at the regal woman who was her grandmother. *"Merde!"* her grandmother had cried. "Go to your room, you stupid child, and don't come down until I call you." Those were the last words she'd heard her grandmother say, the last time she saw her alive.

Sometime later the police had come, but by then she had had no memories. She had erased the past, everything, from her mind. But they told her they'd found her rocking her grandmother in her arms, a long bloody kitchen knife still clenched in her fist.

Deanna shook her head again, trying to chase the past away. Ten years ago, she thought, she was just a child, thirteen years old, and she'd been committed to an institution for a hideous crime she hadn't done. In a sudden flash of self-preservation, she knew she couldn't tell anyone about her innocence or that she had her memory back. That would complicate everything. She took a couple of steadying breaths.

Deanna eased the broom handle from between the door and the jamb and allowed it to slowly, quietly close. She had to pull herself together. If someone found her here, they'd think she was crazy. She almost strangled on a laugh. But the fact was, if someone found her, there would be questions. Endless questions. Maybe even a delay in her release. She couldn't let that happen, not now. Unfolding her body from the crouched position she'd held for so long, was painful, and she had to bite her lip to keep from moaning out loud.

With shaking hands she dusted herself off and tried to straighten her clothes. She had a million things to think about, the past and the future, but now was not the time. She only wanted to get back to her cottage without anyone seeing her.

Slipping out of the janitor's closet, she eased the door shut behind her and headed for the staircase. As she prepared to make a quick exit, Pat's voice halted her.

Deanna whirled around, a sickly smile plastered on her face. "Hi! I wasn't going to disturb your lessons."

Pat leaned across the desk to get a better look at Deanna. "You okay? You look kinda pale."

"You'd be pale, too, if you were about to be booted out of this place." Deanna slowly walked toward the nurses' station, wondering if Pat could detect her jerky steps or notice that she was shaking all over. The closer she got to the desk, the more she seemed to tremble. "You didn't know, did you?"

"What are you talking about?"

"You really haven't heard?"

"Come on, Deanna, it's too late to play games." Patricia Nelson quickly stood up and moved out from behind the desk. She was a tall slim woman in her early forties with short thick black hair and a suntan she'd acquired during her four-day weekend off.

"That's right, you've been away, haven't you? I'm out of here tomorrow, Pat. Judge Jones killed himself last week and a new judge took over his cases. My lawyer got a call that the new judge had reviewed my case, said there'd been a miscarriage of justice. He signed the order to release me immediately, then called Dr. Gresham Monday morning—that was yesterday, right? God, everything's going so fast. Anyway, the judge called Doc Gresham personally to deliver the release."

"Wait, wait," Pat said, her voice low and urgent. She was pale beneath her tan and jammed her shaking hands in the pockets of her white, stiffly starched uniform. "You said Judge Jones committed suicide. Why? What happened?"

Deanna's laughter sounded loud, maniacal, even to her own ears. Her head was going to split wide open if she didn't get away. "Can you believe he'd been under investigation for taking bribes?" She tried to ignore the whisper of French coming from the tape recorder.

She knew she was talking too fast, almost tripping over her words. And as much as she wanted to stay and tell Pat everything, all she could think about was getting away from that voice, escaping to the solitude of her cabin to sort through the memories thronging her mind. "Listen, Pat . . ." She started backing away, and Pat followed her step for step.

"I have to go finish packing," Deanna tried to explain. "Mary's going to pick me up in the morning." She was almost at the fire-escape door, the pain in her head now a dull throb. Pat was staring at her, and Deanna made herself smile, then laugh gaily. "I'll call you tomorrow," she promised. She felt the cold steel bar across the door and pushed her back against it with relief.

"Wait," Pat pleaded, more than a hint of desperation in her voice.

Deanna froze momentarily, her blue eyes round pools.

"Where are you going to live, Deanna? Surely Dr. Gresham's not going to let you out on your own?"

With a backward step, Deanna pushed the door open wider. "I'm going to stay with Mary until I decide what to do." She didn't care if Pat thought she was acting strange. She couldn't stand being there any longer. "I have to go." She stepped sideways as the door slammed shut, whirled around, then sprinted down the three flights of stairs.

Patricia Nelson stared at the fire-escape door for a long time, then turned, her shoulders slumped with disappointment. With dragging steps she walked back to the nurses' station. She glanced both ways down the long hall, making sure there were no doors standing open and no one to hear her. With a hand that trembled, she picked up the telephone and dialed. As she listened to the sound of the hollow ringing at the other end, a cold shiver slithered over her skin.

THE HUMID NIGHT AIR struck her like a wet towel across the face, and Deanna flinched but kept moving, refusing to slow down in case her demons caught up with her. She longed for the shelter of her small cabin, the quiet sanctuary she'd made for herself. All she could think about was getting there, to be alone and sort through all that had happened.

For ten years she'd wanted nothing more than to remember her past; now she just wanted the memories to go away. She'd never thought they would bring so much pain. Yet at the same time she felt exhilarated at the confirmation of her innocence.

The oppressive heat didn't daunt her. Sweat beaded her forehead as she sprinted across the lawn. Panting hard, she finally reached the front door of the cabin and shoved it open. Immediately she slammed it shut behind her and leaned against the cool surface, her heart pounding so hard her chest hurt.

God, she remembered.

Her gaze circled the room, frantically hunting for something familiar, something comforting to focus on, anything to help her calm down. There were boxes everywhere, some taped shut, some still open. Clothes were scattered around, spilling over a chair, piled high on her bed and thrown across her dress form. Her easel was folded up and leaning against the wall. All her canvases, paints and brushes were neatly packed away.

Finally her gaze lighted on the one thing that had been a constant in her life. The one thing that kept her grounded to the real world. She stared hard at her sewing machine, but the serenity she expected, even prayed for, eluded her.

Images from the past assaulted her mind again with such force that she dropped to her knees. She could hear her grandmother's voice as clearly as if the old lady were standing over her, instructing her on the right and the wrong way to make a stitch, showing her how cloth should drape across the breast or hang from the waist. Agatha Fleur Deveraux was a hard taskmaster, and by the age of twelve Deanna could hand stitch a hem only the trained eye of an expert could detect.

With her back to the door for support, Deanna pushed herself to a standing position, closed her eyes and shook her head. *Fleur's.* Over and over the word reverberated in her head. Fleur's, she remembered, was the name of her grandmother's dress shop, and she'd worked there every day after school and on weekends.

Fleur's. A place of gossamer silks, shiny satins and fine wools so delicate they slid though her fingers like warm water. Brocades so rich she could shut her eyes and still remember the feel of the design on the raised surface. All those wonderful colors, a feast for the eyes.

Deanna moaned. Reality seemed to be slipping away from her. She was a grown woman, leaning against the door of her cabin, yet she could see her grandmother's face as clearly now as if the old woman were standing before her. She could make out every line in that stern face with the unbelievably beautiful smile. A smile she had inherited, but one her grandmother rarely bestowed on her.

Deanna's breath caught in her throat. She felt strange, light-headed, then, without warning, through the confusion and darkness of her mind, she could hear a man's voice—harsh, raspy. A loud voice filled with hate. As abruptly as the man's voice had come, it faded away, and she could hear her grandmother's voice, full of fear.

She was remembering, and the disorientation persisted.

She was thirteen again, curled up on the stair landing, shivering from nausea and fear, her eyes squeezed tightly shut. Her grandmother screamed, a high-pitched sound that died as quickly as it had come. She held her breath for what seemed forever, letting it out when she heard a door slam. But it was a long time before she could move, gripping the railing and making her way shakily down the stairs.

She was so dizzy it took her a minute to realize her grandmother was lying in the middle of the Persian rug. "Nana." Deanna whispered the name as she had ten years ago. Stumbling and weaving like a drunk, she had made her way to her grandmother's side. For a second she stood swaying, gazing down, trying to figure out why her grandmother was lying on the floor. Then she collapsed, her muscles giving way at the horror she saw. She fell to her knees beside the old woman, staring at the bright red stain splashed across the white silk blouse.

As if in a dream, she had touched her grandmother's chest, then pulled her hand away at the warm sticky feeling. She held her red fingers up to her face. Her grandmother was the only one left in the world who loved her. Still staring at her wet fingers, she was struck by the realization that she was alone now. Suddenly grief-stricken, she grabbed the limp body and gathered it close, rocking back and forth, back and forth. She picked up the bloody butcher knife and held it tightly—still rocking back and forth, back and forth. She began to scream as loud as she could and was sitting on the floor with her grandmother in her arms when their neighbor, Smithers, hesitantly walked in through the open front door.

Deanna covered her ears with her hands, trying to shut out the sounds and the images—the screams, the feel of her grandmother being pulled from her arms, the way her fingers ached as someone roughly peeled them from the knife. And then mercifully, the darkness had come, deep and thick, and with it a blessed silence. She had felt safe.

When at last she'd opened her eyes again, a man was leaning over her, smiling at her. His name was Dr. Gresham and he told her she'd been catatonic for six months. Later, in the days, months and years that followed, she had learned who she was and what she'd done.

And now she remembered it all.

An insistent knocking on the door jolted Deanna back to the present. Struggling to suppress her sobs, she dried her eyes with the back of her hands. No one should see her like this. No one should know.

She straightened her shoulders and plastered a fake smile on her pale face, then turned around and opened the door. "Mary, what are you doing here?"

Mary Piper was her best friend, Dr. Gresham's assistant, secretary and right hand. She had offered to let Deanna stay with her for as long as she wanted or needed to.

Mary's sharp brown eyes took in everything at once. "You've been crying?"

"Panic," Deanna confessed. That much was true. "Nerves."

Mary's gaze bounced around the room and she grimaced. "I see. If I had to pack all this myself, I'd cry, too. But I've come bearing good news. You're leaving with me right now, so grab your suitcases."

Things were moving too fast. Deanna just stared at her. "But Dr. Gresham said tomorrow." She waved her hand in the air, the gesture taking in the room. "What about all my stuff? I—"

"Taken care of. Raul will load up everything in the morning and deliver it to my house. As for Gresham, he almost insisted that you leave tonight." Mary shadowed Deanna around the room, helping where she could, pulling the heavy suitcases toward the door.

"That doesn't sound like Dr. Gresham. What's with him, Mary?"

Mary ducked her dark head, refusing to let Deanna see her anger and guilt. She decided it was better Deanna didn't know what she'd found out. Better for all concerned that no one ever found out. But she'd made a promise to herself—if anyone ever threatened to hurt Deanna, she wouldn't be quiet then.

They pushed, shoved and manhandled the three borrowed suitcases out of the cabin and down the path to the parking lot. Mary huffed and puffed, and grumbled under her breath about pack rats. Deanna felt her spirits rise and made a few outrageous retorts, and they were suddenly laughing until they were both so weak they could barely wrestle the cases into the trunk of Mary's car. Finally, panting and exhausted, Deanna shut the car door and Mary started the engine. It wasn't until they rounded the corner of the main building that Deanna said, "Stop a second, will you, Mary?"

"Sure."

Twisting around, Deanna rested her chin on the seat and gazed back at the row of ten white-stucco cabins, one of them her home for the past four years. Then she glanced up at the main building with its sterile rooms, where she'd lived up on the third floor for the six years before that.

She turned back around in her seat. "Okay, let's get out of here." The high iron gates swung open, and as they drove through them she waved at Raul and smiled hugely when he gave her a thumbs-up. "I can't believe it," she whispered.

"You're free," Mary reassured her.

"No one's going to come take me back, are they?" That thought had haunted her from the moment she'd been told of her release. She feared that this was all a bad joke, or that she'd no sooner get past those gates than someone would give a yank and, like a puppet on an elastic string, she'd be back inside.

"It's all true." Mary grinned at her, then gave a huge sneeze.

"Bless you.... Mary, what about tomorrow? The judge won't change his mind, will he?" She felt the fear rising again, threatening to overwhelm her, but she battled it down. She had been set free, and she had regained her memory and an even greater freedom. It was just going to take a long time to get used to, she thought.

She realized Mary had been talking. "Sorry, what did you say?"

"Daydreaming, Deanna?"

"Yeah, something like that. What were you saying?"

"From what I understand, your appearance before Judge Harrison is only a legal formality, since he's already released you."

"So why do I have to go to the lawyer's office first?"

"That I can't answer, but it's what Mr. Lambert's office requested." Mary sneezed again, then coughed, a low rattling sound deep in her chest.

"Mary, you're not getting sick on me, are you? You have to be there tomorrow." The fear was creeping in again. Deanna clamped her hands together and squeezed hard.

"I'll be fine. And I wouldn't miss tomorrow for anything."

"Dr. Gresham's going to be there, also, isn't he?"

"Yes." Mary reached over and patted the tightly clasped hands. "No matter how hard you've tried to hide it, and you're pretty good with everyone else, I know you're scared. It's okay, Deanna. It's normal."

"Thanks," Deanna said sarcastically.

Mary laughed. "Sorry, but it's true. Hell, I'm scared, and this has nothing to do with me. Besides, Deanna, only people who care about you will be in the courtroom. The judge obviously does, because he's setting you free. Mr. Lambert's defended you for ten years, and he's believed in you since the beginning. And of course there's me. I'll always be there for you. Always."

Mary had been like a mother to Deanna, albeit, at forty, a young one. Nevertheless, Deanna had cried many a tear in front of her and been comforted by her. Thinking about Mary's love and support made the tension in Deanna's shoulders and neck ease. "Why was it, Mary, that from the first day I arrived at Twelve Oaks you set out to be my friend?"

"The truth?" Mary asked. "Or something you want to hear?"

Deanna smiled in the dark. This had been a long-standing game with them. Over the years as she'd grown up, she'd requested the truth far more often than what she'd needed to hear.

"The truth, please."

Mary studied the road ahead for a few minutes. "I..." She paused, changing her mind about what she was going to say. Deanna was no longer a patient at Twelve Oaks, and she no longer had to be as careful about what she said around her. "I never believed you killed your grandmother. Don't ask me why, I just didn't. Still don't. I even tried to talk to Dr. Gresham about it." She shook her head, then glanced at Deanna. "That was the first time he ever lost his temper with me, so I never brought it up again."

Deanna wasn't sure what to say, but after a moment Mary continued, her tone serious. "You know, if I'm right and you didn't do what you were accused of, someone else did—'' she waved her hand, taking in everything around them ''—someone who might still be out there.''

In the emotional upheaval at getting her memory back, Deanna hadn't thought far enough ahead to realize the truth of her friend's statement. Someone else was indeed responsible for her grandmother's death, and that someone had kept quiet and let her be locked away for ten years. The urge to tell Mary she was right almost overpowered Deanna, and she bit her lip hard. As much as she trusted Mary, she didn't have enough confidence in her own capability to make decisions yet. Best, she thought, to keep quiet.

She stared out the window, watching the Houston city-limits sign whiz past. She could see lights ahead, and the closer they got to the real world, the more nervous she became. She'd been allowed outside the sanitarium grounds to go to a local school once it was determined she wasn't violent. Later, Raul, a member of the security staff at Twelve Oaks, had driven her daily to a community college. But to be out on her own now, knowing that when she had a problem she wouldn't have at least ten people to turn to for help, was both frightening and exhilarating.

Deanna swallowed hard. For years she'd prayed to get her memory back. Now, faced with the horrible truth of what had happened, she couldn't get the memories to leave. Mary was a smart woman, and it wouldn't be long before she began to start asking questions. Better, Deanna thought, to distract her by asking her own questions first.

''How long a drive do you have to work every day, Mary? Do you think I should change my name?''

Mary smiled over at her. "'Bout an hour each way—and no."

Suddenly Deanna was like a glass waiting to be filled. There were so many things she wanted to know. How was she going to get around? What kind of work did Mary think she was capable of doing? Could she even get a job with the stigma of her past? A million questions she'd never had to think of in the protected world she'd just left behind.

CHAPTER TWO

CLAYTON LAMBERT tilted back the big leather executive chair, propped his feet on the edge of his desk and smiled his most charming and sexy smile at the decorative lady perched there. Lynnett Overton Hamilton had both breeding and style. From a very old East Coast banking family with equally old money, she had a classic beauty— pale skin, deep brown eyes and long dark hair that was slicked back and twisted up in some new fashion. Tall and slim, full and firm in all the right places, Lynn reminded him of a graceful, lazy cat. Just thinking about what she could do with that mouth of hers aroused him.

They had been dating exclusively for seven months and sleeping together for the past six. And that was about all they had in common. He knew she was his alone and she wanted to marry him. But was he ready? At thirty, often feeling forty, he'd been thinking it was time to settle down. But did he want to marry Lynn?

There was that doubt again. In the past couple of weeks, every time he thought of Lynn and matrimony, he'd get a queasy feeling in his gut. He'd begun to realize something was missing in their relationship. Did he really want to wake up with her every morning and go to bed with her every night?

Maybe not.

His mind's uncensored response shook Clay hard enough that his feet dropped to the floor with a jarring thud and he stood up, nearly knocking Lynn off the desk.

She stood, too, her fingers reaching out to toy with the buttons of his shirt. "Come on, Clay."

Stifled by her closeness and the overpowering sweetness of her perfume, and irritated by his own abrupt mood swing, Clay walked over to the window. "Come on, what?"

"Lunch. Gregg and Barbara want us to meet them at the country club."

"I told you, Lynn. I have to be in court and I don't know when I'll be through." He had a good view of the street below and watched as a taxi skidded to a stop. All he could make out of the departing passenger as she rushed toward the building was a head of thick, shoulder-length blond hair. He cocked his head, smiling for no reason except for the way the wind took hold of her hair and tossed it around, and the way the sun caught the curly golden strands and made them shine. *Look up,* he thought, trying to send a mental message. *Look up, so I can see your face.* She didn't, and he sighed as she moved out of sight.

"I forgot. It's that Deveraux girl today, isn't it?" Lynn shivered delicately and walked over to where he was standing, wrapping her arms around his narrow waist. "You said last night that court today was just a formality and wouldn't take long. Besides, don't you get the creeps having to defend a case like that?"

"First of all, I'm not defending her, just representing the firm and Grandfather." His breath lodged in the back of his throat at her roaming hands. Catching hold of them, he pulled them back up to his waist and held them there firmly. "Why should this case be different from any other? I'm a criminal lawyer. I've probably defended worse, just didn't know it.''

"Clay! You can't mean you haven't thought about the risk of being in this office, alone, with a convicted, cold-blooded killer?''

Clay laughed. "She won't be alone. Someone from the sanitarium is coming with her.'' He let go of Lynn's hands, moved across the room and sat down in his chair again, watching with an amused smile as Lynn settled on the edge of the desk once more, this time closer to him.

"I want to have lunch with Gregg and Barb.'' Her lower lip jutted out.

Had he never noticed the whine in her voice before or the way she pouted when she didn't get what she wanted? Or had he always thought it was cute, even sexy? Shaking his head, he said, "Can't help it, Lynn.''

"What does she look like, Clay?''

"Who?'' He knew very well who she was talking about, but she always jumped from one thing to another. She actually thought it kept men on their toes. Once, that, too, had amused him. Now, it only irritated him.

"The Deveraux girl. Have you ever seen her?''

"No. She was Grandfather's client. He never talked to me about the case.''

"Oh, come on, Clay. Surely, in all those years he must have said something.'' She scooted across the desk so she was directly in front of him and leaned forward. Her lips were only inches away from his.

"Sorry, nothing.'' Clay backed away just far enough to look her directly in the eye and at the same time be able to take in her entire expression. "Why the sudden interest in the Deveraux case, Lynn?'' When she started to turn her head away, he clasped her chin between his fingers. "Lynn?"

"Oh, hell. I told Barbara I wasn't any good at deceiving you."

"And just what does the queen of fashion have to do with the Deveraux case?" He released her and stood, looming over her. In his best courtroom voice, a voice that could wring the truth out of a hardened criminal, he asked, "And why didn't you just come out and ask me whatever you wanted to know? Why the games?"

"It was Barbara's idea, Clay. Really. And the reason is just what you said—fashion. Barbara is Lamar Maxell's sister-in-law and she was just helping Lamar protect the family interests."

Clay shook his head. "You've lost me. Explain."

"Don't you know anything, Clay? Lamar Maxell was Fleur Deveraux's assistant."

"I'm still standing out here in the dark," he said sarcastically.

"Fleur Deveraux was the woman your client killed, her grandmother."

"So?"

"Clay! Lamar took over Fleur's after Madame Deveraux was killed. She controls one of the most prestigious fashion stores in Texas."

Clay's inner antenna sensed trouble. "You said this Lamar controls the shop? She doesn't own it?"

Lynn's cheeks flushed dark red. "No, and that's what I was supposed to find out. When Fleur Deveraux died, your grandfather allowed Lamar to purchase forty-five percent of the business so she would stay on and run it. About five years ago, Lamar had the capital to buy Fleur's. She'd made money hand over fist, so she approached your grandfather with a deal to buy the shop and the name outright. But your grandfather made it abundantly clear he wouldn't sell under any circumstances. He wanted to keep the yearly income from the business for his client."

Clay smiled, but there was a hard gleam in his hazel eyes. "I see. Lamar had Barbara talk you into using our relationship to find out whether the girl is going to be released and if she's able or capable of taking over Fleur's?"

"Yes."

Clay's voice held no warmth. "Don't you ever, *ever* try to use me again, Lynn."

She had the good sense to look thoroughly contrite. "I knew it wouldn't work."

"I don't care whether you thought it would work or not. Just don't pull a stunt like that again. And by the way, what makes this Lamar, Barbara and you think that just because Grandfather's gone the situation would change?"

"I don't know, Clay. Lamar and Barbara just wondered what this girl's like. If she wants to keep the business, or if she's even capable of having a coherent thought, much less make a business decision."

"I tell you what—why don't you suggest to Lamar and Barbara that they ask her themselves?" His anger surprised him and he had to rein in his temper. What in hell was the matter with him?

"Come on, you don't really think that after ten years in a mental institution she's competent, do you?"

Clay laughed. "That's probably why Grandfather and this firm are her guardians—to protect those interests." He'd spoken more harshly than he'd meant to and had hurt her feelings. "Listen, Lynn. I was just given this case and haven't had time to do more than read the summons from Judge Harrison to appear in court. As to her capabilities?" He shrugged. "I guess I'd have to agree with you. Miss Deveraux..." He didn't even know her first name and flipped open the file on his desk. "Deanna Deveraux was thirteen when she was committed. She's been confined for ten years. I don't imagine she's your average twenty-three-year-old, do you? For all I know, she may be a blithering idiot."

TERROR. PRIMITIVE. Primeval. It swept over Deanna like a flash fire every time the cabdriver swerved in and out of the thick traffic on the freeway. She felt like a lamb being driven into a lion's den by a pack of hyenas snapping at her heels.

Silly, stupid girl, she silently scolded herself as she peeled her fingers off the safety strap and folded her hands in her lap. *Relax. You've ridden in cars before, even driven one.* But she'd never experienced a ride as wild as this, she thought.

Twelve Oaks Valley Sanitarium was located in what some called a satellite city, a small town outside the city limits of Houston. It was a quiet place with a slow and easy pace. As she stared out the window of the taxi, she understood now why Dr. Gresham, Mary and the others preferred to live not in the heart of the city but on the outskirts. The very thought of having to drive every day on this monstrous multilane freeway with its stinking mass of moving steel was absolutely the most frightening thing she could imagine.

"You from out of town?"

The cabdriver had been trying to get her to talk to him ever since they'd left Mary's but all she could do was nod or shake her head. It wasn't that she was shy, but this was her first journey alone in ten years and she was scared to death.

Poor Mary. She'd been so sick this morning yet determined to go with Deanna to the law office and court. After a couple of aborted efforts to get dressed that ended in paroxysms of coughing, both women realized that Mary wasn't going to be able to accompany Deanna, after all.

For what seemed like hours they'd argued—Mary wanted to get Dr. Gresham or Raul to drive her. But now that she was free of Twelve Oaks, Deanna didn't want to take the chance of appearing dependent, needy. She was determined that nothing was going to jeopardize her freedom, and she'd finally convinced Mary that she was capable of going on her own. After all, it wasn't as if she'd be alone for long. Old Mr. Lambert would be with her, holding her hand as he'd done so many times in the past when he was explaining something to her. And Dr. Gresham would be there, though she wasn't as thrilled about the doctor's presence. Mary's reluctance had finally crumbled under Deanna's insistence and the simple fact that she was just too sick to argue anymore. But her dear friend had showered her with a hundred instructions, and Deanna had, as usual, made copious notes.

Deanna was so lost in her own thoughts that when the taxi stopped she had to glance around before she realized they'd reached her destination. She peered up at the rather insignificant-looking six-story brick building—the Lambert Building—where Lambert, Bernard and Lambert had their law offices.

She glanced around, taking in all the steel-and-glass buildings surrounding her. Ten years had changed the downtown dramatically. The buildings were taller and denser, and there were more cars and people. She remembered coming downtown when she was much younger, nine or ten, with her mother. They'd dress up in their Sunday best, sometimes identical outfits, with polished patent shoes and white gloves. They shopped, though they never bought anything, in all the really posh stores, like Sakowitz and Neiman Marcus, but the highlight of each trip, to Deanna at least, was the visit to Woolworth's. The images themselves were blurred, but what Deanna remembered most was the feeling of fun, the laughter. She swallowed hard around the lump of pain in her throat that these memories of her mother brought.

Later, after her mother's death, she'd come downtown one last time, and that was to the Lambert Building with her grandmother. Small, neat and fashionably dressed for a child, she had trailed behind the old woman, staring holes into that ramrod-straight back. She remembered something else, too—the way her grandmother had floated into those richly furnished law offices as if she were a queen, leaving Deanna to sit perfectly still and ladylike in a big leather chair in the reception area.

When Deanna realized where she was, she halted so fast she almost lost her balance. She couldn't recall paying the cabdriver or walking across the sidewalk and through the double glass doors. Quickly she glanced around to see if anyone had been watching.

The lobby was deserted, an empty hull of cold white marble, shiny brass and tall green plants just a little too artfully arranged. The past ten years had not been kind to the once lovely place. A decorator with little taste had done away with the warm wood and thick carpet. Now the lobby reminded her of the third floor of Twelve Oaks.

That mental nudge sent her glance skidding around the area until she found a sign marked Rest Rooms.

Once the heavy door was closed behind her and she'd quickly checked to see that she was alone, Deanna sat down in an overstuffed chair and pulled out her list of notes. She knew them by rote now, but a review wouldn't hurt. She had to smile at the first one. "Be cool," she'd written. "Take a deep breath—concentrate on being calm." She could never let anyone see how scared and unsure of herself she was, or they might make her go back to Twelve Oaks. She quickly scanned the rest of her instructions, then left the rest room and consulted the information board beside the elevator door. "Lambert, Bernard and Lambert," she whispered under her breath, "sixth floor."

This was going to be an adventure, she kept telling herself as she pressed the button and waited for the elevator. Besides, Mr. Lambert was a dear old man and her friend. As the brass double doors slid quietly open, Deanna exhaled then inhaled slowly, screwed up her courage and stepped inside. Before she could change her mind she slammed her hand against the red button marked with the number six.

She wondered if anyone had ever actually died of fright or if she was going to be the first. When the elevator doors smoothly opened again she immediately stepped out while she still had a little nerve left. Her hands tightened their death grip on her purse. Her heels sunk into the lush mint green carpet. There was a delicate scent of roses in the air, and swatches of pastels, like a Monet painting, teased her peripheral vision. But all Deanna could focus on were the two young women standing behind the reception desk, having what looked like a heated conversation.

Were they talking about her? When she told them her name would they stare at her with that strange mixed expression of fear, fascination and distaste? Lord, she'd seen those looks enough over the past ten years to last her a lifetime. As she got closer, relief almost swamped her as she realized the women were caught up in their own problems. And those problems must have been monumental, because as she stood there, silently waiting, they never once glanced her way.

Deanna did the only polite thing she could think of—she coughed softly. When nothing happened, she took heart and said, "Excuse me, I have an appointment with Mr. Lambert."

One of the women glanced at her, then down to an appointment book. "Your name?"

"Deveraux. Deanna Deveraux."

"Oh, sure. Mr. Lambert's office is through there—" she pointed to a set of carved oak doors "—and the last office on the right. I'd take you there, but as you can see, we're having a little crisis at the moment. You don't mind, do you?"

"Not at all," Deanna said. "I'll find it." Well, she thought, the world wasn't waiting for Deanna Deveraux to emerge so everyone could stare and make unsavory comments. Life went on and the past was quickly forgotten. Once she'd made headlines, now she wasn't even an interested gleam in a stranger's eyes.

She pushed open the doors, straightened her shoulders and walked down the long carpeted hall. She hummed a nameless tune in her mind, thinking, *Doors to the right of me, doors to the left...* She'd heard that somewhere but couldn't remember where. Or did it have something to do with guns? Then she was there, the last door on the right.

Bracing herself, she thought of all she'd been through, the injustice of what had happened to her. The rage she'd kept in check ever since she'd regained her memory threatened to overwhelm her. It took a second to calm down. Mr. Lambert was a kind old man. She trusted him. Yet why hadn't he called her personally about the release? He'd left that up to Dr. Gresham, and he knew she'd come to dislike the doctor. Maybe she shouldn't trust anyone.

Through the turmoil that was churning around in her head—indecision, doubts and fear—one thing was very clear. She couldn't take any risks now, not when she had a gut feeling that everything hung on what happened in this office. *Keep cool,* she reminded herself, *as if you were in Dr. Gresham's office. Face blank. No emotion. Look Mr. Lambert and anyone else in that office directly in the eye. Don't ever let anyone see what you're really feeling.*

Deanna raised her hand to knock, then stopped. When she knocked—and someone answered—she would be exposed for who she was, subjected to censure or ridicule, perhaps. But she could also be free. She grabbed the doorknob, twisted and forged ahead.

Oh, Lord, what a boob she was! She'd gotten the wrong office. And judging by the close proximity of the blond-haired man and the lovely brunette and their startled expressions, she'd interrupted more than a lawyer/client conversation.

She was the first to recover. "Excuse me," she said, starting to turn around and retreat as fast as her feet would carry her. "I was looking for Mr. Lambert's office."

"I'm Mr. Lambert."

Deanna stopped. She probably would have kept her mouth shut if he hadn't used that condescending tone. "That's nice," she said, "but you're not *my* Mr. Lambert." This was exactly what she didn't need. An arrogant, smart-aleck male—no matter how good-looking he was. And from the haughty glance and shrug of dismissal the woman was giving her, she was sure she'd stepped into the wrong office. Her sweet Mr. Lambert couldn't possibly be associated with these two.

Before anyone could recover enough to comment, the office door swung open and a stout, gray-haired woman rushed in. "Oh, Mr. Lambert. I'm so sorry. That dim-witted gal at the reception desk and Mr. Bernard had words, and she just walked out a few minutes ago." The woman stopped, looked at Clay and Lynn, then back to Deanna. "She sent Miss Deveraux through without buzzing you."

"Deveraux?" Clay said, totally at a loss for words, while Lynn could only stare at the woman with a mixture of disbelief and fascination.

Deanna ignored their shocked looks. She'd seen them before when people realized who she was, but the hurt she always felt was less painful this time. She reached out and touched the older woman's arm just as she was trying to slip out the door. "This is the wrong Mr. Lambert. I have an appointment with Taylor Justin Lambert."

Clay struggled to recover his wits and good manners, but he had been thrown completely off-balance. This petite young woman with long, curly blond hair, hair that had been carelessly mussed by the wind, was Deanna Deveraux? This was the woman he'd seen exiting the taxi. He remembered how the sun had turned her hair a shimmering gold.

He almost smiled at the smattering of freckles across her nose and cheeks, freckles she did nothing to hide. Then, thanks to the typical man's inner radar when it homed in on a good-looking woman, he sensed more, than actually saw the perfect figure beneath the simple milk-chocolate-colored sheath she wore.

He also noted the assessing look in her blue eyes. A look that told him she knew exactly what he was thinking. He was uncharacteristically ashamed of himself, and because he was, his next words came out harsher than he intended. "Taylor Justin Lambert is—*was* my grandfather. He died suddenly last week. I'm Clayton Lambert."

Deanna felt as if the lush carpet had been pulled out from under her feet. She must have weaved like a drunk, as if about to fall flat on her face. In a heartbeat she felt his hands on her shoulders, his touch gentle as he led her to the nearest chair. There was a loud buzzing in her ears, but over it she could hear him issuing orders for the young woman to pour a glass of water, then leave.

Deanna accepted the glass that was firmly placed in her hand. *Don't show emotion.* She forced herself to smile and take a sip. *Don't let them see they've gotten to you.* When the man—Clayton Lambert—moved away, she heard a whispered conversation behind her and took a slow deep breath. *Keep cool.* The light in the room was getting brighter, her hearing sharper. When she heard the door shut and the muffled footsteps move down the hall, she was composed and ready.

The episode had shaken Clay. So much so that he hadn't bothered to hide his irritation with Lynn when he'd ordered her out of his office. She'd actually wanted to stay. Once the door was closed, he quickly moved back to Deanna. "Are you okay?" She looked at him and he froze. He'd expected tears, hysteria, but instead, was met with a cool expressionless gaze. Wanting to comfort her, he was thrown off-balance again. "I didn't mean to upset you."

"Yes you did, or you wouldn't have blurted it out like that."

Clay blinked. Of course she was right, he had meant to do just that, but he certainly wasn't used to having his nose rubbed in his blunders, either. He straightened and moved rather stiffly behind his desk and sat down. He was in charge again. "I take it no one notified you of my grandfather's death? I'm sorry."

Deanna nodded and swallowed a lump in her throat the size of a basketball. When she felt her voice wouldn't betray her, she asked, "What happened?"

"Heart attack. He died very peacefully in his sleep."

She bit the inside of her cheek so hard she tasted blood. He was staring at her, catching her gaze with his and holding it. Poor Mr. Lambert. He had always been so sweet and kind to her. She would miss him dreadfully, but she couldn't afford to think about him now. She would do that later in private and shed all the tears she was bottling up.

But her eyes filled with tears in spite of herself, and she couldn't stop them no matter how hard she tried. Ducking her head, she searched her purse for a tissue.

Anger slithered over the pain of loss, drying her tears as quickly as they'd fallen. She'd seen the expression on Clayton Lambert's face before. That studied clinical look, as if she were something alien. Some strange creature to be dissected. It was the same expression that Dr. Gresham always wore, and she hated it.

Her peculiar sense of humor kicked in. He'd expected a deranged killer, maybe even a drooling idiot escorted to his office in a straitjacket. He'd expected the worst, and when it didn't materialize, he didn't know what to do or how to act.

Clay saw the tears well up in her eyes and the frantic search through her purse. He was about to offer his handkerchief when she lifted her head and caught him staring. It was her eyes that captivated him. They were dark blue, thick lashed, and though her expression was as still as water, they were laughing at him as if he was the dimwit. He was stymied, and then realized that this woman was nobody's fool. Behind those laughing eyes was a sharp mind, an intelligence he wondered at, was intrigued by. She was an enigma. How a young woman who had spent the past ten years in a sanitarium for the mentally ill could come out with poise, manners, style and intelligence was beyond him.

"If you're through trying to figure me out, could you tell me what to expect today?"

There, she'd done it again. Made him feel clumsy and awkward. And she seemed to enjoy it. At this point, until he knew more about her, the best he could do was stick to business. He realized he was going to appear lacking here, too, since he hadn't had the time or the inclination to read her file thoroughly.

Clay rustled the files on his desk, opened one and cleared his throat. "I have to apologize..." Damn, he hadn't meant to start that way, and she just sat there quietly looking at him. "I hope you'll understand that since Grandfather's death, things around here have been rather chaotic. All his clients are being shuffled around." He closed the file with a thump. Why didn't she say something? "Actually, Miss Deveraux, I'm a criminal lawyer, and I simply haven't had time to thoroughly review your case."

Her breath was cut off as efficiently as if her heart had stopped. "Do you mean we won't be going to court today? That my release has been delayed?"

Bingo. For a second before it was quickly masked, there was dismay in those beautiful blue eyes. It was the first real emotion, other than amusement at his expense, that he'd seen. "No, no. We're still set for Judge Harrison's court—" he glanced at his watch "—in about thirty minutes. The thing is, Miss Deveraux, I don't have the slightest idea what the judge wants other than to officially release you from the sanitarium. With the death of the judge who had been overseeing your case for the past ten years, the charges of misconduct, then Judge Harrison taking over... To tell you the God's honest truth, I don't know what the hell's going on."

"Thank you for that," she said.

"For what?"

"Honesty. People tend to tell me only what *they* think I need to hear."

Clay noticed that she'd relaxed a little and even managed a sincere smile. "And I'm truly sorry for the way I broke the news of my grandfather's death. You obviously cared for him."

"Yes, I did. He was a sweet man." Her smile widened when she saw his startled expression. "He was, you know. No matter what Dr. Gresham or the others said, Mr. Lambert never believed I was guilty, or if he did, he never let me know. He sent candy and flowers on my birthday, and brought me a gift and came to see me every Christmas Eve." For some reason she didn't feel comfortable telling Clayton Lambert of his grandfather's unofficial visits. Those times were precious to her and not to be shared with a stranger.

"Grandfather?" He couldn't believe it. His grandfather was the original curmudgeon. If his grandfather had stuck with this case for ten years, maybe there was something more to it. Deanna Deveraux intrigued him more and more. "Tell me something."

Here it comes, she thought with a sinking heart. The old question—*Did you really kill your granny?*

"I didn't think institutions such as Twelve Oaks were in the educational system, but you're obviously well educated."

"Mr. Lambert saw to that, and a lot more." She couldn't help smiling at his incredulous expression. "I was never considered dangerous, Mr. Lambert. I—"

"Clay, please."

"I just don't have any memories . . . Clay. I went to public schools and a community college." Deanna scooted forward in her chair. "Do you have any idea why the judge is releasing me so soon?"

"None, and we'd better get going." He stood up and pulled on his jacket. "Is whoever brought you waiting in the reception area?"

"I came alone."

Clay nodded, though he didn't understand at all. He grasped her arm and led her out of his office. "The court is only a block away, so we'll walk."

The trip to the courthouse was a silent one. After a few attempts at conversation, Clay realized that his client was actually scared speechless. When he thought of what was at stake for her, he stopped trying to hold her attention. He did make one silent promise to her and himself before opening the door to the courtroom, though. Before this day was over, he was going to know all there was to know, all his grandfather knew, about Deanna Deveraux and her past.

KEEP COOL. The reminder wasn't working. Her palms were sweaty and she had to work at controlling her labored breathing. She'd thought her legs were going to give out when they entered the courtroom. At that moment she wanted only one thing in the world—to turn and run. Her knees had even locked up on her for a few seconds like a stubborn mule's, and it took Clay's tugging hand to get her moving again.

"Relax," Clay whispered as he led her down the aisle, through the waist-high swinging gate and to a chair behind a long oak table. "This is all in your favor, remember."

"I hope so." She wouldn't look at Clay, but asked, "He couldn't change his mind, could he?"

He desperately wanted to tell her no, but there were no guarantees in the courts, especially with Judge Harrison. He was a tough and honest man, but he was also prone to making examples of certain cases.

Clay squeezed her hands, which were clasped tightly together under the table. "Everything's going to be fine."

Despite the old "Trust no one" warning in the back of her mind, Deanna was relieved by his encouragement and relaxed enough to look around. There were only three other people in the courtroom, all men. Two were sitting on her side of the room and the third was on the opposite side. She couldn't see the faces of the two men closest to her; they seemed to turn away whenever she glanced their way. But the third, a young man about her age, grinned rather engagingly and nodded. She briefly wondered where Dr. Gresham was. She hadn't seem him anywhere.

Deanna quickly twisted around, realizing that Clay had been trying to get her attention. "Sorry. Who's that man smiling at me as if he knows me?"

He glanced around and scowled. Leaning close to Deanna, he whispered, "He's a reporter." As he moved his mouth away from her ear, he unconsciously inhaled the clean scent of soap on her skin. "Listen to me, Deanna." Why was she such a distraction, he wondered, puzzled by his reaction to her. "Whatever you do, don't say anything to the judge unless he directly asks you a question. Do you understand? Don't volunteer any information."

"Why?"

"Because if you lie, you could perjure yourself."

"Why would I lie? What would I lie about?"

"Don't ask questions," he ordered. "Just do as I say. If he asks you something directly and we have to answer, wait until I give you the okay. Have you got that?"

She had a real aversion to being told what to do. Up until now she'd always had to sit, smiling, and submit. But no more. Yet one look at the angry determination in those hazel eyes, that stubborn glint, and she could feel the need to assert her independence sink like a stone in a pond. "Yes, but—"

With startling speed, everything seemed to happen at once. The courtroom door behind them flew open. Clay told her the tall thin man almost running down the aisle was an assistant district attorney and was here only as a formality, since the state wasn't contesting the decision.

Then another door opened, this time at the side of the judge's raised bench, and a deep baritone voice said, "All rise." Clay pulled her to her feet, but she didn't feel his hand on her arm, nor did she hear the rest of what was

being said. All her attention was focused on the short
balding man dressed in a long black robe as he floated up
to his domain. Once seated, he nodded to the clerk,
folded his hand in a neat pyramid and surveyed his court
while the clerk read the case number and name.

The numbness was leaving, and she even felt Clay's
touch as he urged her to sit back down. She managed to
stop visibly shuddering when the judge settled his gaze on
her. With a decisiveness she'd been unaware of, she met
his piercing eyes straight on with honesty and strength.
Then she jerked a little and wondered if she'd imagined
it or if he had actually given her a wink of approval.

Judge Harrison was angry beyond words. He'd reread
the Deveraux case three times to make sure that he was
correct in his decision, that there wasn't an important
detail he'd missed. Someone was going to account for this
horrific miscarriage of justice. He'd see to it personally.
His gaze slipped away from Deanna's wide blue eyes and
scanned his courtroom. A deep frown cut across his shiny
brow. "Gentlemen, these proceedings are closed to the
public. Bailiff, see them out."

The delay was painful, and the three men Deanna had
noticed earlier left the courtroom. Deanna felt the weight
of Clay's hand on hers, and she looked up at him. There
was no use trying to fool him—he knew she was terrified—so she grabbed his hand and held it as tightly as she
could. Then she realized the judge was speaking.

"Deanna Deveraux, after a careful review of your
case, it's the findings of this court that the murder case
and verdict brought against you by the state prosecutor
was a miscarriage of justice, with insufficient evidence to
prove without a doubt that you took the life of your
grandmother, Mrs. Agatha Fleur Deveraux.

"It is therefore the decision of this court that you are hereby cleared of all charges against you and are free to go."

The sound of the wood gavel was like the opening of locked gates.

She was free—but so was the killer.

CHAPTER THREE

WHEN THE COURTROOM DOORS were flung open and Clay and Deanna hurried out, two men watched from opposite sides of the wide rotunda. Though both men were far enough away that their intense interest wasn't noticed, neither missed the radiant smile on the young woman's face.

Both men were professionals, with lengthy careers behind them, but they were so absorbed in their target that neither was aware of the other's pursuit of the same woman. As soon as Deanna was out of sight, they stepped from the cool shadows, each with one goal in mind—to confirm what they already knew before placing their telephone calls.

One man was short, bowlegged, in his early sixties, with a shiny bald pate and thick black-rimmed glasses; he headed for the door marked Stairs and slipped behind it. After a few minutes, Judge Jones's old bailiff walked through the same door. Before it had time to shut completely behind the bailiff, he was backing out and stuffing a wad of money into his pants pocket, then he turned around and rushed off.

A few minutes later, the bowlegged man exited the stairwell and with slow, leisurely steps started down the corridor for the phone booth at the end of the hall. Closing the door, he dropped in a coin, dialed a number, then dropped in a few more coins and eased himself carefully down onto the hard wooden seat. He was getting too old for this nonsense, he thought. His arthritic knees were killing him, and his feet were swollen, making his shoes pinch.

Harry Dobbs sighed deeply with fatigue. He leaned his head back and closed his eyes as he listened to the hollow ring of the telephone. When a male voice, soft and slow with a distinctive Texas drawl, came on the line, Harry relaxed.

"Harry. Glad you called. How's Houston?"

"Oh, hell. Gil, it's a poor excuse of a town even if it is part of Texas. You know that." Harry had to smile. He knew his boss and longtime friend was dying to know what had happened, but good Texas manners and small talk always won out first.

Gilbert Foley was the wealthiest man in Texas. Hell, if you put all of old Gilbert's corporations together, he'd probably be listed as the wealthiest man in America. Oil, gas and an uncanny instinct for making money had built the Foley empire. Gilbert Foley was a crafty old redneck, masquerading as a gentleman in his three-piece suit and Stetson hat. But once crossed, he was as lethal as a rattlesnake. Harry had seen his boss destroy more powerful men, some taken down with his money and position, a few almost beaten to death when Foley lost that tightly controlled temper of his.

"How's Dallas?" Harry asked, trying to hide the longing in his voice.

"Hotter than hell, drier than your dead mama's old bones, but home, Harry."

The only things genuine about Gilbert were his Texas drawl, his love for his two sons and his devotion to his few true friends. And over the past thirty years Harry had earned his boss's devotion, and he returned it in kind.

Ailing as he was, he had spent ten years chasing around this town on Gil's behalf. Now, maybe, it was all over and he could go home.

"Like we thought, Gil, the judge let the girl go." There was silence at the other end, and Harry waited patiently. Though Gilbert had yet to confide just why he'd assigned Harry to be the girl's watchdog, Harry knew it was important to the boss, and that was all the reason he needed. Over the past ten years he'd managed to put together the whole story of Deanna Deveraux and her connection to Gil. Or at least he thought he had.

He'd received monthly reports from that woman at the sanitarium, then sent her generous cashier's checks. Judge Jones was also one of Foley's paid contacts. Harry was privy to this knowledge, since he'd personally passed money to the judge. But he was never allowed to question or talk to him. Hell, he was just the bread man, and the amount of dough that had rolled from his hand to Judge Jones's had been staggering.

Yet even after all the years he'd been Foley's top security man, and all the sticky situations from which he'd rescued Gil, the company and even Gil's two boys, his friend and boss still didn't trust him enough to tell him why he'd kept a ten-year surveillance on the Deveraux girl. And that hurt.

But old Harry wasn't anyone's fool. He'd made it his business to know Gilbert Foley's business. After all, how could he protect his boss, the family or the company if he didn't know what was going on? Over the years he'd managed to put his own spin on the Deveraux case and was pretty sure he knew all there was to know.

So now, Harry thought, it was over. The ten years of protecting Deanna Deveraux were at an end. She was out, free and clear, and on her own. He wondered if Gil would go see her now that she'd been released. After all, it wasn't as if Gil had a wife's tender feelings to protect, and his sons were grown men. As for publicity, if there was any, hell's bells, Gil thrived on making headlines.

Harry jerked out of his stupor, realizing that for as long as he'd been lost in his thoughts, Gil had also been silent. "Gil— Gil, you still there?"

"Listen, Harry. I need you to stay in Houston and follow the girl, make sure she's okay on her own. Would you do that for me?"

Harry wanted to get back home, but he owed the man. "Sure, but for how long, Gil? And what am I supposed to be looking for?"

"Just watch her closely and let me know everything she does, will you?"

Harry didn't even have time to answer before the telephone line went dead. He sighed and stood slowly, stiffly, testing his knees before he pushed open the door and hobbled out of the phone booth. Damn, he thought. What was going on? As far as he could see, the case was closed. Harry had a gut feeling of unease. Something wasn't right. He needed a drink—a couple of stiff ones— and time to think. The girl could wait. It wasn't as if she was going anywhere. He knew where to find her.

Dallas, Texas

GILBERT FOLEY hung up the phone before Harry could ask him any more questions, then sat staring at the top of his desk as if he was hypnotized. The past always found its way back to the present, he thought. So far he was okay, but if anything with Deanna changed, he'd have to take steps to remedy the situation.

A bone-deep chill made Gilbert shiver. For comfort, he lifted his gaze to a silver frame on the edge of his desk. Two, tall, handsome boys. His sons. Fortunately they looked like his ex-wife, but they were all his when it came to business and women. Twenty-two and twenty-one, they were smart, sophisticated and hungry.

He'd given each boy his own company to run when they turned eighteen and nineteen respectively, and both had been successful. Gilbert smiled at the photograph on his desk and his eyes darkened with pride. His sons had turned into a pair of corporate sharks. The problem was they'd recently turned on each other in a frenzy of dirty tricks and underhanded deals as each plotted to take over the other's company. Gilbert thought he'd give them room for a while longer, then put a stop to their shenanigans before they caused real harm. God, he was proud of his boys!

He'd been born dirt poor, but with the exception of a few unfortunate episodes, life had been good to him. He was smart, and his mama had raised him to be polite. She'd even stolen a book on manners at the local five-and-dime and taught him from it. All the while his old man had sat across the dinner table, stuffing his face like a pig and belching beer like a locomotive. But he guessed he was a little like his pa, had a tad of the old man's temper, because no one ever crossed him but once.

He'd learned about the oil business at a very early age, and the hard way—in the oil fields, breaking his back and getting his hands dirty. But it hadn't taken him long to realize he had a talent for sniffing out untapped oil, for making deals and talking his way in and out of any situation. Those gifts had taken him far and given him his start, that, and marrying the banker's daughter.

Memories of his family, of the past, brought Gilbert back to the present and the problem of Deanna. He looked around his opulent office, thought about everything he had—the money, private jets, homes in all the right playgrounds, beautiful women at his fingertips, his family—and knew he could lose it all.

He mentally shook off his feelings of doom and gloom like a dog shaking water from his coat. Memories were all very fine and good for him, but if Deanna had memories, she could end up very dead.

THE SECOND MAN to exit the courthouse was tall and thin, a dapper dresser with a full head of dull brown hair just beginning to turn gray at the temples. He was in his late forties and carried himself with military stiffness and confidence as he headed for a door with a nameplate that had as yet to be changed. When he entered the chambers of the deceased Judge Jones, the secretary glanced up from her desk. All the blood drained from her face, leaving her skin a pasty white.

She'd dealt with this man many times before, but mostly over the phone. Now she glanced nervously at the closed door of the new judge's private chambers, then back to the man standing before her. Without a word, she quickly wrote something on a scrap of paper, then pushed it to the edge of the desk, refusing to look up and meet the man's too-knowing eyes. Her heart almost stopped completely when she saw the folded one-hundred-dollar bill being pushed toward her. She snatched the money up, stuffed it in her bra and waited for the sound of the door to close. When it did, her shoulders sagged and she let out a long sigh of relief.

Once outside the courthouse, the man headed for the nearest public telephone. Sidney Sawyer dropped his money into the slot and dialed a series of numbers, then waited for a special dial tone and added another string of numbers. As he listened to the ringing at the other end, he leaned against the phone booth door, wondering when his boss was going to tell him what the hell was going on. For ten years he'd kept tabs on the girl, getting updates on her physical and mental condition and reporting back. Those reports were always verbal, either by telephone on a secure line or face-to-face. He thought he knew why his boss was so obsessed with the girl, but he didn't dare voice it.

There was a loud double click on the telephone line, and Sidney straightened as he heard, "General Fitzpatrick's office."

"Sawyer here," he said.

"Hello, Major."

The sound of that particular female's surly voice on the secure line angered him beyond reason. It was bad enough that the bitch was sleeping with the general, but now she was trying to push *him* out and take over his duties. "Let me speak with him, Betty." There was no question that the general would be in. He'd probably been waiting beside the phone for hours.

There was a long irritating pause, then the deep vibrant voice of General Franklin Concord Fitzpatrick, chairman of the Joint Chiefs of Staff, adviser, right-hand man and personal friend of the president of the United States.

"Sid, son. What's going on down there? I've been waiting for your call for hours."

But not alone, Sidney thought grimly. "Just as we expected, General. This new Judge Harrison's a real stickler."

"I don't give a damn about the judge. Judges can be had one way or the other. What about the girl?"

"She's free and clear of all charges. Gresham didn't show up in court to make any statement, either, but I found out Deanna's been released from his care and left the sanitarium." Sidney grinned when he heard the growl of displeasure on the other end. They never called Deanna by name. The general seemed to have a real aversion to using her name. Instead, he preferred to refer to her as "the girl" or just "she."

"Did the girl make any statement? Did the judge ask her any questions?"

"No, sir." He wondered for the millionth time in ten years why his boss was interested in Deanna Deveraux and her problems. He'd been personal aide to the man ever since he'd made general those ten years ago, and had worked side by side with him on a daily basis at the Pentagon.

It hadn't taken Sid long to realize that the general was going places, and if he was loyal and made himself indispensable, he'd climb that ladder right behind him. He'd also made it his business to know everything, every personal detail, about the man.

Sidney had been in navy intelligence, made a name for himself before the general offered him the position as his aide. He knew all the tricks of the trade and felt confident that there was very little, if anything, about the general's life that slipped by him—except this Deveraux business.

Sidney snapped to attention as he realized the general was speaking. "Sorry, sir. You were saying?"

"Sid, do me a favor, will you? I want you to stay in Houston awhile longer. Check up on the girl, shadow her a little longer. See where she goes. What she does. Who she talks to."

There was a tone in that strong voice Sidney had never heard before, and he was instantly alerted, sensing a weakness in his leader. "I don't see what good I can do, General. Shadow her? What's she supposed to do? What am I looking for? To tell you the truth, sir, I just don't think there's anything else left to do here."

Sidney deliberately let the silence hang between them. For ten years he'd passed cash around to certain parties, including that pompous ass Ernest Gresham, that had added up to a staggering amount. Was it hush money? He thought so, but hush money for what? Or was his boss genuinely concerned about the health and welfare of Deanna Deveraux? And just what did that strange girl with her weird past have to do with the general? Of course, he thought he knew, but he'd never been able to confirm his theory even after years of searching.

"Sid, I'm well aware you know all about the girl's past—what she did all those years ago and why she was confined to an institution." The general cleared his voice, then went on. "She could ruin me—us, Sidney. I need you there, son. I need you to watch the girl closely and let me know if she starts asking questions or looking into her past."

Sidney figured he was gaining on the old man, snapping at his heels, but he wasn't there yet. He also knew he'd pushed as far as he dared for now. The general's dire prediction made his blood run cold. How could a twenty-three-year-old girl destroy a man with the general's power and influence? The thought of his own future in ashes stung like a million bees. He'd do whatever it took to protect the general and his position. "If I'm to help you, sir, you're going to have to tell me what hold Deanna Deveraux has over you."

"Soon, I promise. You'll do this for me, though? You'll stay, Sid?"

"Yes, sir."

"Thank you, son. I won't forget what you've done ... what you're doing."

You bet you won't, Sidney thought, *because I'll never let you.* He hung up and smiled at the pleading note, followed by relief, that had been in the general's voice. A feeling of power rushed through him. He was going to stand beside his boss in the Oval Office of the White House yet.

Washington, D.C.

GENERAL FRANKLIN Concord Fitzpatrick gently put down the telephone and switched off the scrambler. He sat behind his ornate antique desk, and after a couple of seconds of staring blankly, he focused his gaze on the wall lined with photographs. It was a pictorial chronology of his achievements over the past ten years. Photographs of him with foreign dignitaries, with political movers and shakers, some of the most powerful and richest men in the world. There were more than ten pictures of him with his boss and close friend, the president of the United States. It was rumored that when the president's term was up, the vice president wasn't going to run for office. Rumors were as reliable as the gospel in Washington, and the mill was abuzz with talk that the president was going to endorse his good friend, General Fitzpatrick, for the presidency.

Goose bumps sprouted from his skin and he almost shivered in anticipation. President Franklin Concord

Fitzpatrick. The very thought was as satisfying as sex—almost. A small surge of guilt swept over him as his gaze settled on the silver-framed photograph at the corner of his desk. His wife and son stared back at him, as expressionless as they were in real life.

He'd made a good marriage. His wife was a Jefferson, of the New York Jeffersons. Barons of industry. Estates in Virginia and on the banks of the Hudson. They were a family of both wealth and fine lineage. Franklin thought back to his first meeting with Alice's grandmother. The memory still managed to bring a smug smile. The old matriarch thought she'd put him in his place by dragging out the Jefferson-family history and slapping him in the face with it. She'd snootily told him her husband's family had come over on the *Mayflower* in 1620. To hear her tell it, you'd have thought the Jeffersons had single-handedly colonized the Americas.

Franklin remembered nodding to show his appreciation, then watching gleefully as he told her that the Fitzpatricks had been in Virginia some fifteen years earlier, since 1605 actually, even before the Royal Jamestown Charter. He'd told her that his mother was a leader of several prestigious family-lineage organizations—here he had the old bitch, because his mother had made it her business to know just what organizations the Jeffersons were involved in and which ones had turned them down.

With absolute delight and with as straight a face as he could manage, he'd told her that his mother was of the royal Stuart line, but it was through the Fitzpatricks that they claimed their membership to Americans of Royal Descent, Signers of the Magna Carta and Descendants of Charlemagne. That had shut the old gal up and brought a glimmer of respect to her rheumy eyes.

Franklin remembered the silent prayer of thanks he'd sent his mother, grateful for the first time in his life for her obsessive interest in genealogy. He was sure it had been the deciding factor for the family's stamp of approval when he asked Alice to marry him. The Fitzpatricks weren't as rich as the Jeffersons—few people in America were—but the firstborn Fitzpatrick men had all been in the military service and distinguished themselves for their country, even in the American Revolution.

Franklin studied the photograph of his wife and son again, and the bitter bile of disappointment filled his mouth. His son, Henry Jefferson Fitzpatrick, was twenty-one, a lazy bum with no ambition other than to paint, visit museums and hang on to his mother's apron strings. He'd given up long ago on Henry.

As much as he'd have loved to divorce his cold fish of a wife, he knew he never could. No taint of scandal must touch his life or reputation. He'd worked too hard covering the past and getting where he was today to turn back. Now that his goal was within reach, no one—*no one*—was going to ruin his chances.

DEANNA AND CLAY had walked about two blocks before she realized that not only was she still holding on to Clay's hand, she hadn't heard a word he'd said to her. She halted abruptly. "I'm sorry. It's just... I'm so..."

"Happy?" Clay asked. She was totally uninhibited in her happiness. Her eyes sparkled. Her smile was wide and genuine—and damn contagious. She seemed to bounce along beside him, her hand firmly in his and her hair blowing freely in all directions. Suddenly Clay realized he didn't want to end this time with her. He glanced at his watch. "How about an early lunch?" In the back of his mind he was already planning which restaurant to take her to. There'd be a nice secluded table, softly lighted, and a chilled bottle of wine. A quiet place where they could talk.

All of a sudden Deanna felt panicky. A public restaurant. She glanced around frantically, then forced herself to calm down. It wasn't as if she'd never eaten away from Twelve Oaks, or that her table manners weren't impeccable. It was just that Mary had always been with her, and they'd had tons of things to talk about. What could she possibly have to say to Clayton Lambert that would interest him? Then she decided, what the hell. He was a lawyer like his grandfather, and she'd always got along well with the senior Mr. Lambert. Besides, he'd probably do all the talking, anyway.

That faint childhood memory of lunching downtown with her mother drifted through her mind. She didn't think the lunch counter at Woolworth's was a regular eatery of Clay's, but there was one other place her mother had taken her. "Is James Coney Island still open?" she asked, then immediately regretted it. He looked shocked and surprised, then his expression melted into a wide smile, as if she'd just made his day.

"You're sure you want a hot dog?"

Deanna laughed. "Yes. With lots of cheese, onions and relish and absolutely sloppy with chili. I haven't had a good hot dog...in years." She'd been about to say, "Since I was a child and Mother and I used to eat there," but caught herself. In her excitement she'd almost slipped up about the return of her memory and reminded herself to be more careful in the future. Then she noticed Clay's rather quizzical look and said, "I wasn't locked away in a padded cell, you know. We did get outings at the sanitarium."

At that moment Clay wished the ground would open up and swallow him whole. "I wasn't thinking that," he lied.

"Sure you were, but it's okay."

Her straightforward manner confused him, threw him off-balance. When the traffic light turned and they started across the street, Clay thought fast for a way to change the subject. "Do you want to head back to the office and get my car," he asked, "or are you willing to walk a couple of blocks in the heat?"

"Let's walk." She wanted to look at everything at once, to experience this new gift of freedom, but she knew she'd have to put a damper on her enthusiasm to keep from appearing the total bumpkin. A silence settled between them as they strolled down the street, and Deanna took advantage of it to gaze around her. She tried hard to keep up with Clay but was constantly slowing down, checking the displays in the store windows, judging the fashions there.

After a while Clay chuckled and suggested that maybe they should skip lunch altogether and go shopping, instead. He watched with delight as Deanna's color heightened, staining her freckled cheeks with two spots of bright red. He couldn't help laughing out loud at her embarrassment.

James Coney Island was a hole-in-the-wall sort of restaurant that literally packed the lunch crowd in, and though no one in the establishment would ever hurry you along, it was an unspoken law that you ate your lunch and left immediately. There was no lingering over a cigarette or enjoying long conversations. They served the best hot dogs in Texas, and you were likely to share a table or sit at one of the old school desks lining the wall with construction workers, the cream of Houston society, the mayor or even the governor when he was in town.

Except for people giving their orders, the room was relatively quiet as everyone went about the business of eating lunch. Clay studied Deanna closely, and the more he saw, the more he wanted to know. He promised himself that as soon as he returned to the office he was going to cancel his appointments for the rest of the day and read the Deveraux files.

Deanna felt his gaze on her and looked up, wiped the last vestige of mustard and chili from the corners of her mouth and stared back. "Why don't you just ask me what you're wondering?"

Clay wadded up the soiled paper napkin, tucked it under the edge of the basket the food had come in and stood up. He held Deanna's chair while she rose, then escorted her out of the restaurant. "Listen, Deanna. There are probably a thousand questions I'll ask you, but not until I read my grandfather's files." They walked down the sidewalk, the sun hot on their heads. "That is, if you still want the firm to represent your interests."

"Can you?" she asked. "I mean, your grandfather told me most of the firm's clients were either criminal or divorce cases."

Clay laughed, remembering his grandfather's sour grumbling over the state of affairs and the morals of the younger generation. "Grandfather was of the old school. He believed children should been seen and not heard. He was appalled at the war protesters, the violence, the sexual freedom of the flower children, the whole 'Make love, not war' generation. He believed we were all going to hell. I can remember him looking over his half glasses at me and in that deep voice filled with disgust saying—"

"What goes around, comes around," Deanna finished for him. "Mr. Lambert used to say I was the lucky one to be where I was, protected from the ugliness that was happening. When he visited me, we talked for hours. He said the world had gone crazy."

Clay felt strange listening to a stranger quote his grandfather. Then he reminded himself that Deanna probably had had longer conversations with his grandfather than he'd had. He felt suddenly ashamed that in the last couple of years he'd become so wrapped up in his own life, in day-to-day living, that he'd neglected the one person he truly loved.

"Mr. Lambert was very proud of you, you know."

"What?" They were close to the office. Clay stopped and pulled Deanna out of the crush of people. "What did you say?"

"Mr. Lambert loved you very much. He talked about you all the time. How you'd done your duty to your country and gone to Vietnam even though you were against the war. He told me, as proud of you as he was, he wished you'd run off to Canada, because you came back changed, you had suffered too much."

Clay didn't know what to say or if he could say anything, even if he wanted to. To know that one person in his family had realized what the war had done to him, how it had changed him forever. For three years he'd built a wall around himself to keep the daily horrors at bay. That wall had never completely come down. The fact that his grandfather had recognized his pain caused a lump in his throat. He grabbed Deanna's arm and started off at a trot across the street.

"I'm sorry," she said rather breathlessly as he practically dragged her along behind him.

Clay stopped abruptly. He didn't want her to know how moved he had been by what she'd said. "What the hell are you sorry about?" he growled as he opened the door to the office building, scowling down at her as she walked past him.

"I'm sorry you had to go to Vietnam," she said softly as her shoulder brushed his chest. She stopped and gazed up at him. "Sorry when you came home they spit on you. Sorry you had to endure so much."

"You watch too much television."

"Actually I didn't. Dr. Gresham carefully supervised what we saw. He thought the evening news coverage of the war was too gruesome. Mostly I read newspapers and magazines that his assistant, Mary, slipped me. One way or another, I managed to keep up with what was happening."

Clay suddenly realized just how isolated Deanna had been, and yet she recognized the shame and anger he'd felt when he'd come home. Those who'd sent him off with proud cheers had welcomed him home with either bitter recriminations or, like his family, with silence.

Clay was struggling to express how moved he was when Deanna smiled sweetly at him and said, "I need a taxi. Could you call me one?"

"Sure. You're a taxi." The joke was so old, so childishly stupid, that they both started laughing. When he recovered sufficiently to speak, he said, "If you don't mind getting your hair blown, I'll drive you wherever you need to go."

Deanna soon discovered the reason for the strange question concerning her hair. Clay owned a brand-new, fire-engine red Corvette convertible. He stood there with a silly grin, glancing from the car to her, obviously waiting for her reaction. With a female instinct she hadn't known she possessed, she started professing awe and admiration for a car she knew absolutely nothing about. From Clay's goofy grin she was sure she'd done the right thing, though. Just wait, Deanna thought. Just wait till she told Mary she'd become a gushing female.

She wondered what else she might have said but was stopped from making a complete fool of herself by the sound of footsteps echoing in the parking garage. Suddenly there was a chill in the air and she shivered. In the nightmare of her memories, she'd heard footsteps.

Deanna turned as the sounds came closer. With a gasp she shouted, "William!" then ran toward the tall black man, whose hair was white, whose walk was slower, but whose smile was as wide and friendly as she remembered.

"Miss Deanna." He hugged the small woman, then realized that Clay was watching and stepped back. "I heard you was free."

Deanna sensed William's stiffness and glared at Clay. "William drove your grandfather to Twelve Oaks. He taught me to drive."

Clay shook the man's hand and laughed. "William and I know each other. But please don't tell me he taught you to drive in Grandfather's limousine?"

William grinned. "To tell you the truth, Mr. Clay, I lived in fear she'd take my job, she was that good at maneuvering that tank around the place."

Deanna didn't want to talk about cars or driving. She wanted to know how he was. And how his wife and their seven children were. Clay stepped back and let them reminisce, but not so far away that he was totally excluded from their conversation.

"What are you doing now that Mr. Lambert's gone?" she asked William. For the first time she noticed he was wearing a different uniform than the one he wore as a chauffeur.

"The firm's kept me on as security guard. Now don't go saying nothing bad. I get to sit almost all the time in that nice cool lobby." He chuckled. "And don't go turning your nose up, either. The decorating kinda grows on you."

"What's wrong with our lobby?" Clay demanded to know, all the while trying to keep a straight face. It was a running joke between him and William.

Deanna shuddered with distaste and both men laughed. Then Clay clasped her arm. "We'd better go, Deanna. I need to do some work this afternoon." He made a mental note to meet with William later for a long talk.

Deanna agreed, but before she could be pulled away, she gave William her phone number at Mary's with instructions for him to call her so they could chat.

CHAPTER FOUR

DEANNA STOOD at the picture window, the curtains pulled back, like a brazen Peeping Tom as she waited for Clay to back out of Mary's driveway. She stood there, watching, until his car was out of sight, then sighed and turned around. "Did you see him? Did you get a good look?"

"Yes," Mary said.

"Isn't he pretty, Mary?"

"Men are handsome, not pretty." Mary laughed as she pried the crushed material from Deanna's fingers and tried to straighten it out.

"Yes, but handsome doesn't seem to fit. How about beautiful?" She grinned at her friend, her eyes sparkling. "And did you see his car?" Deanna tried again to smooth her wind-tangled hair. "I want one just like it. Oh, Mary, you should see his smile!"

Mary wheezed in reply, then glanced at Deanna. She blinked her watery eyes a couple of times to make sure she wasn't seeing things. But there was no mistaking the glazed look on the girl's face, a look that cut her amusement dead. If anyone knew how sheltered Deanna had been, it was Mary. She began to wonder just how much she'd taken on. "Maybe we should have another birds-and-bees discussion?"

"What?" The question jolted Deanna out of her happy daze. "Don't be ridiculous."

"I'm serious." Mary motioned Deanna away from the window and toward the couch. "I'm talking about...you know."

Sometimes the age difference between them gaped wide. Deanna feigned a shocked expression and whispered, "The dirty deed? It? A roll in the hay? Oh, that dreaded word—*sex*. Mary, Mary, this is the seventies, and I might have been locked away for ten years, but even I know what's going on. The pill has given women their sexual freedom and the right to openly say the word S-E-X without whispering behind their hands or glancing over their shoulders." Deanna laughed, but when she realized Mary was serious, she sat down, straight-faced. "Mary, I'm twenty-three years old, you know, and it's not as if I've never been kissed."

Now it was Mary's turn to be struck speechless. She dropped like a stone into the chair across from Deanna and was overtaken by a fit of coughing. When she could finally speak again, she asked, "Are you telling me you've had sex? How? When? And for God's sake, with whom?"

Deanna loved to tease Mary, but she'd gone a little too far with her joke this time. Mary was the only person who truly cared for her. "Not sex, Mary. But I've been kissed. As a matter of fact, I was getting quite good at it." Even with Mary's red and puffy eyes, Deanna could tell that her friend was horrified and confused. "Come on, you remember Ned Durrand, don't you?"

Mary closed her eyes and blew her nose. "I wish I didn't. Please don't tell me you let that despicable boy touch you."

"Kiss, Mary. He taught me how to kiss." The look of distaste she received shook Deanna. Mary had come through the sixties, the era of flower children and free love, surprisingly straitlaced. She was appalled at the indiscriminate sex and use of drugs of Deanna's peers.

Mary didn't like Ned, either. Actually no one cared much for him but Deanna. He was good-looking, charming, rich, and his parents had spoiled him into thinking that anything was his for the taking. He took too much, though—too many drugs, too much alcohol and too many girls. Finally, in utter despair, he tried to take his life. A judge committed Ned to six months at Twelve Oaks. After two weeks, everyone there believed the judge had condemned them to six months of pure hell.

"You know very well, Mary, that once Ned was clean and sober and bored, he began looking around for some amusement. I guess he heard about me from one of the nurses he'd charmed. Actually I think he set out to cause more mischief, but after we talked awhile we became friends. He opened up, told me all about his family life. I felt sorry for him, you know. His parents didn't care a fig for him. They were too wrapped up in each other to share their feelings with anyone else. I told him I didn't think *he* had a problem, his parents did, and if he was as smart as I thought he was, he'd wise up, stop acting like a spoiled brat and do something constructive with his life."

Mary stared at her for a long moment. "You told him that, did you, Dr. Deveraux? And what did he say?"

"He was his usual belligerent self—for a while. Then we were friends again and he changed. Really he did, Mary, and that's when he taught me how to kiss and was willing to answer my questions. We were just friends. You needn't look at me like that. We kissed, yes, but just *talked* about sex."

Mary buried her face in her hands. "And that's who you obtained your great kissing experience and knowledge of sex from—a nineteen-year-old boy?"

It took a minute for Deanna to realize that Mary was trying to hide her smile. "Ah, but you forget—a very experienced boy," Deanna laughingly told her. "Besides, nineteen or forty, how old do you have to be to be a great smoocher? That sort of thing kinda comes naturally, doesn't it? Of course, I don't have anyone to compare him with. But I'll bet Clayton Lambert could make my toes tingle. That's supposed to be a good sign, isn't it?"

Mary nodded and decided it was best to change the subject before Deanna launched into one of her intense questioning sessions. She steered the conversation back to the day's events. "You said Dr. Gresham wasn't in court?"

"No, and I thought for sure he'd be there."

Mary blew her nose and tossed the used tissue in the wastebasket, then took a long swallow of water, all the while thinking about a small item tucked away in a box in the top of her closet.

Deanna realized she was sitting on Mary's makeshift bed and jumped up, helped Mary out of her chair and back to the couch. She made her lie down, tucked her under a pile of quilts, refilled her glass of water, then sat down on the edge of the coffee table and proceeded to relate every detail of her day.

"I'm sorry to hear about Mr. Lambert. He was a good man, Deanna, and he thought the world of you. Are you okay?"

"I think so. I can't cry for him yet. Maybe it'll sink in later, but I know I'll miss him dreadfully, Mary. Did I tell you I saw William?"

They talked for a while more, then Deanna picked up the portion of the morning newspaper she'd been studying before she left for court. The classified-advertising section. It was a dismal feeling to realize that Dr. Gresham had been right when he'd said the only jobs available for a woman were secretarial or bookkeeping. She hadn't found one ad that professed a need for an artist, dress designer or seamstress. The thought of sitting behind a typewriter, taking orders, making coffee and generally being a servant made her feel ill.

"I have to find a job, Mary," she said, desperation in her voice. "But even if I was qualified and wanted to be a bookkeeper or secretary, who'd hire me once they learn who I am or where I've lived for the past ten years? What if I never get a job? Do you realize you could be stuck with me for a long time?"

Mary reached over and pulled the crumpled newspaper from Deanna's grip. "You're worrying yourself into a fever. Stop it! You know you're welcome here as long as you like. As for a job, we'll find you one." But she wasn't so sure. What Deanna said was true. Any prospective employer was sure to do a background check, and that would end her chance of being hired.

"But, Mary, I can't mooch off you. I need to pay rent while I'm here. Where am I going to get that kind of money?" Mary was quiet for so long that Deanna thought she'd dropped off to sleep. She quietly stood up and was about to slip away to her room and do some deep thinking when her slumbering friend came alive.

"What about the money for the sanitarium?" Mary demanded.

"What do you mean?"

"Deanna, keeping you at that place cost an arm and a leg. I know the monthly checks were always signed by Mr.

Lambert, but where'd the money come from originally?"

"I have no idea." Deanna perched on the edge of the coffee table again. "I asked Dr. Gresham about my financial situation a couple of times, and he told me all I needed to worry about was getting well, not money. I even asked Mr. Lambert, but he said I wasn't to worry my pretty head, that everything was taken care of. Why do men do that, Mary, treat us like we don't have a brain?"

"Probably because it makes them feel good."

"Maybe. But I wish someone had told me something."

"Wait a minute, wait a minute," Mary said. She scooted up to a sitting position, which brought on another coughing fit. When it subsided, she continued, "It seems I remember something Dr. Gresham said about your owning part of your grandmother's dress shop."

"Fleur's."

"Mmm, yes." Mary jumped when Deanna quickly stood up. "Where're you going? What's wrong?"

With her back to Mary, Deanna closed her eyes, took a deep breath, forced a smile, then turned around. "You're exhausted and I'm worn out myself. I think I'll go lie down." She left the room with a puzzled Mary staring after her. But she couldn't help it. Merely hearing the name Fleur's brought back all the memories and pain.

She'd allowed herself to live in a different world all afternoon. It was so wonderful to pretend to be normal. She'd let her imagination run away with her. But now came a deep foreboding, fueled by a sense of self-preservation, a feeling that she couldn't trust anyone, not even Mary, until she learned why she was convicted for a crime she didn't commit. The seriousness of her situation struck her anew.

Deanna quietly but firmly shut her bedroom door, dodged the boxes in her path and flopped down on the bed. She rolled over onto her back and stared at the ceiling. Only fools lived in a dreamworld, and she couldn't afford the luxury of being a fool right now. It was time to reflect on her newly recovered memories, to examine the past.

But where to start? A home of warmth and laughter? A soft voice filled with love? No. Although she wanted, needed, to remember her mother, to think of every loving detail she could, she was skirting the real issue—which was what happened ten years ago.

Those ten years seemed both like a lifetime ago and only yesterday. The memories felt like those of someone else's life, memories of a child of thirteen who was forced to live with a grandmother she respected, but disliked and feared.

She remembered waking up sick with the flu one particular morning. Her grandmother, Agatha Fleur Deveraux, had become angry and agitated because she had to stay home from school. Agatha had given her some of her own medicine, something to make her sleep.

Everything had become fuzzy after she'd taken the pills. She lost track of time, and when she opened her eyes, the room spun, as if she were riding a twirling top. Her throat was dry. She was thirsty and sick, and wanted someone to hold her even if it was her grandmother. Getting to her feet and walking was another matter, but she'd finally managed to crawl to the door.

Deanna saw herself clearly in her mind's eye. Envisioned herself as that sick child and wanted to cry. She'd been alone and lonely ever since her mother had died when she was eleven. Her grandmother didn't love her, she knew that, and the old lady definitely didn't want a child to raise when running her business was the one burning desire in her life.

She remembered hearing voices, shouting, arguing, and though she could hear them, she couldn't understand what was being said. The stairway landing was her refuge, and she reached it with her last spurt of strength. The voices sounded louder there, but as hard as she tried, she still couldn't understand.

One of those voices was a man's, filled with rage and threats. Her grandmother's voice was raised, also. Oh, she knew that loud accented voice, a voice that could cut her off in midsentence, cut her dead with words of contempt. But there was something strange in her grandmother's voice this time. It took a few minutes for her to realize it was fear she was hearing.

Suddenly the voices came closer, louder. Something evil moved with them, changing the very air around her. Deanna remembered cringing and shoving herself into a corner on the landing, trying to get as far away as possible from the noise of footsteps on the hardwood floor. It was dark and cold and safe there in the deep shadows. She was scared and sick, her head hurt, and she was burning up inside.

She didn't want to hear the voices anymore, couldn't stand to hear her grandmother's fright and the cry of pain. She wanted the voices to stop and covered her ears to block them out. It was a long time before she lowered her hands. The grandfather clock was chiming and the house was still.

Deanna realized after all these years that she must have fallen asleep on the landing. She remembered waking, stiff and cold. Her head had ached dreadfully and she was so thirsty. She'd made her way down the rest of the stairs, holding on to the banister. It was at the bottom, just as she was turning toward the kitchen, that something in the living room caught her eye. Her grandmother was lying on her back, unmoving, silent.

On legs that wobbled and threatened to collapse, Deanna made her way to her grandmother's side. Dropping to her knees, she gently shook the thin shoulders. Her hand felt wet and she held it up before her eyes. For what seemed forever, she stared at the smear of bright red, then glanced back down at her grandmother and realized that her chest was covered with the same color.

In her fevered and drugged state, everything had taken longer to sink in, and it wasn't until she'd picked up the butcher knife beside her grandmother that she realized what was wrong. Agatha Fleur Deveraux was dead. In shock at the sudden realization that everyone she cared about was gone and that she was alone, she'd gathered the limp body in her arms and rocked back and forth, screaming her grandmother's name.

Deanna opened her eyes. Those were the last memories she had of that day. She would have cried for that thirteen-year-old girl, cried for her grandmother, but she couldn't. She'd been an emotional child back then, and it had cost her her sanity for ten years. Now she had to be stronger and wiser. She had to learn the identity of the man who'd killed her grandmother, who'd let her take the blame and lose so many years of her life.

Where to start?

The killer had known her grandmother personally, that much was apparent. Was he still alive? Did he know she was free? Was she a threat to him? Deanna realized that, before she could find the answers to her questions, she had to know everything there was to know about that day ten years ago. She had to know everything that had happened to her back then. A private detective would be helpful, a professional, but she didn't have the money to pay one. Nor was she sure she wanted to divulge what she knew to anyone just yet.

She was going to have to do it on her own. Maybe the best place to start was with the newspaper accounts from ten years ago. That meant a trip to the public library. And that created another problem. What would she tell Mary? She didn't want to lie to her, but she wasn't ready to confide in her, either.

Deanna sat up, swung her legs over the side of the bed and stood. She slipped out of her wrinkled dress and into a robe, then walked over to the window. The afternoon was fading, and Mary's backyard was a haven of cool shade and shadows. It was a time of day Deanna usually found soothing, but she was afraid she wasn't going to find any peace of mind until all her questions were answered.

She turned away from the window, scanned the piles of boxes and unpacked luggage in her bedroom and frowned. Her sketch pad was buried somewhere underneath the mess, but she wasn't in any mood to draw, either. With a sigh she left the bedroom before she lost her nerve. The lies she was about to tell Mary rode heavily on her shoulders.

Mary looked as if she was sleeping. Guilt almost convinced Deanna she should wait, let her friend rest, but then Mary opened her eyes and smiled.

"Deanna, you okay?" Mary grabbed a tissue and sneezed. "I didn't know that mentioning Fleur's would be so painful for you."

Deanna shrugged and lied. "I don't know why, but every time I hear that name it gives me the willies. Like

someone running their fingernails down a chalkboard."
She now knew why. Fleur's had been her grandmother's
dress shop, her dream and her life, and the woman had
never let Deanna forget that the shop was what sup-
ported her. Even at thirteen Deanna had worked there,
listening to that voice, so gracious with her customers, yet
full of barely suppressed anger with her granddaughter.

Once again, Deanna made herself comfortable on the
edge of the coffee table. "Mary, what would you say if I
told you I wanted to find out about Agatha's murder?"

Mary sniffed. "I'd say it's about time."

"Would you?"

"Indeed, yes. For too many years you've taken Dr.
Gresham's word, and everyone else's, about it. I think
you need to find out for yourself. Maybe doing so will
help you remember something." She pushed herself up
into a sitting position. "Just as soon as I get over this
damn cold, we'll start looking."

The weight of the guilt on Deanna's shoulders was
getting heavier. Mary, being Mary, wanted nothing more
than to help her. "I'm going to the library tomorrow,
Mary." She hurried on before her friend could say anything else. "Please. This is something I want—have to do
on my own."

A silence settled around them, broken only by an occasional sniff and cough from Mary. Deanna was sure
she'd hurt her friend's feelings and was surprised at the
answer she got.

"You're right to want to do it on your own. It's time
you started standing on your own two feet." She smiled
at Deanna. "And if I sometimes treat you like you're still
thirteen, you'll just have to overlook it." She reached out
and patted Deanna's clenched fist. "You're like a

daughter to me, Deanna. Please don't forget that you can talk to me, tell me anything, and I won't judge you.''

Oh, God. She didn't think she could feel any worse than she did at that moment. Mary deserved to know that she'd remembered everything. She decided then and there that she would tell her as soon as she found out all she could about that horrible day ten years ago.

Mary was frowning. "How are you going to get downtown? I'd let you take my car if you had your license. Your research will take a couple of days, and taxis are damn expensive.'' She sighed, leaned back and closed her eyes. ''Of course, you can always take the bus. Not the fanciest of transportation, slow and hot as hell this time of year.'' She glanced at Deanna, sitting so attentively beside her, waiting to be told what to do. ''I guess you'd better decide, hadn't you?''

Deanna smiled gratefully. ''I still have about three hundred dollars of the money you paid me, so I'll go by taxi.''

Mary nodded. "That's one of the reasons I would never want you to pay me rent. All those beautiful clothes in my closet that you designed and made for me. They're worth a fortune, you know. I've always felt guilty that you've never allowed me to pay you more than a pittance of what they're worth.''

''It was enough, really, Mary. Besides, if Dr. Gresham found out I was making a living designing clothes, he'd have had a heart attack.'' She'd sewn not only for Mary but for a few of the other nurses, and the doctor never discovered she had her own bank account.

''I still feel badly,'' Mary protested.

''Well, you shouldn't. You were the only one who was willing to take my advice and buy the best material and notions. I was proudest of what I made for you.''

Mary's sniffles, this time, had nothing to do with her cold. "Okay. You're going to the library tomorrow. Do you have any idea where to start looking for information on your grandmother's death?"

Deanna began to map out her plans for Mary, but it wasn't long before the cold medication she'd taken started to work and the older woman fell sound asleep. Her light snoring didn't bother Deanna at all, and she continued to outline her plans. Speaking them aloud only seemed to cement her determination.

CLAY SAT among the mountain of papers stacked on his desk. He'd read and reread the transcripts of Deanna's trial until he thought his eyeballs would fall out of his head. This case was the worst miscarriage of justice he'd ever seen. The state's prosecutor was a joke, and his statements were often led by Judge Jones. He could see that his grandfather and the young lawyer who'd helped him had done an adequate job, but something sinister was going on behind the scenes, Clay was sure of that. Every motion his grandfather made was overruled. The trial, which should have been delayed because of the physical and mental state of the accused, was held only one month after the murder of Agatha Fleur Deveraux. The law might state entitlement to a speedy trial, but lawyers were notorious for dragging their feet, either to let things cool off or to use the news media to sway public opinion.

The whole case was a classic example of railroading. Someone had been manipulating the law to fit their own means. That thirteen-year-old girl hadn't had a snowball's chance in hell. But why? If she was indeed guilty of murder, this travesty of a trial had been to her benefit. But if she wasn't guilty...

Clay stood up and stretched to get the kinks out. He glanced at the stack of file boxes he'd brought from his grandfather's office and sighed. What bothered him most was why his grandfather had defended Deanna in the first place. If he'd wanted the firm to keep the case, as he obviously had, then why hadn't he turned it over to someone more competent? His grandfather had been a tax attorney, not a criminal lawyer.

Clay couldn't remember the old man talking about the case, either, which wasn't at all like him. As far as he could recollect, his own thoughts at the time weren't geared to much more than women and law school, women and parties, and then Vietnam.

He rubbed his eyes and the back of his neck and stared out the window. It was beginning to get dark. He was tired, but he felt a driving urge to keep at this. His grandfather hadn't fought all those years to get Deanna free if he hadn't believed in her. He glanced down at his notes and the disheartening short list of people who were involved in the Deveraux case. Most were officials who'd probably retired and moved away. But there was one name that kept popping up in his mind—Bob Spencer—and he couldn't figure out why.

Something clicked in Clay's head. He squatted beside a cardboard box marked Deveraux, then began rummaging frantically through it until he found the stack of invoices he'd been looking for. He flipped through them, then grinned when he found what he wanted. A copy of a bill from a company called Spencer Incorporated for six hundred dollars—ten hours of investigation at sixty dollars an hour. Clay had seen enough of this type of bill to know without a doubt that Spencer Incorporated was a private-detective firm. What intrigued him was that the last invoice was dated three weeks before his grandfather's death.

Without thinking, Clay dialed the phone number on the invoice, but after a few rings realized the place was probably closed for the day. He was just about to hang up when a deep voice growled an irritated hello. Clay explained who he was and started to say why he was calling when he was interrupted.

"Heard about your grandfather. Sorry for your loss. You know he was convinced Deanna was innocent, don't you? Hired me to help him prove it. That and the fact that Judge Jones was being paid off to keep her locked away. Your grandfather knew the judge was dirty and was sure His Honor also knew who the killer was and was being paid to protect him. So he tipped off the feds—put a little bug in their ear about checking the judge's finances for the past decade.

"The problem was, my hands were pretty much tied as far as interviewing certain parties. I couldn't question the doctor out at the sanitarium or the judge. Mr. Lambert was careful how big a stick he used to stir the hornet's nest. He was always afraid for Deanna. That's why he was forever just dropping in at the sanitarium—odd days, odd times. He thought the doctor out there and the judge were just a little too friendly. But now that the judge's croaked and our little lady's free, don't think it's over."

It was as if bombs were being dropped all around him. Clay felt shell-shocked, flinching each time the detective told him something new. The last volley brought Clay to full attention, and he sat upright in his chair. "For God's sake, Spencer, what are you talking about?"

"Why, money. The good judge's bank account—his portfolio, if you like—was bulging with blue-chip investments made in the past ten years. A judge's salary doesn't lend itself to those sorts of investments. Someone was paying him big bucks, Lambert. Think, man. An old woman was murdered. A thirteen-year-old, who was catatonic and couldn't begin to defend herself, was tried and convicted for murder, found insane and committed to a mental institution.

"By the way, did you know that Judge Jones originally committed Deanna to the state mental hospital up at Rusk, Texas? She probably wouldn't have survived two months there. It took your grandfather four weeks of daily petitioning the court, badgering and finally threatening the judge to obtain a transfer to Twelve Oaks Valley Sanitarium.

"The point I'm trying to make, Lambert, is the judge and whoever was behind him worked hard and paid out a lot of money over the years to keep Deanna where she was. Now the girl's free, and whoever was working behind the scenes doesn't have the inside track anymore. Say Deanna gets her memory back and remembers who murdered her grandmother. Put yourself in his shoes. What would you do?"

"You're saying Deanna's life is in danger?" Clay felt as if someone had just punched him in the gut. He sagged in his chair.

"I'm saying it could be. Then again maybe not. After ten years she's never regained her memory. What're the odds she ever will? You know, it must have been a real shock for whoever was paying off the judge to find out that the girl probably has as much or maybe more money than he did. Your grandfather was too honest a man to use her money to grease palms."

Clay's head hurt. Deanna's money? He didn't have the faintest idea what the detective was talking about, and the strangled sound he made must have alerted the other man.

"You don't know much, do you, Counselor? Your client's one very rich lady. Mr. Lambert personally supervised all the investments, watched over everything. He was convinced someday he'd get Deanna out of that place, and he wanted to make sure she'd never have to work, that her life would always be financially secure. So what now?"

"What now what? How the hell do I know? I've just taken over the case. My office is full of Grandfather's files. I've only had time to go over the trial transcripts." As Clay talked, he glanced down at the notes he'd made after reading the transcripts. There was a list, short as it was, of the people who'd testified at the trial. About five names down was Detective Robert Spencer, HPD.

"Wait a minute. Spencer, were you with the Houston Police Department ten years ago?"

"Yeah, and it's a long story. I'll tell you about it when we get together and discuss what we're going to do. You do want to know who was behind the judge, don't you?"

"Damn right I do. So you're still interested in working on the case?"

"Hell, man, I've been on this case one way or the other for ten years. When do you want to get together?"

Clay glanced at the four file boxes stacked against one wall. "Make it tomorrow. Lunch. Here. We'll have time to talk."

After he hung up, Clay threaded his fingers through his hair. He was dead-dog tired and would have called it a day if not for a thought that kept running around in his head. His grandfather, even with his health failing, had never given up the fight to free Deanna. Now that was done, but he didn't believe his grandfather would have stopped there. He would have wanted the true culprit to pay, not only for the murder of an old lady but for the conspiracy to keep Deanna locked away.

Clay agreed with his grandfather. He intended to pick up the investigation. There was only one problem—his very determination might backfire. He could be setting the wheels in motion to do away with the one person he was trying to protect.

CHAPTER FIVE

PANIC SET IN the moment Deanna stepped through the doors of the public library. The place was intimidating, cavernous and cold with the subtle scent of old books and wood polish. She wanted nothing more than to turn and run. Instead, she forced herself to move forward to the nearest table and chair.

A clammy chill settled over her. What she needed was a rest room where she could lock the stall door and have a long talk with herself. She was free, she told herself, and if she continued to be terrified of every little thing, she was going to be spending half her life in rest rooms. It wasn't a particularly appealing thought.

After a couple of calming breaths, she felt her heartbeat return to normal. She began to study her surroundings, the people at the table where she was sitting, those around her. She took particular care to watch and figure out how the system worked, and tried to think of a story to cover her ignorance. The librarians looked friendly and more than helpful, as they answered questions and checked books in and out. They even led people down aisles to find what they wanted.

Feeling somewhat calmer, she got up and approached the long desk. She ignored the nice-looking man and with a sweet smile approached the stern-faced older woman. "Good morning," she whispered. "I wonder if you could help me, please?"

Deanna watched the frowning expression settle into stony acceptance and wavered in her choice. But she remembered what her mother had once told her: you catch more flies with honey than with vinegar.

Deanna's smile widened. "I'm from out of town," she began, which wasn't exactly a lie, "and not familiar with the library—" She didn't get to finish.

"What are you looking for?" the woman demanded, her attention on the small group of teenagers seated at a nearby table. "Have you checked the file catalog?" she asked.

This was going to be a hard nut to crack. Deanna figured the truth might be the ticket. She glanced around, then whispered, "To be honest, I don't have the foggiest idea where to start." That brought the librarian's full attention back, and Deanna even received a tight smile. "I need to find two Houston newspapers, about ten years back—say, 1966. Is that possible?"

"Of course." The librarian shot another disapproving glance at the group of teenagers, whispered something to one of her co-workers, then moved quickly out from behind the desk. She grasped Deanna's arm and guided her up the stairs to the secluded area of the reference section on the second floor, all the while giving instructions. "The local newspapers are on microfilm. I'll show you how to look up what you want and how to load the machine, then you're on your own. If you want copies, make a note of the number on the top of the film and bring me the roll and the numbers and we'll make you a photocopy."

Deanna listened carefully as the woman rattled off her instructions like a drill sergeant with a raw recruit. She doubted she'd remember half of what the woman said, but nodded as if the librarian's words had been engraved on her mind. Once she was left alone with the spool of microfilm in her hand, the reality of what she was about to read hit her. All the details would be there, she thought, but not the truth.

She was more adept at listening and following directions under stressful situations than she'd thought. And it didn't hurt that the instructions were clearly diagramed on the machine. After a few tries she got the hang of the controls and began looking for dates to guide her. When she reached November 1966, she slowed her search down. The days clicked by, and suddenly she came across the date she was looking for. She closed her eyes a second.

Thirteen-Year-Old Girl Stabs Grandmother to Death was the headline on the evening edition. She scrolled down to the next day's morning paper, which was even more gruesome: In a Drugged Frenzy, Teenager Slashes Grandmother to Death.

Deanna felt sick. If this was just the headline, what would the rest of the piece say? She wondered if she could continue. But the thought that someone had killed her grandmother and let her take the blame was like a dash of cold water in the face, a quick cure. Angrily she continued reading and taking notes, making a list of every name connected to the case. She felt somehow detached, as if she had no connection to the girl in the article.

Suddenly one name seemed to leap out at her. She was so startled to recognize it that she flinched. Bob Spencer was a homicide detective. Now how, she wondered, did she know that? She'd spent the six months after her grandmother's murder in a catatonic state, and that time was totally lost to her. Yet she had an elusive memory of the man.

Deanna put her elbows on the table and her chin on her fists, and stared blankly at the screen. She could see him in her mind's eye—he was very tall with thick black hair and a mustache. He'd been rather intimidating but not threatening or accusing as so many had been. Why in the world did she remember him? Then it came to her. Bob Spencer had visited her a couple of times the first year she'd been at Twelve Oaks. He'd asked her endless questions for which she'd had no answers, then he'd stopped coming. And there was something else. Bob Spencer didn't believe she'd murdered her grandmother, she was certain of it.

Her eyes were tired from the strain, and she rubbed them, wondering where that certainty had sprung from. He'd never said a word to her about it or intimated in any way whether or not he thought she was guilty. But she remembered an honesty about him, a kind of gentleness in his questions and a sadness in his gaze when he looked at her. Bob Spencer liked her.

Deanna struggled to return her attention to the screen and even started reading another article concerning her trial when she was unexpectedly paralyzed by the strangest feeling. A creeping sensation slithered slowly up her spine and made the fine hairs at the back of her neck stand on end. She jerked around, sure she was going to find someone staring at her. There were only five people near enough to have caused that feeling, and none showed the slightest interest in her. Two women sat huddled together over a large book. A bald-headed old man was seated at a distant table, intently reading. At the far side of the room a man was engrossed in a newspaper, and the only thing she could see was a head of dishwater brown hair.

Deanna decided she was imagining things and turned her attention to the only other person close by. He was working at the microfilm machine next to hers and must have noted her strange behavior, because when she glanced at him, he was staring back. She smiled and explained, "A possum ran over my grave."

He smiled back. "I know what you mean. Weird feeling, isn't it?"

"Yes." If she was any judge of age, he wasn't much older than she was, and had a boyish grin with peekaboo dimples. His green eyes sparkled with amusement and his mass of reddish blond hair seemed to stick out in all directions. Deanna quickly looked away. She returned her attention to her work, but the words on the screen wouldn't focus and she fiddled absently with the controls, all the while trying to remember where she'd seen the man beside her. She'd almost shrugged it off as her imagination, then glanced at him once more. He grinned again, and the answer came to her. "You were in Judge Harrison's court yesterday, weren't you?"

He gave a start, and Deanna realized she'd surprised him. "The judge asked you to leave the room," she said, musing out loud. "Why would he do that? Who are you?" A little wide-eyed ignorance was called for here. She knew very well that he was a reporter. She just didn't know his name or what he wanted. What she did know was that seeing him twice in such a short span of time was suspect.

He'd been caught off guard and made a quick recovery, obviously deciding partial honesty was called for. He stuck out his hand. "Hi, I'm Danny Hudson. Funny, the way we ran into each other today, isn't it?"

"Yes." He was lying. Any fool could see that. "But it wasn't a coincidence, was it?"

Danny Hudson put on his best you-found-me-out face and shrugged eloquently. "No, to be honest, I was on my way to talk to you this morning when I saw you getting into a taxi. I . . . sort of followed you."

"How'd you know where I was living? Why would you want to talk to me?"

Danny could feel the sticky wetness under his arms. He didn't know what he'd expected. "Look, I'm a reporter for the *Post*. I cover the courthouse. Yesterday I didn't even know who you were," he lied. "I just happened to be in Harrison's court and got interested when he ordered the room cleared." She was staring at him with those pretty but icy blue eyes. His smile widened to his most charming as he quickly went on, "Hey, so shoot me. I'm just trying to do my job."

Deanna had a feeling she shouldn't talk to him anymore and finished writing down some page numbers. "You know who I am?"

He was about to lose his mark and decided to play his last card. "Listen, I see you've been researching the murder. I spent all yesterday doing the same thing. Personally I think the whole case was rather bizarre even for the sixties." He gathered up his pen and notepad and stood, then, in what looked like an afterthought, handed her one of his business cards. "If there's anything I can help you with, answer any questions, give me a call." He was only three steps away when she called to him to wait. He almost fainted with relief.

Deanna had decided he was right. He knew more about the murder investigation itself than she did. She smiled at him. He could, after all, be a help to her, but on her terms, not his. "I didn't mean to be nasty. You do know who I am, don't you?"

"Yes. Deanna Deveraux."

"Are you out for a story? Because if you are, there isn't one. I've never remembered what happened that day."

"Hey, I was just curious why the judge closed his court, that's all. So I did a little digging to find out what the secret session was."

"I've been trying to learn what happened to me that day." It was working, she thought. He was soaking in everything she said. Maybe if she played her cards right, she could get him to reveal what he'd learned. "You said you've already researched what's here?"

With a great show of reluctance, Danny moved back to the table and sat down. "Yes. There's not much there, you know. Just old articles by reporters who believed that sensationalism, whether true or not, was the way to sell newspapers. What you really need to read, like I did, are the trial transcripts."

"How do I get them?"

"Well, you need to be a lawyer, an officer of the court or have some pull with the county clerk. I have one of the three." He leaned forward and whispered as if they were conspirators. "Why don't you wrap up what you need here, then we'll go have lunch and I'll tell you all about the trial."

Deanna didn't trust him, but she had to admire him for his effort. Gathering up her notes, her purse and the soft leather briefcase Mary had loaned her, she said. "I noticed some nice shaded benches out front." She patted the briefcase. "I brought plenty of sandwiches. You could join me for lunch."

Danny had pictured a quiet table in a restaurant. Maybe a glass of wine to loosen her tongue. But he nodded, deciding not to look a gift horse in the mouth. What he desperately wanted at the moment was a telephone to call his editor, but he wasn't sure how to explain the delay. Then he noticed the spools of microfilm in her hand and mentally danced a jig of joy. "You finish up here and I'll go find a soda machine and meet you out front."

By the time Deanna made her way outside, she discovered that others had had the same idea. Most of the benches were occupied, but she saw some people leaving one and hurried over to lay claim. The bench was situated under the spreading limbs of an old oak, its thick canopy of leaves making the afternoon breeze feel almost cool.

Deanna busied herself laying out the three pimento-cheese sandwiches and a bag of now crushed potato chips. Mary must have thought she was going to work up a real appetite. After a twenty-minute wait, she was hungry and beginning to wonder if Danny had decided not to join her. She was just about to give up and go ahead and eat when she saw him hurrying down the library steps.

Danny was all apologies and barely suppressed excitement. The conversation with his editor had enlightened him with undercurrents of the Deveraux story he hadn't previously known about. Instead of a simple human-interest story buried on the third page, he was looking at a major front-page exclusive.

He waved a couple of Cokes, condensation beading the bottles. "Did you think I'd skipped out on you? There was a long line at the machine." He set the bottles down and wiped his damp hands on the seat of his jeans before accepting the wax-paper-wrapped sandwich. He didn't know if he could calm down enough to eat.

Deanna took a sip of her drink. "How long have you been a reporter?"

She didn't seem like someone who'd been locked away for ten years, he realized he was going to have to watch what he said. "About two years," he replied, trying not to choke on the sandwich. "I've written a couple of feature stories." Something about the way she was staring at him made him uneasy. He reminded himself that she had been institutionalized for a long time. He could probably tell her anything and she'd believe it. Hell, he could take advantage of her and the situation if he had a mind to. But what he really wanted was to get his story—whatever it took.

Deanna felt the change in his attitude, recognized it for what it was and sighed. A wave of hot anger welled up inside her. She ducked her head to keep him from seeing it and began eating her sandwich, unaware the move made her appear shy and vulnerable. Why not use his prejudice and ignorance against him? she thought. Keeping her head down, she glanced around. People sat enjoying their lunch and companionable talk. Some were simply basking in the afternoon sun. She pulled one of Dr. Gresham's tricks and let the silence become uncomfortable. When she noted Danny's nervous shifting, she looked at him and asked softly, "What are trial transcripts, Danny?"

Danny explained as simply as he could so she would understand. And because she was gazing at him as if he was the most handsome and intelligent person she'd ever met—which was probably true, he thought, since she'd been locked away for so long—he began to tell her everything he knew about her trial.

After he was through, he wondered how much comprehension there was behind those beautiful, empty blue eyes. "Now it's your turn," he said, smiling as he boldly reached over and patted her hand.

Deanna's eyes widened with surprise. "My turn?" she asked. "What's my turn?"

"You were going to tell me all about your grandmother's death, remember?"

"But I told you, didn't I?" She gave him a lazy smile. "I can't remember that day or anything prior to it."

"Oh, come on. Surely you must remember something. You know your name. You know about the murder and the trial."

"No. The doctor at the sanitarium told me my name. He also told me the story of my grandmother's death, how I was tried and convicted of her murder and placed in an institution. That's all I know." She glanced at her watch. "Oh, my. Just look at the time, would you? I'm going to be late if I don't hurry."

Deanna jumped up, grabbed Danny's hand and shook it hard. "It was nice meeting you. If there's anything I can help you with, give me a call." Then she scooped up her belongings and walked quickly toward the library steps.

Danny watched her in a daze. He watched as she skipped up the steps, watched as she disappeared through the door, all the while asking himself why he felt used when there wasn't a chance he could have been outsmarted by a psycho like that.

Deanna felt like laughing and dancing at the same time. She was free and felt happy and truly alive. How many times had she wanted to turn the tables on Dr. Gresham? Do exactly the same thing to him that she'd done to the reporter? Leave him with his mouth hanging open, feeling confused.

Her grandmother had repeatedly told her that she was too much like her mother, who had drawn men to her the way flowers drew bees. She'd said that Deanna would only invite trouble. But it wasn't true. She had used her brains, not her charm, to handle the reporter. And besides, what really irked Agatha Fleur Deveraux had been the fact that she couldn't control her daughter—or her granddaughter.

Deanna remembered her mother as a beautiful, graceful lady, a sweet-natured woman few men could or would say no to. Her grandmother had warned Deanna that if she wasn't careful she would end up the way her mother had—pregnant, unmarried and abandoned.

Deanna stared blindly at the microfilm screen. The powerful memories had obsessed her all the way into the building. She didn't have the slightest idea how she'd gotten here, only that she hurt. For the first time since her memory had returned, she realized there were going to be many more painful recollections besides her grandmother's death.

But there were going to be memories of happier times, too, memories that would make her heart ache in a different way. What she hadn't planned on were the vivid pictures that played in her mind like a movie. In ten years she'd had no recollection of her mother's image. The past had been wiped clean, and as far as she knew, Dr. Gresham had never made any effort to find any photographs for her. For so long her past had been like a blank screen, and reliving these newfound memories brought both joy and excruciating pain.

Deanna pushed away from the table and left to find a public telephone, where she called for a taxi. Then she waited outside, sitting on the steps of the library with the sun beating down on her. Heat had melted the tar in the cracks of the sidewalk, making it bubble. The breeze had stilled, and the air was hot and suffocating, but she didn't notice. Her mind was going wild, jumping from scene to scene of her childhood.

All she could think of was getting back to Mary's, digging out her sketch pad and recording what was in her might be the only likeness of her mother she'd ever have. Memories, like everything else, faded with the passage of time, and time was ticking away.

Deanna was startled by the blast of a horn and quickly gathered up her purse and briefcase. In her flight she almost ran over a short bald-headed man and absently apologized, then hurried on. The cold blast of air in the taxi was like a sobering slap in the face. She reminded herself to be careful. It was fine for Mary to read all that she'd found at the library, she could even amuse her friend with her triumph over the reporter. But she'd have to do her sketching alone in her room during the evening or when Mary returned to work. She closed her eyes, summoning up the image of her mother once again.

The sudden swerve of the taxi and her shoulder slamming against the door snapped her back to the present. The driver seemed more intent on his rearview mirror than what was ahead. "Is there anything wrong?" she asked.

"I could swear... Never mind. Sorry."

The driver's uneasiness broke the thread of her thoughts. For the rest of the trip to Mary's she remained alert to her surroundings. That creepy sensation was crawling up her spine again. Several times she caught the driver's eyes glancing in the rearview mirror. After a few nervous minutes she realized he wasn't peeking at her but checking out the road behind them. She twisted around to discover what it was that kept distracting him, but all she could see was cars.

"MARY, DO YOU BELIEVE instinct or intelligence heightens the senses?"

Mary was reading the photocopies Deanna had made at the library and replied absently, "What do you mean?"

"It seems to me that primitive man used and depended on his senses—his instincts—more. As time passed he relied more on his intelligence to understand the world around him and his feelings. So, if one is ignorant of the modern world, could it heighten the senses? Make a person more alert to what other people are feeling, things like that?"

"What have you been up to, Deanna?"

"I haven't the faintest idea what you mean."

"I know you. You start with all that Dr. Gresham psychobabble just when you're about to drop some bomb."

Deanna told her about the reporter, and they had a good laugh. "Do you think I'm getting my womanly wiles late in life? He was so easy to read and leave twisting in the wind."

Mary smiled. It was wonderful seeing Deanna so happy. "You'd better be damn careful with these newly acquired talents and who you pull them on. By the way, Clayton Lambert called just before you came in. He wanted to know if he could drop by."

Deanna felt the room rock beneath her feet. It was a new and strange sensation. "Well," she demanded, "what did you tell him?"

"Deanna, I'm not your mother. I told him yes, but that you were out. He said he was coming right away, that he'd wait for you."

Deanna didn't know what she felt. Excited and nervous at the same time. Then she reminded herself that it wasn't as if she was going on a date. She started out of the room, then stopped. "Do you think I should change?"

Mary studied the peach linen slacks, the crisp white shirt with the sleeves rolled up to her elbows. Deanna was a fan of old movies. She liked the casual Carole Lombard look and had the willowy thinness to carry it off. "You look fine, except for your hair. Why don't you put it up for a change?"

Deanna sighed as she stared into the bathroom mirror. Her hair was the bane of her life—blond, curly and tending to kink in the humidity. She'd tried a shorter style and to her dismay had lost all control over it, ending up for months looking as if she'd stuck her finger in an electrical socket. The only way to manage it was to keep it long, which gave it some weight and straightened the curls. As she secured the knot on the top of her head, she was surprised to see that her hands trembled.

When she joined Mary again, however, she looked refreshed and calm. Mary's muffled laughter startled her, and it took her a few seconds to realize what she was pointing at. She'd forgotten to zip her slacks, and if that wasn't bad enough, a long trail of toilet paper had stuck to her shoe and been dragged across the floor.

"Well, that would have convinced him of my sanity, wouldn't it?" They were still grinning when the doorbell rang.

Deanna was shocked at Clayton's condition and could only stand aside as he passed her. His clothes were rumpled, and she realized they were the same ones he'd worn yesterday. There were dark circles under his eyes as if he hadn't slept, and he was in need of a shave. Her introduction of him to Mary was a little hesitant, and he must have sensed that his appearance had startled them, because he immediately began apologizing.

"I'm sorry about the way I look, but I haven't been home or slept since I left you."

Both women were seated on the couch and he was in the overstuffed chair across from them. He ran his fingers through his hair, wanting to say the right thing, but he was so tired all he could manage was, "I've been reading the transcript of your trial and most of my grandfather's files."

"You mean you haven't been to sleep at all?" Mary asked.

"No, ma'am." His weary gaze settled on Deanna and his focus sharpened. "I want you to know that from the minute you were arrested, my grandfather did everything he knew how to get you released. He believed in your innocence, you know, and never wavered in his convictions."

Deanna couldn't say anything and nodded as a lump formed in her throat. It was wonderful to know that someone had believed in her all these years. "Why didn't he ever tell me?"

Clay settled himself more deeply in the downy softness of the chair, leaned his head back and stared at the ceiling. "I don't know. Maybe he didn't want you to think less of him because he couldn't get you released." He fell silent as he remembered those hand-scribbled notes of his grandfather's, which made him realize just how much the old man had thought of Deanna Deveraux and her spirit, humor and honesty. If his grandfather had been younger, Clay would have sworn he'd been in love with Deanna. But that was disrespectful. His grandfather was a wonderful man and a great attorney, but not a criminal lawyer. Clay could only speculate about why he'd defended Deanna in court.

He'd been lost in his own thoughts far too long. Both women were staring at him, and he forced himself to sit up straight. "I think a great miscarriage of justice was done. If you'll allow me, I'd like to clear your name— take your case on. I'd—"

"No!" Deanna said firmly.

He was surprised at the explosive answer. Obviously so was her friend.

"Deanna," Mary admonished, "let the man finish."

"Why? And what happens if his meddling does something to put me right back in Twelve Oaks, or worse, jail. No, no. Just let it be."

Clay realized she didn't understand how the legal system worked and was terrified of the judge's decision being reversed. "Deanna, you're not going back to the sanitarium or to jail. Listen to me. Even if you admitted to me or the judge that you cold-bloodedly killed your grandmother, you can't ever be tried twice for the same crime."

Deanna stared out the window. She should be happy that she could never be retried, but there was something about what Clay said that bothered her. She wanted desperately to assure him that she was innocent, but something inside her held her back. She would seek to prove her innocence on her own terms, and she had taken the first step just this morning.

"I don't think I did it, you know." It was the closest she was willing to come to the truth at that point. She glanced at him and found him studying her closely, but she knew her expression disclosed nothing.

"Deanna, no one who knows you thinks you could have killed your grandmother," Mary said. "Think about what Clay's offering you. A chance, Deanna. A chance to clear your name and find out once and for all what happened that day ten years ago. Besides—" she paused to delicately blow her nose "—I don't like the idea of you talking to that reporter, no matter how stupid you thought he was. I would—"

She never got any further. Clay was towering over them, staring down from his considerable height and looking as if he were having trouble speaking.

"What did you say?" he finally asked in a gruff voice. He knew what damage the media was capable of. God, they'd crucify her! Before Deanna or Mary could say anything, he demanded, "What reporter? Where'd you see him? What did he ask you?" His fatigue was making his temper short, and his frown was ominous. "What the hell did you tell him?"

Mary cringed, thinking that this man could be formidable and very dangerous, then she glanced at Deanna and ducked her head to hide her smile. Oh, dear. She'd seen that cool stare before. Clay Lambert just might have met his match.

Any other time, Deanna thought, she might have sat quietly and answered the questions, but she was free now and not under a doctor's microscope. Suddenly she was standing, too, the coffee table the only thing separating them. "I told him I was another ax-wielding Lizzy Borden. Lizzy got away with murder, too, didn't she?" She punctuated her next words by poking his chest with her finger. "Let me tell you something. I might have been locked away, but I'm not a dummy. Don't ever talk down to me or use that arrogant, condescending tone of voice. I've had ten years of it."

Deanna took a deep breath and dropped her hand. "Now sit down and act like the intelligent man you are, instead of someone who just crawled out of a cave, and I'll tell you all about my adventure today.''

Clay sat.

Deanna smiled sweetly as she took her own seat. ''I went to the library this morning to read newspaper accounts of what happened on the day Grandmother was killed. You know I never knew what went on or anything about the trial.'' From the way his frown was etching deeper lines into his forehead, she decided she was pushing her luck. ''Do you remember yesterday when the judge made everyone leave the courtroom?''

''Vaguely,'' Clay said.

''This morning while I was working at the microfilm machine, I got the feeling I was being watched, and I was right. One of the men who'd been in court and had to leave was at the other machine. His name's Danny Hudson.''

Clay groaned and Deanna quickly went on, ''But I didn't tell him anything. How could I? I don't know anything.''

Clay stared at the floor, praying for strength. She was a babe in the woods. Easy prey. A ripe plum ready to be picked. She was every cliché he could think of. The problem was, he didn't want her asking questions or talking to anyone. If she wasn't guilty of murder, then someone else was. What Deanna was doing could be dangerous.

He looked at her for a long moment, made an effort to lower his voice to a sane, persuasive tone, then said, ''Deanna, let the professionals handle this reporter. The next time you see him or if he calls, just tell him to come see me.'' Damn, but she could stare daggers. ''Please.'' He tried charm and threw in a smile with his plea.

The sparks seemed to be flying between the two young people. Mary decided some cool-headed intervention was required here. "Mr. Lambert, would you mind telling us why you would want to handle this case?"

Clay never removed his gaze from Deanna. "Because my grandfather believed in Deanna. He also knew something dirty was going on. He had a plan, rather long-range for my taste. I just intend to speed it up. We're going to clear your name, Deanna." He didn't want to tell her about Bob Spencer or what they'd talked about during their lunch meeting in his office. He didn't want her to know that someone had conspired to keep her in the sanitarium all those years.

Since Deanna seemed determined to sit stubbornly silent, Mary asked, "How would Deanna pay you? What's your fee?"

"Fee?"

"Come, come, Mr. Lambert. Fee—as in money. Deanna's looking for a job, but I'm sure even you must realize it's going to be difficult with her background."

It was as if he'd been suddenly dropped into a foreign country. She was speaking a language he didn't understand, and it left him feeling disoriented and confused.

"I know this is the seventies and women are more career-minded, but why would Deanna want to work? She's a very rich young woman."

"I don't understand," Deanna said.

"I don't, either." Clay glanced from one to the other. "You really didn't know you were wealthy? I thought—"

"Mr. Lambert," Mary interrupted, the anger in her tone unmistakable. It was so like men, she thought, to keep the important facts from women as if they didn't have the intelligence to understand. "Neither Dr. Gresh-

am nor your grandfather, for whatever reason, saw fit to
discuss Deanna's financial situation with her. She knows
very well the obstacles the past ten years would put on her
chances to be gainfully employed, and believe me, it's
been one of her major concerns. So why don't you tell
her everything now."

"I don't know everything yet. But the tax department
at the firm is pulling all her files." He could see he hadn't
made any headway with Mary, and from Deanna's expression, she was beginning to doubt his ability. "From
what I can tell, the financial statements show that your
grandmother's estate was considerable, and with my
grandfather personally overseeing the investments, it's
grown by leaps and bounds over the years."

Nothing was making sense. Deanna shook her head.
"My grandmother owned a dress shop, Clay. She worked
hard all her life, but . . ."

Deanna couldn't tell him that she remembered the long
hours her grandmother had worked both at the shop and
at home. The old lady had been a skinflint, the original
Scrooge, who never failed to let her granddaughter know
what a burden she was. Deanna hadn't thought there was
much money.

"I don't know yet what the initial investment from the
estate was, but I do know Grandfather never sold Fleur's.
You still own fifty-five percent of the shop, and believe
me, over the years the money has rolled in from that
quarter. By the way, Grandfather didn't sell your grandmother's house, either. He leased it. I have a feeling he
must have known something was going to happen soon,
and you'd need a place to live. From the records and bills
I found, it looked like he canceled the lease on the ten-
ants and had the house cleaned and painted. Then he had

some of your grandmother's furniture, which had been in storage, moved in."

It was all too much to take in for Deanna. Her peaceful existence had been shattered with the return of her memory and she'd been thrust back into the outside world, ready or not. Everything was moving too fast. She hadn't had a chance to catch her breath, let alone think things out carefully or make plans.

She walked into her bedroom and shut the door, leaving behind the urgent murmuring of Mary's and Clay's voices. She frantically dug around in a couple of the boxes until she found her sketch pad and pencils, then she settled down in the chair beside the window. For ten years, drawing had been the only way she could capture her feelings and emotions. She'd always put her thoughts down on paper in the form of pictures. Now she felt strangely compelled to draw. She began to sketch, the lines and swirls recreating the interior of the library. All other concerns were put aside, past and present, as she lost herself in her work.

CHAPTER SIX

DEANNA HADN'T DREAMED in years, ten years to be exact.

The return of her memory had meant the return of dreams, but instead of being a comfort, they'd taken on a nightmarish quality. Several times during the night she'd awakened, heart pounding, short of breath, in a cold sweat and unable to go back to sleep. She'd picked up her sketch pad, drawn what she'd seen in her dreams, then fallen back into a sound sleep, only to repeat the process an hour later.

When she heard the distant ringing of the telephone, she was awake, having just finished drawing. Exhaustedly slumped against her pillow, she watched the dawn light creep across the ceiling. Papers littered the bed, and she picked up two of the sketches, smiling sadly. One was of her mother, the way she remembered her. The other was of Clay. Her smile turned thoughtful. If Clay was a barometer by which to judge how men were going to react to her, the prospect looked bleak. Was her life always going to be tainted by her past? Was she going to wear that invisible label— murderer—forever? One day she hoped someone would look at her and see her simply as Deanna—only Deanna.

She rested the drawings on her chest and picked up two more. Why, she wondered, would the library be in her dreams? She had felt strangely compelled to draw it in her waking hours, but that was after spending the better part of a day there. One sketch showed the two women hunched over a large book, their expressions alight with excitement. To the left of the women was a side view of the bald-headed man, his elbow on the polished table, his hand propping up his forehead as if he was about to fall asleep. Then there was a man seated in a comfortable-looking leather chair reading a newspaper. He must have been tall and thin from the way she had sketched in the position of his crossed legs. She'd even added herself and the reporter as they talked together at the microfilm machines.

Funny, Deanna thought, that she had caught so much detail. Then she glanced at the other sketch in her hand and frowned. Something about the drawing bothered her, but she couldn't put her finger on the source of her discomfort. The picture showed her seated on a stone bench, surrounded by others on their lunch hour. She was staring at the library steps, waiting for the reporter.

A couple of her subjects were stretched out on the soft grass, taking a catnap in the shade of the oak trees. Others were busy eating and talking to their companions. She'd added the two men from the reference section to the scene. Still, she was unable to figure out what it was about the drawing that disturbed her.

She was glancing through more of the sketches when Mary knocked on her bedroom door. She gathered up all her drawings and slipped them between the cover of her pad. "Come on in, Mary." Her smiled faded when she saw Mary's worried expression. "What's the matter? Do you feel worse?" Throwing the covers back, she started to get up but Mary motioned for her to stay put.

"I just got a call from your attorney." Mary sat on the edge of the bed.

Deanna didn't like the seriousness of her friend's expression, and the alarm she felt robbed her of any further questions.

"Clay's on his way here."

Deanna nodded, her mouth dry with panic. The first thing that popped into her head was that the judge had changed his mind and she was going back to Twelve Oaks. But that couldn't be. Clay had promised she'd never have to go back. Deanna mustered up the courage to ask, "Why is he coming here?" She glanced at the clock, saw it was only six-thirty and knew something horrible had happened.

"You remember the reporter you met yesterday at the library?"

"Sure. Danny Hudson. Why?"

"Deanna, Danny Hudson was found stabbed to death behind the library late yesterday evening."

"Oh, my God! That's awful." Silence settled over them like a dark shroud. "But why's Clay coming here?" Deanna asked at last.

Mary looked even paler than usual, and her expression was graver than Deanna had ever seen it. "Mary, what's the matter?" she demanded.

"Clay said his office has a source in the police department, and as soon as your name was mentioned, Clay was notified."

"My name?"

"Deanna, you were the last person seen talking with the reporter."

"So?"

"Possibly the last person to see him alive."

"Except for whoever killed him." That ominous quiet blanketed the room again. Deanna suddenly went icy cold all over. "I don't want to hear any more, Mary. Please."

"Clay said the police know your name. They questioned the librarian."

"I see. I was the last person to see Danny Hudson. I was the last person to see Grandmother. Danny Hudson was stabbed, Grandmother was stabbed, and I'm immediately guilty." Deanna threw back the covers, rolled out of bed and stood across from Mary. "I'm *not* going back to the sanitarium. I'm *not* going to jail, because I didn't do anything wrong."

Then, as if she'd been kicked hard in the stomach, Deanna doubled over and was forced to sit down on the edge of the bed. She put her face in her hands and groaned. She hadn't done anything when her grandmother was murdered, but she'd been the one to pay for the crime. Dear God, what was she going to do?

Mary's hand on her shoulder made her look up. "Why, Mary? Why is this happening to me again?"

"I don't know, but we're damn well going to find out."

"We?" Deanna whispered. She'd been alone for so long that "we" was almost a foreign word.

"Me. Clay." Mary patted Deanna's shoulder one more time. "You'd better get dressed. Clay'll be here soon. By the way, he's bringing someone with him, someone he says is going to help you."

With shaking hands Deanna was still trying to put on a little makeup when she heard the ringing of the doorbell. She quickly applied some pale peach lipstick, then stood back from the mirror and attempted to slick back the wisps of curls that had escaped the smooth French twist. Her sundress was a muted pastel print, almost like an Impressionist painting. She wondered if the dress made her look too young, but she didn't have time to rummage through the unpacked suitcases for something else to wear.

An unwelcome thought stopped her at the bedroom door, and she was too paralyzed with fear to move. Danny's death had to be an appalling coincidence. Surely reporters made enemies. But what if it wasn't a coincidence? What if...?

God, Deanna thought, she couldn't think about what ifs anymore and forced herself to open the door and concentrate on walking to the living room. When she lifted her head, her calm facade was immediately shattered. It was a long second before she could catch her breath. "I know you," she said to the big man standing between Mary and Clay.

Oh, he'd changed over the years, gained weight, so that now he looked barrel-chested instead of broad-chested; his stomach, once flat, hung slightly over the wide Western-style belt; and his close-cropped beard was graying around the edges, where once it had been jet black.

"You're the detective who came to visit me a couple of times at Twelve Oaks." Then she remembered the photocopies of newspaper articles lying on her bedside table. "You were involved in my grandmother's investigation." She looked at Clay. "Is he here to arrest me?"

Clay felt the anger twist deeper in his gut. She looked like an angel, a frightened angel. Someone was going to pay for doing this to her, he thought. "Deanna, this is Bob Spencer. He's not here to arrest you. He's not even with the police department anymore. Bob's a private detective, and like my grandfather, he thinks you're innocent. He's been working on your case a long time and was recently partnered with Grandfather."

"Can any of you tell me what's going on?" Deanna asked. The telephone started ringing and Mary rushed over to answer it. "What's going to happen?"

Both Clay and Bob were watching Mary, and from their expressions they were not at all happy. "What's the matter?" Clay asked her.

"That was your office calling. The media's gotten hold of the story. Pretty soon they're going to be swarming the place." No sooner had Mary hung up than the telephone rang again.

Deanna knew by Mary's expression that the caller wasn't a reporter but someone her friend was acquainted with. Then Mary turned her back to the room and spoke quietly so no one could hear. When she finally hung up, she looked guiltily at Deanna. "That was Dr. Gresham, Deanna. He wants you to come back to Twelve Oaks."

"Oh, no. No way will I ever go back there. You know that, Mary." Fear made her voice high, frantic. She knew she must sound as if she were losing control and forced herself to calm down.

Deanna studied Clay and Bob Spencer, expecting to see some sort of verification in their eyes that she was as crazy as a loon. But they were gazing at her with worry and compassion. It was Clay's compassion that almost did her in. "I didn't kill my grandmother and I didn't kill Danny Hudson."

"We never thought for a moment that you did," Clay said. "But what you have to realize is that on the surface it looks bad. The reporters only skimmed the facts in their stories." The telephone started ringing again. Clay frowned. "What we need to do is get you someplace they wouldn't think of."

"You want me to hide? Wouldn't that make me look guilty? Sorry," she said firmly, "but I'm not hiding."

Until that point Bob Spencer had been quiet, studying everyone and their reactions to what was happening. Now he focused solely on Deanna. "I admire your determination, little lady," he said. "But let me tell you something. The media played a major part in convicting an innocent girl of murder ten years ago. It could happen again. Oh, maybe not in the courts, but a public crucifixion can be just as damning. Do yourself and everyone else trying to help you a favor. Don't talk to reporters under any circumstances.

"Now, Mr. Lambert and I—that is, old Mr. Lambert—worked hard over the last year to spring you, kid. I ain't so sure we did the right thing. Mind you, not for one moment did it occur to us you were guilty, but you were safe out there in la-la land. I don't believe in coincidences, and this reporter's murder, the way he was killed, points to you. It's a little to pat for me to swallow. Besides, whether you were guilty of your grandmother's murder or not, someone went to a lot of trouble to keep you locked away."

Finished with what he had to say at the moment, he set his jaw stubbornly and marched over to Mary, who was dealing with another pesky caller. Gently he took the phone from Mary's hand, hung up the receiver, then yanked the cord from the wall. Without a word he put his arm around a shocked and silent Mary, led her to her nest on the couch and tucked the blanket around her, then handed her the box of tissues.

"Clay," Deanna said, almost smiling as she watched Mary's expression shift from indignation to pleasure. "How could the police know my name or that I even knew Danny Hudson?"

Bob answered for Clay. "The librarian, the one who helped you. She remembered your interest in the Deveraux case. She told the cops about helping you find the microfilm, then making copies of the pages pertaining to your case. She also recalled Danny Hudson and his interest in you. Then to clinch it, she identified your photograph from one the police obtained from Dr. Gresham."

"Good old Dr. Gresham," Deanna said sarcastically, "always willing to help." She glanced at Clay. "Are the police going to arrest me?"

"When hell freezes over," Clay said. "Let me tell you something about Texas law—it's not what you know but who you know and how much money you have. But in this case that adage doesn't necessarily hold water. Lambert, Bernard and Lambert have been around for a long time. We've handled more than our share of high-profile cases over the years, won a lot of them, too, and kept a lot of secrets." He didn't tell her he had wondered where the firm's influence had been at Deanna's travesty of a trial.

"I've called in some favors," he went on. "You're not going to be arrested for three reasons, Deanna. One, the coroner placed the reporter's time of death after you were already home. Two, the taxi driver identified you, and his log shows what time he picked you up from the library. Three, Mary and I are your alibis. Money and influence are important in this state, Deanna. Lady, you're loaded, and you have friends this time who believe in you."

Deanna remembered something Bob had mentioned earlier. "You said you thought someone was keeping me at Twelve Oaks. Do you know who or why?" It was obvious from their shared glance that the men preferred not to answer her. She was about to voice her objections when the doorbell rang.

"That'll be the police, Deanna." Clay could see the sudden flicker of fear in her eyes and quickly added, "I promise they're not here to arrest you but just to ask a few questions." He motioned for Deanna to sit, then he took up a position directly behind her and rested his hand firmly on her shoulder. He nodded to Bob to answer the door and said, "Let me do all the talking."

Over the years at the sanitarium Deanna had taught herself how to outwardly relax while she might be seething inside. The trick then had been on Dr. Gresham, and it had amused her immensely to see him lose his patience. But now was different. This wasn't a joke, and she struggled to regain her composure. The comforting pressure of Clay's hand helped. She looked up and found him smiling at her. How, she wondered, could Mary not think he was beautiful?

She folded her hands in her lap, her face calm, her gaze direct. Two men, both dressed in street clothes and not uniforms, as she'd expected, greeted Bob Spencer. The older man was short and round with a deep voice and dark puffy bags under his eyes, and throughout the introductions his sharp gaze stayed fixed on Deanna. The younger officer was tall, with a spit-and-polish appearance. He tried to appear stern like his older partner, but his baby face could only manage a weak scowl.

The older man's greeting was friendly, and Deanna realized that he and Bob were old associates. Her fear escalated. Ugly thoughts of a trap ran through her mind. Hadn't she seen enough television shows—like "Hawaii Five-O," "Mannix," "The FBI," "Kojak," "Cannon"—to know that cops always stuck together?

"Miss Deveraux," the man said, "I'm Detective Howard Haskel. It's good to see you again." He waited.

Deanna blinked and stared.

Clay's hand tightened in warning. "You've met my client before?"

He ignored Clay and directed his attention solely at Deanna. "Ten years ago, Bob and I were the first homicide detectives at the scene of your grandmother's murder. You were a little spaced out at the time, so I guess you don't remember me. I was the one who pried your fingers off the knife you used."

Deanna didn't blink. This man was a real bastard. What scared her was his bulldog attitude. She knew as surely as if he'd told her that he would never forget seeing her covered with blood, holding her grandmother, the murder weapon still in her hand. And he believed she was guilty.

"That'll be enough, Detective," Clay said, his voice both angry and authoritative.

Haskel shrugged, pulled out a small notebook and scanned what he'd written. "I understand you met the victim, Danny Hudson, yesterday. Would you tell me about that meeting?"

Clay squeezed Deanna's shoulder. "Detective, did your boss tell you Miss Deveraux has not one but a couple of solid alibis for her whereabouts at the time Hudson was killed?"

"Yeah, sure. But you know very well, Counselor, that I need her statement."

Deanna patted Clay's hand to reassure him. "I didn't set out to meet the reporter, Detective. I was doing research and he was there. Just as he was in court the day before yesterday. He wanted a story. My story."

"And you didn't want to give it to him?"

"That's right."

"What exactly were you doing at the library?"

"Reading about my grandmother's murder." She watched his expression of feigned surprise.

"That's right," he said. "You're supposed to have lost your memory all these years."

"Yes. And I was interested in reading how the police conducted their investigation." She'd gotten under his skin, and she felt wonderful at the sense of power it gave her. The warning pressure of Clay's hand almost took her breath away, but she knew she couldn't or wouldn't stop.

"What's that supposed to mean?" the detective growled.

Clay knew the pitfalls of verbal debate with the cops. Haskel was no dummy, and Clay had a feeling the man could be a vindictive SOB. He was toying with Deanna and Clay was going to put a stop to it. It was better to have the detective's wrath directed at him. "What she means, Haskel, is that your department was on the take then and probably still is." Clay smiled, a predator moving in for the kill. "I'm going to prove it, and when I do, you're going to go down so hard you'll wish you never heard the name Deveraux. Do I make myself clear?"

"Crystal. Maybe we should finish this questioning downtown. What do you say, Counselor?"

"When pigs fly." Clay hadn't been prepared for the detective's viciousness, and he lost his temper for the first time in more years than he could remember. He moved so fast no one noticed what he was about to do except Bob, who intercepted him before any damage could be done. Clay knew he should have kept his mouth shut, but he'd never wanted to hit anyone so badly before.

"Howie, Howie," Bob said as he kept Howard and Clay separated. "Before you go off half-cocked and make an even worse fool of yourself, listen to me. Scuttlebutt around the department has it that you're chest-deep investigating the Ford murders. Don't you think it's odd that, busy as you are and after all these years, you get assigned this case again? You might want to follow the line of command. Find out where those orders came from. 'Cause my friend, someone's pulling your chain." All the while he was talking, Bob was slowly moving the detectives toward the front door.

Haskel knew very well what his old partner was doing and shot one last look at Deanna. "You're a real cool piece of work, lady. If I find your story doesn't check out, I'll come down on you so fast it'll make your head spin. This time you'll go to jail, instead of that country club you were in."

The door shut on the last part of the detective's threat, but everyone heard. Mary had been silent too long. She flipped the blanket off her, adjusted her robe modestly and stood.

"I don't believe I've ever seen such lack of self-control as I have today. Deanna I can understand, but you two..." She scowled at Clay and Bob. "What're you trying to do, get her arrested? You practically started a brawl." They all began to talk at once, but Mary waved them immediately silent as if she were wielding a magic wand.

"Oh, don't anyone say anything to me yet. Deanna, take Clay to the bathroom and have him splash some cold water on his face. Maybe that'll cool him off. As for you—" she turned to a rather sheepish-looking Bob Spencer "—you reconnect my telephone this instant, then just take it off the hook so it won't bother us any longer."

Deanna was shaking all over. She'd never felt so alive in her life. Clay's anger, his violent reaction to the police

detective, had destroyed the cool facade she'd worked
hard to maintain. She was on an emotional high and
wasn't sure how to come down. Biting her lip to keep
from laughing wildly, she led Clay down the hall and
pointed to the bathroom.

Clay couldn't believe what he'd almost done. He
glanced sideways at Deanna, trying to figure out what she
was thinking. She must be paralyzed with fear and
loathing at his actions. He touched her arm as she turned
to leave, and when she looked up, he saw her beautiful
eyes shining with excitement and laughter. He was so
startled, and without stopping to think what he was doing, he gathered Deanna in his arms and kissed her. It was
a wild kiss, a passionate kiss, and left them both breathless.

Clay felt like a heel. "God, I'm sorry." She was such
an innocent. Isolated for so many years, she would have
no idea what passion was. He'd probably scared her to
death—though he had to admit she'd kissed him back
with a certain enthusiasm. He held her away from him,
frantically trying to decipher her smile. Where to start
explaining his actions? "I didn't mean that to happen."

"Then why'd you do it?"

"Because . . . because . . ."

"Yes?"

At least she was still smiling. "Because you're an irresistible little thing, and you've got such a kissable
mouth."

Deanna laughed, then shook her head and walked
away, leaving him more confused than ever. She thanked
heaven for all the old movies she'd watched, or she'd
never have recognized the line. Clay's rendition wasn't as
convincing as Cary Grant's, but there was hope. She was

still smiling when she returned to the living room and was met with a sharp glance from Mary.

Deanna couldn't help herself. She walked over to her friend and whispered in her ear, "A real toe tingler." Then with a quick wink and a secret smile, she turned her attention to Bob Spencer. "Will I have to talk to that obnoxious detective again?"

Bob shrugged. "Maybe. Depends on how his investigation goes."

Deanna noticed that he seemed less talkative, almost distracted, and it took a minute to realize his attention was focused on Mary.

Clay reappeared and made his way toward the windows that looked out onto the street. He parted the curtains, then let them fall back. "Reporters are parked outside."

"Well, go tell them to move," Mary said. "My neighbors won't like it and I don't, either."

Bob's laughter rumbled like a drumroll. "They're leeches, ma'am. They won't go away until they get what they want."

"And that's Deanna," Mary said. "They can't have her, and I'm holding you personally responsible, Bob Spencer."

"Yes, ma'am."

Somewhere in the back of Clay's mind he realized there'd been a not-so-subtle change in Bob, as if his gruffness had lost its edge. He wondered if Mary had anything to do with the change. But he didn't have time to dwell on it now. All he could think about was keeping Deanna away from the reporters until he and Bob could dig deeper into her case. Like Bob, he didn't believe in coincidences, and his gut feeling told him the reporter's death was too closely connected to Deanna. How was he going to keep her safe without telling her she could be in danger?

"Deanna," he said, "I know reporters. They're going to make your life and Mary's a living hell unless we can put you someplace safe." He could have taken her to his apartment, but knew that would be the first place they'd look for her. Then it came to him. "I know a place they'd never think of." He didn't know how she would respond to his suggestion, but he asked, anyway. "How do you feel about returning to your grandmother's house?"

CHAPTER SEVEN

DEANNA WATCHED with a mixture of shock and amusement the fireworks Clay's question set off. The room fairly rocked with the raised voices of Clay, Mary and Bob, each seemingly determined to keep the other from finishing a sentence. It was like an episode of "I Love Lucy," where everyone was arguing at once. The problem was, the three of them were talking about her as though she wasn't there. They were treating her like a child who was incapable of making a decision on her own.

"Excuse me!" She raised her voice to be heard over the commotion, but they still ignored her. "Hey!" she yelled. Mary was the first to glance her way and stop talking, then Bob and finally Clay. Deanna deliberately let the quiet settle before saying, "I think going to Grandmother's house is a good idea."

The explosion started all over again, this time with Mary and Bob firing a barrage of questions at her. Clay smiled with satisfaction. "Mary, please," Deanna said. "Listen to me."

"Deanna." Mary couldn't keep quiet. "I don't think this is a good idea. You don't know what being there might do to you."

"What could be worse than this, Mary? This not knowing. My grandparents bought that house. My mother was born and raised in that house and I lived there."

"And your grandmother was brutally murdered in that house," Bob ruthlessly reminded her.

"That's right," Deanna said. "But why should it bother me? I didn't do it." It was getting harder and harder to hide the fact that she'd recovered her memory. She'd slipped up by mentioning that her mother was born in the house. But Mary and Bob were so wrapped up in their objections, and Clay obviously so pleased with himself, that no one caught her blunder.

"I'm going. As a matter of fact, I've mooched off Mary long enough. I think I should move into Grand-mother's house permanently." That statement caused another outburst of protest, with Clay voicing his mis-givings even louder than the others.

Deanna listened patiently, shifting her attention from one to the other. Finally she said, "Hush, all of you, and listen to *me* for a change. I'm sure you all think you know what's best for me, but you don't. I know what's best for me."

She looked around her friend's house, a warm cozy place that was a reflection of Mary herself. As much as she loved Mary, this was not her home and never could be. Nothing here was hers, and she had a sudden long-ing to be surrounded by things that had belonged to her family. "I appreciate your concern, all of you, but don't you see? For ten years, actually all my life, someone has dictated how I was to live. I need—no, I *have* to take control of my life." She moved over to Mary and put her arm around her. "Mary, I love you dearly. Please don't be hurt. This is really something I must do."

Deanna could see she'd won. Mary had many admi-rable qualities and one was the willingness to let Deanna make her own decisions, no matter if she got hurt or not. "Trust me, Mary."

"Okay," Mary said, "but I want you to know I think it's too soon."

"Well, I don't think it's okay," Clay objected.

Bob snorted. "Man-oh-man, that's rich. You're the one who started this mess. You suggested it."

"Only as a hideout. A stopover to give us some room to regroup and think clearly until we can come up with a better place. I didn't mean she should live there, alone, for heaven's sake." He was sorry he'd ever told her about the house being cleaned and ready for her to take over.

Deanna tried a smile to take the sting out of her next words. "Clay, I've lived alone for the past ten years. It's nothing new."

Deanna's statement stopped Clay cold. His pleading glance in Mary's direction only got him a shrug, a look that told him not to push his luck, so he gave up and nodded at Deanna. "Okay. We'll do it your way." He scowled, then shifted his attention back to Mary. Maybe guilt was the way to thwart Deanna's plans. "Are you sure you're feeling up to a trip outside? You don't look very well."

"No, I'm not sure, but I'll do anything I can to help." Mary coughed, then sat down heavily on the couch. "What do you want me to do?"

Bob scowled at Clay. "She's got no business leaving the house, Lambert. Can't you see she's sick?"

Clay wondered if everyone was going to be disagreeable. "Have you got a better plan? Take a look outside. There must be four cars out front that I recognize as belonging to reporters. If we take Deanna out of here, they're simply going to tail us wherever we go."

Bob's frown deepened. "So we lure them away on a false trail?"

Clay nodded. "The reporters know me and my car. They'll follow me. Deanna and Mary are about the same height. If Mary puts on a scarf to cover her dark hair and I hustle her into my car, maybe they'll fall for it. Then you could take Deanna in Mary's car once it's clear." He turned to Deanna and said, "If you agree, Deanna?"

For as long as Deanna could remember, there had always been someone making decisions for her. The sudden realization that everyone was waiting for her to make up her own mind was heady stuff, and frightening. Mary wasn't as well as she pretended, but she was nodding her agreement to the plan. Deanna was the last to cast her vote. "Sounds good to me."

Mary had to try one more time. "Deanna, please, think carefully about this."

"I have, Mary. It's what I have to do." She watched her friend throw up her hands in defeat, then leave the room, telling everyone she was going to get dressed.

Deanna followed closely on her heels. "I'll go pack a bag, then call Raul, so he'll know where to deliver the rest of my stuff."

Clay wasn't sure how he should feel. His plan had backfired. He was so deep in thought that it took a tap on the arm from Bob to bring him back to earth.

"You got a right to look worried, friend," Bob growled softly. "Someone out there's a killer, not once but likely twice. Leaving that poor little girl alone in that house is just begging for trouble."

"No," Clay said. "Up till now, Grandfather, you and I only guessed that Deanna didn't kill her grandmother. No one had any solid proof that she didn't. But yesterday that reporter was murdered after talking to Deanna at the library. We've got a cold-blooded killer on our hands. I think Deanna's probing into her grandmother's murder may have set the ball in motion, and she could be his next victim."

"That's what I've been trying to get through your thick skull," Bob snarled at Clay. "What we need to do is find the killer, and the only way we're going to do that is pick up a trail that's been cold for ten years and find out why someone would have wanted to murder the old lady. We need the whys, not another body, for God's sake. And that's not all we—"

"Right, we need time to move around—time to dig deeper and still keep the killer off guard," Clay interrupted. "Bob, use your head a minute. No matter what she thinks, I don't plan to leave Deanna alone in that house. But you and Grandfather have had ten years to discover who killed Agatha Deveraux and have come up blank. If Danny Hudson was stabbed to death because of his meeting with Deanna, then our killer's still on the prowl, and he's a lot closer than he's ever been. Let's reel him in."

Bob couldn't believe his ears. Coldest bastard he'd ever met, he thought. "You're going to use that sweet gal as bait?" he whispered.

"I don't like that word." Clay began searching through his pockets and finally came up with a set of keys, which he held out to Bob. "These are to the Deveraux house."

Bob shook his head and backed away a step. "Tell me something, Counselor, will solving this case be another feather in your cap? Maybe you've got an agenda all your own."

"Absolutely, and the first thing on that agenda, Spencer, is to make sure Deanna doesn't end up in jail or back at the sanitarium. You know very well that accidents can happen in those places—deadly accidents." He leaned closer to the angry man. "And keep this in mind—I've never lost a case."

Bob whispered back, "This ain't the polite world of the courtroom, Lambert."

"That's right, Spencer, and it's not the jungles of Vietnam, either, but I won there, too. Do you want to know how?"

Bob hesitated. There'd been a lightning-quick change in those hazel eyes. He recognized that ruthless look and knew there was more to Clay Lambert than a pretty face and a fat bankroll. He took the keys and stuffed them in his pocket just as Deanna entered the room. She was struggling with a suitcase and he rushed over to help.

"If you'll get me the keys to Mary's car, I'll put this in the trunk." Bob shot a thoughtful glance at Clay, then followed Deanna through the kitchen, where she plucked a set of keys off the counter and showed him the door to the garage. Before he passed her, he paused and said, "You be real careful, kid."

Deanna jumped as if guilt had poked her in the backside like a sharp stick. "What do you mean?"

"Games can be real dangerous. Be careful who you play with." He deliberately cut off her next words by closing the door.

Now what, she wondered, was that all about? She worried about the warning all the way back to the living room. Clay was standing in front of the picture window, the curtains slightly parted as he studied the street. He was so handsome, she thought, then wondered how involved he was with the woman who'd been in his office. She remembered one of Dr. Gresham's pearls of wisdom—if you want to know, ask. Laughter bubbled up and she struggled a moment to battle it down.

Clay turned in time to see Deanna's smile and smiled, too. Guilt over the kiss gnawed at him, but he didn't know how to explain why it had happened. "Deanna?"

She felt the weight of his gaze, the way his eyes lingered on her face, her mouth, then moved downward. Her cheeks heated and she felt suddenly nervous, edgy, surprised that one look could cause such a reaction. She eased the curtain back in place. "Are you in love with the woman you were kissing in your office the first day I met you?"

"You mean Lynn? No, I'm not in love with her." His quick denial came as a shock, and he wondered where her line of questioning was leading.

"Then kissing doesn't mean anything to you? It's not special?"

"Yes, it is, sort of. There are different types of kisses." He began to feel uncomfortable.

"I see. And what type of kiss was the one in the hall?"

"Listen, I'm sorry. I don't know what in the hell possessed me to act like that."

"You didn't want to kiss me?"

"No—yes."

"You didn't like it?"

"Yes—no." He felt frustrated and was astonished that he was more than a little embarrassed and practically tongue-tied.

"Then why did you kiss me?"

"Because." He caught a flash of amusement in her eyes and wondered if she was putting him on, but he dismissed the notion. "Deanna, sometimes a man's hormones kick in. I was angry, excited, and you're beautiful." That was the best he could do at the moment, since he wasn't sure himself how he felt.

One thing he was sure of, though—the undeniable excitement he felt every time he got close to her. She was a dangerous temptation, and as hard as he tried, he kept losing control. "You're far too sexy for your own good," he said softly, knowing full well he should keep their relationship impersonal. But dammit, his thoughts could only be categorized as pure lust. "What's keeping Mary?" he asked, and glanced around, wishing she'd magically appear.

"So you kissed me," she persisted, "because you were angry at what that detective said?"

He wanted to drop the subject, and fast, before he did something else to feel guilty about. "I kissed you... because I wanted to."

"Then you're saying you're sorry, but you're really not?"

"Deanna, the only thing I'm sorry about is the way I kissed you, not that I kissed you. I shouldn't have been so— Aha, here comes Mary." Clay didn't even try to hide the relief in his voice as he hastily moved away from Deanna and inspected Mary's scarf. He made a few adjustments, pulling it forward a little to conceal her face more.

Deanna watched him fuss over Mary's disguise, then glanced at Bob, realizing as she did that he'd been standing in the kitchen entry eavesdropping all the while she'd been talking to Clay. It was a safe bet he'd heard their entire conversation, but Bob's attention didn't seem to be on her or Clay but on Mary.

With everyone's focus elsewhere, Deanna had time to calm down and collect her thoughts. Her heart was pounding hard. She was short of breath and there was still heat in her cheeks. But the excitement went deeper and she couldn't describe it. She'd deliberately set out to needle Clay. To get under his skin like a grain of sand, but only as an irritant, she told herself. Or was it simply that? Had she been pushing him into kissing her again? What an interesting concept, she thought.

Obviously female wiles were inbred. The game of flirting came as naturally to her as if she'd taken instructions. Maybe her grandmother had been right and she *was* like her mother. Deanna didn't think it was such a bad thing, after all, if the sensations and emotions she felt simply came with being a woman.

"Deanna?" Mary said. "It's time to try this scheme. Are you sure you want to do this?"

She had to quit daydreaming and pay more attention to what was going on. "As sure as I can be. Don't look so worried, Mary. I'll be fine, and as soon as you feel better you can help me settle in. Oh, and don't let me forget to call Raul and have him pick up my belongings here before he delivers the rest of my things." She was blathering like an idiot and bit her lip to stop.

Deanna and Bob went to the window where they could peek through the curtains and watch as Clay and Mary hurried out and down the path to the driveway. The opening of Mary's front door set the hounds on the scent. The reporters stirred, ready for blood, but before they could get out of their cars, they realized their quarry was fleeing and took up the chase.

Deanna counted five cars trailing behind Clay's Corvette. Suddenly his tires screeched like the cry of a bird of prey, and abruptly the Corvette was nothing but a red blur in the hot morning sun. Deanna watched until the street was quiet and empty. She dropped the curtain back in place and turned to Bob. "When do we leave?"

"Give 'em enough time to get clear of the neighborhood. A couple of minutes. They're a smart bunch. It

won't take some of them long to realize they can't keep
up with Clay and that he's leading them on a merry
chase. They'll be back, staking out Mary's house in no
time." He began moving toward the kitchen and motioned for Deanna to follow. "Can you drive?" he asked.

"Yes. Well, sort of. I don't have a license, though."
Deanna locked Mary's door securely and hurried to the
car. Bob moved quickly, with easy fluid motions for such
a big man. She sat quietly and watched as he raised the
heavy garage door with one hand, backed the car into the
driveway, then closed the garage door and secured the
lock.

Once they were on their way, Bob glanced over at her.
"You can't get around in this town without a car. Want
me to look around for one?"

He was sweet, Deanna thought. "Thanks, but I know
what I want. One just like Clay's. But I'll need to get a
license first."

"Not to worry. I have a friend down at the Department of Motor Vehicles. I'll get you all fixed up tomorrow."

"You mean I won't have to take a test? How can that
be?"

"I told you, I got friends."

"Oh, well, I don't think..."

Bob sighed as he pulled onto the freeway. "If you tell
me you know how to drive, I believe you. Don't be too
quick to be independent. Let me do something for you,
Deanna."

The change in his voice and the gentleness there made
her turn in the seat and look at him. "Why? Why would
you want to do anything for me?"

Bob's hands tightened on the steering wheel. He cleared his throat loudly, then said so softly he had to repeat his answer, "Guilt."

"What?"

"Guilt. When you were doing research yesterday, did you happen to read the article about your drugged state when they found your grandmother?" He couldn't look at her. Couldn't face what he'd done even to this day. Old man Lambert was the only person who knew the guilt he'd carried all these years. He was ashamed of what he'd done and was determined to make up for his mistake. A mistake that might have made a difference if it had surfaced during the trial.

"Do you mean the article that ranted and raved about the depraved youth of the sixties? The one that said I was spaced out on drugs and hinted at a hallucinogen as the reason I flipped out and killed my grandmother? Is that what you're referring to?"

"Yep."

She couldn't figure him out. For a man who usually talked without taking a breath, he suddenly seemed at a loss for words. "So. Yep what?"

"You were no drugged-out kid like the press let on. I knew that, my partner knew it, and so did the powers that be at that time. When we got the test results back they showed you'd been on a mixture of antibiotics, aspirin and antihistamines, so we figured you'd had the flu. But there was another drug in your system, Darvon, and a strong dose of it. We found the prescription in your grandmother's medicine cabinet. I think the combination of all those drugs made you act strange. Then, after witnessing your granny's death, you went catatonic and couldn't tell us anything."

She remembered that day so vividly now, how her grandmother had been angry that she was sick and begging to stay home from school.

"It took too long to get the blood work back. So without telling anyone I made a trip to the lab, only to find that my partner had picked up the reports. When I grilled him about it, he told me he'd picked them up on the chief's orders and turned them over. But he'd taken a peek and there wasn't any evidence of hard drugs in your system. There was nothing there that we didn't already know."

"Why didn't that fact come out in court or the newspapers?"

"Well, kid, that was something I wanted to know myself. I had a funny feeling about those reports, the way they were handled. You know, it kept bugging me, but we were busy and I let it ride until the trial. When nothing was ever mentioned in your favor, I told the district attorney something was wrong and why. A couple of hours later I got a call to go see my chief. The meeting didn't last long, but the meaning was clear. Keep my mouth shut about the drug report or I'd be back walking the streets." Guilt made his shoulders slump. "Man, I was madder than hell. But the outcome of the trial was a done deed by then."

Deanna listened, and when he fell silent she said, "Bob, from what I've read about the trial, I don't think that information would have made any difference."

"Yeah, but I've always felt guilty I didn't do anything. I'd been with the force long enough to make waves. Hell, I'd made them before, but there was something weird about your case." He didn't think he could put into words what he felt, but he was going to give it a try. "You ever see a wheel rolling downhill? Ever watch it pick up momentum as it went, running over and smashing anything in its path? That was the Deveraux case—step in the way of the political machine behind it and you'd get crushed.''

"So you never said anything and kept your job?"

Bob flinched. She didn't mince words. "That's it in a nutshell. But I never forgot you, or the case and when old Lambert contacted me a couple of years ago, I was eager to help."

"I remember you came to see me when I was at Twelve Oaks? You thought I was innocent even way back then, didn't you?"

"Yep." He concentrated on maneuvering through the narrow side streets. "Couldn't prove it then. May never be able to prove it. You're going to have to be prepared for that." He'd pulled up in the driveway of her grand-mother's house and switched off the engine, but neither seemed to notice they had reached their destination.

Deanna's smile was sweet and forgiving. "I think this time you and Clay'll do it, Bob." She realized they'd stopped and she looked around. For a second her breath caught in the back of her throat. She groped blindly for the car-door latch, found it, then was out of the car with Bob's warning ringing in her ears.

Deanna didn't stop until she was standing in the front yard. Amazing, she thought. The two-story brick house hadn't changed in all this time. Maybe the trees and shrubs were larger, but everything else seemed the same. The house had weathered the years remarkably. Then she remembered that Mr. Lambert had diligently overseen the care of the property.

Her gaze roamed over the front of the house, search-ing the long wide windows until she found the one that had been her room. She expected to see a water-colored paper cutout of a turkey taped to the inside of her window, but that had been a cold November day ten years ago.

Slowly she moved up the curved stone steps to the front porch, then turned around and glanced up and down the street. If she remembered correctly, the house was only a few blocks from Rice University and the Village, where her grandmother had had her shop. This was an older, rather elegant subdivision, and from the looks of it, nothing much had changed there, either. She shivered as the horrifying thought flicked across her mind that any minute Agatha Fleur Deveraux was going to yell at her to get in the house.

She mentally slammed the door on her memories, then almost jumped out of her skin when she saw the front door. It was painted Chinese red. A sad smile touched her lips. Mr. Lambert had made sure nothing had changed. That particular shade of red was her first triumph over her grandmother. They'd discussed the color loudly for days. Finally Agatha had given in, but only if Deanna scraped and painted the door herself.

Now, of course, Deanna realized she hadn't won, after all. Her grandmother had wanted her to do the work. She was a sharp, ruthless, mean-spirited old lady who always got what she wanted, and woe to those who stood in her way.

"Are you okay?"

She'd forgotten about Bob and was about to explain, then stopped herself, remembering she wasn't supposed to have any memories. "I'm fine. May I have the keys, please?" His worried expression made her smile. "Really, I'm okay."

But she wasn't okay. Weird things were happening in her head. Pictures were flashing in and out, as if she was flipping through a family photo album. She slipped the key into the lock. If the inside was the same, she thought, she just might run screaming from the house.

The first thing to greet her was the heat. It was like opening an oven door, and the shock robbed her of her breath. The house smelled musty and it was dark. Deanna reached for a light switch. Nothing happened.

Bob swore under his breath. "Electricity's off. Stay put a minute."

Deanna stood in the gloom of the entryway, listening to Bob cautiously moving around. The sound of his shoes clicking on the hardwood floor jerked her back in time to that fateful day.

She cringed and bit down hard on her lip to suppress the scream that wanted to escape. The dark. She'd always hated the dark. Now her fear was worse, and she was in a deep pit, suffocating. She had to get out and was just about to turn around and slip out the door when the room lightened significantly, taking away some of her fears.

Bit by bit the house grew brighter as Bob yanked the curtains back from the windows, and she could see the stairs and the first section of the landing, then the doorway to the dining room on the left and, across the entry, the closed doors of the living room. Light began to illuminate the hallway, and a little hesitantly she was drawn there like an insect attracted to light. She could see a corner of a kitchen cabinet and stopped. Footsteps were echoing hollowly above her and she glanced up, following them first to her bedroom, then to her grandmother's room, the two bathrooms and finally down the hall to the top of the stairs. She knew it was Bob. Still, she stood frozen to the spot until the glimmer of light caught his shadow as he made his way down the stairs. Deanna let her breath out slowly and smiled.

"I think there's enough light to see. There's furniture in two bedrooms, the breakfast room, dining room and the den at the back of the house. But you can't stay here until the electricity's on."

"How long will that take?" She knew he was carefully watching her, gauging her reactions.

"Normally it could take a couple of days, at least one, but I'll take care of it right now if you want."

"How?"

"I can jimmy the lock off the meter. I've done it before."

"Is that legal?"

"No, but I know someone who'll cover for me." Bob glanced at the closed living room door. "Thing is, I need to call this guy before I tinker with the meter." He couldn't stand it any longer. He had to ask the question that had been on his mind since Clay had come up with the lame idea to bring her here. He nodded toward the closed door. "You want to go in there?"

She was being tested, Deanna realized, and knew she had to walk into the living room as calmly as if she'd never seen it before. At first the heavy pocket doors resisted her efforts, then they slowly began to slide open. Her heart jumped in her throat and her head began to throb. For a second she hesitated and squeezed her eyes shut. Maybe she wasn't as strong or as brave as she thought. But before what courage she had fled completely, she shoved the doors apart until her arms were fully extended, then she opened her eyes.

Darkness. The mustiness of stale air was all she could detect. The tinny smell of fresh blood was gone. The scent of gardenias, her grandmother's perfume, had faded away.

Bob touched her shoulder. She stepped aside, letting him enter the room first, then waited while he felt around the walls. As he hunted for the windows, it gave her time to pull herself together.

When all the curtains were parted and sunlight filled the room, Deanna glanced around, knowing Bob was watching her. If he'd known she'd spent the better part of the past ten years learning to hide her true feelings, he might have looked harder and deeper. What surprised Deanna was that she truly didn't feel anything but anger.

The room was empty of furnishings. There wasn't even a stain on the hardwood floor where the blood must have soaked through the rug. "From the way you've been watching me," she said, "I take it this is the room my grandmother died in?"

"Yeah. Sorry, old habits are hard to break." Ten years hadn't dulled his memory. Details of the murder scene were as vivid in his mind as if he'd been dropped back in time. The room gave him the heebie-jeebies, and seeing Deanna there unnerved him. He wanted out, fast. Taking Deanna's hand, he pulled her back into the entryway and shut the heavy double doors. "Come on, there's a convenience store a couple blocks away. I need to go call that friend of mine."

"I'll stay here."

"No. That won't do. I told Clay—"

"For heaven's sake, I don't need a baby-sitter. I'm a big girl. I intend to live here. Alone."

What the hell was keeping Clay? he wondered. Arguing with her was useless, he realized, so he handed her the key and told her to lock the door. Besides, Clay would probably be there before he returned. "I'll be back in about twenty."

Well, Deanna thought when he'd left, she'd gotten her wish—she was home, and alone. But her bravado quickly evaporated in the numbing silence. She remembered the cool peacefulness of the backyard and headed toward the back of the house at a trot. What a fool, she thought, and slowed her steps, even forcing herself to pause to inspect a piece of her grandmother's furniture.

The brilliant sun almost blinded her as she stepped out into the yard. This time when her breath caught in her throat it was with delight. The last tenant must have been a real gardener, for the yard looked lovingly tended. The oak tree had grown to such a height and width that half the yard was in shade. A white wrought-iron bench made a semicircle around the massive trunk. There were flowers everywhere and neatly trimmed boxwood hedges. At the back and lining the fence were her grandmother's beloved gardenia bushes, tall as the fence now, with a few scattered flowers. She longed to see them in full bloom.

She'd always enjoyed working in the garden, putting her hands in the warm earth, planting flowers and watching them grow. Drifting in a gardener's dreamworld, she mentally began designing and planning where she'd put some of her favorites.

In an instant her dreams were shattered. Her heart seemed to stop and she froze, a familiar chill shimmying up her spine. Nothing moved. For a second she thought maybe Bob had returned. But she knew that if he hadn't found her in the house, he would have checked the backyard.

She listened, trying to figure out what had alerted her. The muffled sound of a twig broken under a heavy shoe, followed by, in her imagination, a slow, carefully placed backward step. There it was again, but she couldn't decide where it was coming from.

Deanna remembered that the neighborhood was old and one of the few in Houston that had alleys. Her head went up like a bloodhound's, and without thinking what she was doing, she made a dash for the back gate. Some things never changed, she thought. The gate reacted as it had ten years ago. The corner dug in the ground. The trick was to pull up, then push on it hard. But it took her a moment to remember, and she struggled a few precious seconds before she applied her shoulder to it.

She almost ended up being dragged out into the alley as the gate swung free. She teetered to a stop and looked both ways. At the far end, nearest the street, was a parked car.

Deanna shaded her eyes, trying to see its occupants, but the sun shone on the windshield, making its surface like a mirror. She started walking toward the car but was shocked motionless to see it back up. When she stopped, so did the car. She took a few steps, fear making her cold in the hot sun. The car backed away again.

It was a stupid childish game and it made her angry. This time she didn't stop but kept walking. The car sped up, backing rapidly down the alley. When it was halfway out in the street, it made a sharp turn, and with a squeal of tires was gone.

Deanna stood staring for a long moment, then, her knees shaking, turned around and walked back to the house. Fool. She should have been scared silly, she told herself. But she wasn't. She was mad and elated at the same time. From the moment her memory had returned she'd known the truth of her grandmother's murder, that the killer had let her take the blame. Maybe now that she was free, the killer was concerned she might remember.

When the car had backed out of the alley, the direction of the sun had shifted and she had gotten a good look at the driver. What made her shiver was that she'd seen him before, a couple of times, actually. She'd even drawn him.

The driver of the car in the alley was one of the men who'd been at the library—oh, Lord, she'd even bumped into him!—the older, bald-headed man. She knew what he looked like but had no earthly idea who he was. One thing was for sure, though. She wasn't crazy.

She was being watched.

She was being followed.

CHAPTER EIGHT

DEANNA TURNED and headed back up the alley, then stopped abruptly. Out of frustration and her own stupidity she kicked at a discarded can and missed. She should have gotten the license number or at least the make and model, but the only thing she remembered was that it was a big green car. Great.

Kicking at the can again, she watched with satisfaction as it skipped and hopped down the alley, then she made her way through the gate, careful to pull it securely shut and double-check the lock. Her hands were shaking. Maybe she wasn't as smart or as brave as she'd let herself believe. She'd been kidding herself that she could find out who killed her grandmother on her own.

The grandstand play she'd envisioned where she'd single-handedly brought the killer to justice so everyone would know the truth was a childish dream. She'd read too many mysteries over the years and had a talent, a knack, for figuring out whodunits long before anyone else. She thought she could unravel her own real mystery.

Even after the murder of Danny Hudson, it still hadn't sunk in what she was up against. But it became crystal clear after the incident in the alley. There was something sinister about the way the car had backed up and advanced as she did. Fear, real fear, was sobering.

She was a fool.

For the first time since she'd regained her memory, the realization hit her that she needed help, and there were only two people she trusted—Mary and Clay. Of course Mary was going to be hurt that she hadn't confided in her earlier, but she'd get over it.

Clay.

She stopped and thought about him for a minute. Yes, she trusted him, even though he was high-handed and still a little unsure of her, but yes, she could trust him.

She was just entering the house when she heard a loud knocking that sent her heart hammering wildly. The pounding, then the sound of a familiar masculine voice, made her smile and she hurried to the door. She was about to open it when another voice joined the first and a loud argument ensued.

Deanna yanked the door wide. "What's the matter with you two?" Clay and Bob fell silent. "All I need is for the neighbors to call the police." As she fumed, she looked around for her friend. She glared at Clay. "What did you do with Mary?"

"I'll tell you in a minute. After you tell me what the hell you're doing here alone." Clay glared at Bob. "I can't possibly guess why you'd go off and leave her by herself."

There was that tone again, but she was too concerned about Mary's absence to say so. She tugged at Clay's shirtsleeve. "Stop acting like a Neanderthal and tell me where Mary is."

But it was as if both men were deaf as stumps. Bob pushed past Clay into the house and waved his arms. "Take a good look around, Lambert. Your plans leave a lot to be desired. No electricity means no lights and no air-conditioning. The gas and water's off, too. Did you want Deanna to stay here like this? And answer the kid—where'd you stash Mary?''

Kid? The term made the hackles rise on the back of Deanna's neck like a porcupine's quills. But she couldn't have objected if she'd wanted to. The men wouldn't give her a chance.

''Mary's in the hospital,'' Clay continued quickly before they could throw any more questions at him. ''She had a coughing spell in the car. I thought she sounded awful, but when I suggested I take her to her doctor she wouldn't hear of it. Since we were already on the freeway, I just headed on downtown to Memorial Baptist Hospital emergency room.''

Deanna smiled. She would love to have seen Mary's face when Clay ignored her wishes and drove her to the hospital.

''The doctor had an X ray taken, diagnosed pneumonia and immediately admitted her.'' Bob and Deanna were closing in on him at once with a barrage of questions. He backed up a step and held up his hand as he tried to answer them. ''No, she shouldn't have any visitors today. They have her on antibiotics and oxygen and she's resting. Yes, tomorrow. And yes, Mary's going to be all right. She just needs rest.''

Deanna sighed with an overwhelming sense of relief. ''I'd be lost if anything happened to Mary. She's been my rock for years. Thanks.'' She touched Clay's arm, a gesture of gratitude, and was surprised when he quickly pulled away. Something was wrong. He usually had a reassuring smile for her, but now his expression was solemn, even grim.

Second by second she felt him slipping away from her until the distance yawned between them like a chasm. How many times had she caught him watching her when he thought she wasn't looking? Now he didn't even bother to glance her way, his gaze totally avoiding hers. Surely she hadn't been crazy when she'd thought his voice softened each time he talked to her. Now his tone was cool, impersonal, the way he must sound in court. That damn kiss, Deanna thought. He was feeling guilty, and her teasing hadn't helped.

"You got a screwdriver in your car, Lambert?" Bob asked.

"No, and what do you need one for?"

"To pry off the lock on the meter."

Deanna sighed again, hugely. They seemed determined to stand there glaring at each other. "Mary keeps a tool kit in the trunk of her car," she offered.

"Fine." Bob turned to leave. "While I get the juice turned on, why don't you do something useful, Lambert, like seeing to the water and gas."

In awkward silence, they watched Bob stomp down the porch steps. Deanna wanted to say something but was at a loss for words, the distance Clay had put between them suddenly feeling insurmountable.

Her throat ached with suppressed tears. But that was ridiculous, she thought. That would mean he'd hurt her feelings, and she'd never allowed anyone to get close enough to hurt her.

"He's right," Clay said. "You can't stay here."

That old saying of Dr. Gresham's came back to her. *If you want to know, ask.* "What's the matter, Clay?"

He leaned his shoulder against the door frame, watching Bob open the trunk of Mary's car. "Matter? This was a stupid idea. I didn't give a thought to the utilities or what staying here might do to you."

"That's not what I meant, and you know it. Staying here was a wonderful idea. It's an anchor for me, Clay."

She was on the verge of telling him about the return of her memory and the man in the car, but his next remark robbed her of words.

"You're not strong enough to be left alone."

She stared at him, unable to believe what she'd heard, as he continued to gaze straight ahead. There was a sharp pain in her chest and a stinging behind her eyes. She wasn't strong enough—meaning she couldn't take care of herself. Wasn't that what Dr. Gresham had always told her, that until she faced what she'd done she would never be well? No one would ever trust her, it seemed, or be totally convinced of her innocence. But Dr. Gresham was wrong, and so was Clay. She wasn't quitting. She damn well wasn't a weak sniveling female.

So Clay was like all the rest, she thought sadly. It had simply taken him a little longer. Well, she wouldn't trust him, either. "What did you just say?" Her voice was soft with pain and anger.

Clay realized what he'd said and how it sounded, but he wouldn't back down or apologize. Mary had accused him of being bored with his life. She'd said that he was playing emotional games with Deanna and that Deanna wasn't equipped to handle them. She'd warned him to stick to Deanna's legal problems and leave the girl alone. Mary's accusations had made him face some cold, hard truths, and he hadn't particularly liked what he'd seen.

Mary had been right about him. He'd been spoiled, he admitted, and had never taken life very seriously. There'd always been plenty of money and never a shortage of women. Hell, law school wasn't even particularly difficult, and he'd breezed through with top grades. He'd been carefree and reckless, a true hedonist. But after the war he had changed; he'd come home a different man.

And Mary was dead wrong about one thing. He did care about Deanna.

Clay gave Deanna a sideways glance, saw the angry sparkle in those beautiful blue eyes that contradicted the sweet smile. "I'm going to take you to my sister's home. You can stay with her until Mary's out of the hospital." He was more than a little relieved to see Bob rounding the side of the house.

Deanna's eyes narrowed a fraction and her smile widened. "How old am I, Clay?"

"Around twenty-three." His answer was offhand, as if her question was trivial, unimportant. He was about to walk away and intercept Bob at the bottom of the porch stairs when her next question made him pause.

"I believe that's over the legal age in Texas, isn't it?"

"Right. But what does that have to do with anything?"

"I'll tell you," Deanna said between clenched teeth.

Bob caught the anger and tension in the air, feeling it almost crackle with electricity, and pulled up short at the first step.

"Twenty-three means I call the shots. Twenty-three means I do what I want, and I intend to stay right here. As my attorney, I want you to do the following, Mr. Lambert." In the past few minutes it had become even clearer to her that freedom meant independence.

"One, I want my money. Now. Today. If that means you have to take me to the bank to do whatever is necessary for me to get it, then let's go."

He was staring at her as if he'd never seen her before, as if she'd sprouted horns and a tail. Then he smiled, and the smile infuriated her.

"Two, I won't be dependent on you or anyone. I want my own car. And three... three... I'll think of something else in a minute."

Clay couldn't help it, he started laughing. She was magnificent when she was angry. Mary still saw Deanna as that helpless, lost thirteen-year-old, but she was mistaken. Deanna wasn't an emotional cripple, unable to take care of herself. Inexperienced in some areas, yes, but she was as sharp as anyone he'd ever met. Deanna Deveraux knew what she wanted and went after it. She was just a little more direct and honest in her approach than most women.

A feeling of joy washed over him, and he wanted nothing more than to reach out and give her a hug. When he tried, she turned away, and he realized he'd hurt her. He would have said something then, but she was talking to Bob and he was forced to wait.

"Since you have friends in high places, could I ask a favor of you, Bob? Would you get the water and gas turned on?" Asking for help wouldn't lose her bid for independence, Deanna thought. After all, it was only those who assumed she was helpless that ticked her off. She slanted a look hot with anger in Clay's direction.

"Be happy to." Bob twirled Mary's key ring around on his finger for a second. "I'll have to take your friend's car."

"I don't think she'll mind. Maybe you could go see her—return her keys. Say you're family if they won't let you in." She bit back a smile at the way his stern face dissolved into a shy grin.

"Good idea," Bob said, and hurried off. He was almost to the car when Deanna hailed him and he swung around, waiting for her to catch up to him.

"Bob, if you were in my place and wanted to talk to someone . . . someone you could totally trust, who would you pick?"

"You mean someone besides Clay or me?"

"Yes. Sorry, but . . ."

"You really don't trust any of us, do you?" He opened the trunk of the car and pulled out her suitcase.

"I thought I did. Now I don't know." He didn't seem upset with her answer.

"Let me think a minute." Something about Deanna kept nagging at Bob like a sore tooth. He just couldn't pin down what it was yet. She was obviously leery of everyone and he couldn't blame her. Still, he had the feeling that she was playing her hand very close to the chest. Not that he could blame her after what she'd been through.

"If I were you," he said, "and I was looking for someone to confide in, or even just talk to, who was honest and had an impeccable reputation, I think I'd have to elect Judge Harrison. Old Mr. Lambert trusted him totally."

"Thanks, Bob." She grabbed her case with both hands and started off.

"Don't be too hard on Clay, Deanna."

"Why not?"

"Because he's out of his element and doesn't even know it yet." He could see she didn't have the faintest idea what he was talking about. He shrugged, then opened the car door and slipped behind the wheel. She was a bright kid, she'd figure it out. As for Clay, well, he planned to keep his eye on that one.

THE SUMMER SUN hung low in the sky as the light began to fade. A sudden breeze kicked up, sending dried leaves and dust dancing around in crazy circles. Deanna sat in her grandmother's driveway, her hands caressing the steering wheel of her brand-new cherry red Corvette.

She ignored the other red Corvette parked on the street in front of her house and refused to think about the man sitting on the top step of the porch, glaring at her wordlessly. Instead, she inhaled deeply, closed her eyes and savored the scent of new leather.

For a while she'd allowed herself to forget everything. For a while she'd simply been Miss Deveraux, wealthy, catered to and pampered. Money did that, she'd quickly learned once Clay had introduced her to the vice president of the bank where part of her inheritance was drawing interest. The banker had been polite and authoritative, and she'd let him run on about interest rates and the bank's brilliant investment record. Then, tired of listening, she'd stunned both men by asking what the bottom line was—she wanted the dollar figure of her investment.

Once she'd recovered from the shock of her monetary worth, Clay had quickly pointed out that the bank's holding was only about a quarter of her estate. His grandfather had invested wisely, and the dividends had been left to draw interest.

She almost gave the banker a heart attack when she sweetly told him half of the savings were to be converted to a checking account with immediate access. Then she'd listened to him moan a protest and allowed him to try to fast-talk her into being more reasonable and responsible. The boom was lowered when she told the banker she could always draw her investments from the bank and put them elsewhere.

She chuckled and caressed the soft leather of her seat. A hot breeze ruffled her wildly tangled hair and made her sun-touched cheeks sting. Buying the car had been fun. She leaned back, remembering her feeling of elation at the shock on the salesman's face. Then she thought of a certain face in the rearview mirror and could only imagine how angry he must have been when he realized she'd purposely disappeared.

It had taken her more than a couple of wrong turns before she'd finally ended up in front of the courthouse. She was lucky she hadn't been stopped, driving without a license. It had been one thing convincing the car salesman to let her take the car off the lot; she didn't think a police officer would be as willing to swallow her fabricated tale.

After an hour and a half she'd left Judge Harrison's office feeling relieved and apprehensive at the same time. Bob was right. She'd trusted the judge the minute he'd greeted her. There was something honest in his eyes. And though she balked at following his orders, she knew she wouldn't disappoint him, either.

Deanna glanced in Clay's direction and sighed. She'd judged him without giving him a chance to prove himself, exactly as so many others had done to her.

Clay had been waiting for Deanna for more than two hours. He'd abandoned the heat of the car and made himself as comfortable as he could on the shaded porch of the Deveraux house.

He tried not to think about their afternoon together or he'd have to face the truth that every time he'd looked at her he'd ached to touch her. He'd spent the afternoon seesawing between worry, shock, amusement, anger and fear, and he was exhausted.

After an initial attempt to instruct Deanna, Clay realized she was doing fine on her own and decided to sit back and enjoy the entertainment. If she'd done something truly stupid, he would have stopped her, or at least protested. But once again, Deanna had shown him she was nobody's fool. A sweet smile, a soft voice and her politeness only intensified the firm request.

After the bank, he'd taken her to the same car dealership he'd bought his car. But before he'd allowed her out of the car, he'd tried to explain the complicated business of dealing with a car salesman. He should've known better.

She'd breezed into the showroom, found exactly what model and color she wanted, asked the price, pulled out her checkbook and started to write. Then she'd paused. He'd been stunned speechless as he'd watched the drooling salesman when she smiled that sweet smile of hers and told the man her friend—she'd looked pointedly at Clay—had told her to deduct one thousand dollars. Before the salesman could protest, she'd signed the check and handed it to him.

Done deal. Deanna had paid exactly 550 dollars less than he had, and he'd spent three hours at the same dealership haggling with the same salesman.

He watched her from his vantage point and enjoyed the familiar blissful expression. There was something special about a first car; he'd just never thought women felt the same. Obviously he was wrong. Let her savor the moment. A smile touched the corner of his mouth, then his expression turned grim.

He'd followed her from the dealership, thinking she was returning to her grandmother's house, but she'd slipped away and he'd spent an hour cruising the city in search of her. He'd even visited Mary, only to find that Deanna hadn't been there. Finally he'd given up, deciding that if she wasn't dead, or in jail for driving without

a license—something he'd have to talk to her about—
she'd eventually end up back at the house.

Deanna opened the car door and climbed out.

Clay watched her, his eyes missing nothing. There was
something wrong, he realized, a hesitancy in her step. As
she drew closer, he rose to his feet. "I'm not your keeper,
Deanna. But I was worried when you disappeared. There
are things going on that you're not aware of."

"I know," was her response, and she continued
quickly, "I need to talk to you, Clay. And you need to
listen to me and not ask a bunch of your lawyer-type
questions."

"May I ask one?" He wanted to smile, the way she
stood there like a disheveled queen in a wrinkled dress,
her hair a mess and her cheeks bright red from the sun
and wind.

"Sure."

"Where'd you go?"

"I went to see Judge Harrison."

Once again she'd managed to render him speechless.
His mouth worked soundlessly for a second, then he finally managed to say, "What? Why?"

"Because I don't think you believe in my innocence, or
my capabilities. It's made me suspicious of you and your
motives. So—" she shrugged her shoulders "—I don't
trust you."

Those four words cut deep, deeper than he wanted to
admit. Yet when he thought about it, he'd given her little reason to trust him. He'd treated her at times as off-
handedly as if she were a dim-witted child. He'd
deliberately kept things from her, telling himself he was
protecting her, but in reality he didn't trust her to understand. He'd tap-danced around the truth, skirted issues
she should have been advised of, because, he told him-

self, it was for her own good. And all the while she'd seen through him. She didn't trust him, and he'd brought it on himself.

Clay held out his hand. "The house must be cooled off by now. Let's go inside and talk."

Deanna took his hand, then unlocked the door. There was a sadness about him that puzzled her. If she hadn't known better, she'd have thought her declaration had hurt him. But to be hurt, he'd have to care about her, and she doubted she was more than a job or an obligation to him.

Clay squeezed her hand reassuringly and followed her inside, picking up the suitcase that stood in the entry-way. He gave a grunt of surprise at its weight. As they were passing the living room, Deanna abruptly stopped and he almost ran up her heels. He was about to ask what was wrong when it suddenly came to him.

Agatha Fleur Deveraux had been murdered in that room. Deanna didn't know. She had no memory. Yet he observed silently and with a puzzled frown the way her whole body seemed to stiffen; the way her head jerked up like a trapped animal's. From her profile he could see her eyes widen a fraction, her lips part and the color drain from her face. He wondered if it was all coming back.

He couldn't stand it. She was so still. Her fear vibrated through the air. He didn't want to frighten her further with any loud noises or sudden moves, so he lowered the suitcase to the floor. Then he moved up beside her and gently wrapped his arm around her shoulders. Her absolute stillness, not even the flicker of an eyelash, worried him.

"Deanna," Clay whispered, but she didn't answer or move. Her unblinking gaze was riveted on an area of the floor, and though he was loath to take his attention away from her, he shifted his eyes to the spot, then immediately glanced back.

It took a second for what he'd seen to register, and when it did, his head whipped around again. "What the hell?" Lying in the center of the floor was a beautiful white gardenia. For the first time he caught its pungent fragrance. It was like a splash of cold water in the face.

"Deanna," he said, turning her around to face him. But he wasn't getting any response. From the blank look in her eyes, he realized she was in another world, another time. "Deanna," he shouted, "look at me!" When she didn't react he said, "Don't you dare slip away from me." Grasping her shoulders, he shook her. "Deanna!"

From some far-off place, Clay's voice reached her and dragged her back to the present. She blinked a couple of times to clear her vision, inhaled deeply and whispered, "I'm okay. It was just a shock, that's all."

"A shock! You're shaking all over." He turned her around so she wasn't facing the living room. "Would you mind telling me what that flower means and what it's doing there?"

"The gardenia was my grandmother's favorite flower. She loved them and used it as her personal signature—her trademark. All of Fleur's boxes, bags and advertising had the gardenia on it. Those black shiny boxes, like patent leather, with the white ribbon and flower in the center were so beautiful. I must have wrapped a million during the holidays." She'd slipped, but it didn't make any difference now. She was going to tell him everything.

Clay wanted desperately to ask questions but didn't dare interrupt. Her voice was emotionless, a monotone, but some of her color was coming back and her eyes were losing that vacuousness. She was still shaking though, and he wrapped his arm around her shoulders and led her through the house, looking for someplace comfortable. The den offered an arrangement of nondescript old-fashioned furniture, and he guided her to the couch and urged her to sit.

"Deanna, how did that flower get there? Do you know?"

"I think so." She didn't want to look at him when she told him, didn't want to see his disbelief. The thought of lying crossed her mind, but she remembered her conversation with Judge Harrison.

Taking a strong hold of her emotions, she said as calmly as possible, "When I talked to Judge Harrison, he advised me to tell you everything I know. Clay, someone's been following me and watching everything I do. He was at the library. He followed me here and he was definitely in the alley today. Maybe he even killed Danny Hudson and wanted to blame me for it."

"Wait a minute, wait a minute. Who's following you? And what does Judge Harrison have to do with this?"

"When I gave you the slip this afternoon, I did it on purpose so I could go see the judge. I told him everything, Clay, and he said he'd help me all he could, but I was to talk to my attorney."

In one terrifying second Clay remembered telling Deanna that even if she admitted she'd murdered her grandmother, even if she told the judge or announced it publicly, she couldn't be prosecuted.

Deanna saw the doubt and the question in his eyes and looked away. "I remember, Clay. Everything." She turned back and gazed directly at him. There was nothing for her to lose, nothing to be ashamed of. "The day I was to leave Twelve Oaks, my memory returned."

He wanted answers and details, but she waved him silent. "It doesn't matter how or when or why. I'll tell you

all that later. The thing is, Clay, I didn't kill my grandmother. But I don't know who did, either."

Clay kept silent, knowing he had to let her get it out in
her own way, her own time.

She told him everything, every detail she could remember about the day Agatha Fleur Deveraux was murdered. Reliving that day in her mind always made her feel
a little detached, almost emotionless. Now, as she re-
counted the details out loud, putting her emotions and
feelings into words, the warmth of his hands squeezing
hers and his sympathy washing over her were almost her
undoing.

"And you told Judge Harrison all this?"

"Yes, and about the man following me."

Clay glanced down at their hands. Somehow they
looked right together, their fingers entwined, the strength
of his, the delicate elegance of hers. There'd been a black
hole in him since he'd returned from the war, but at this
moment it didn't seem quite so big or so dark. Mentally
he shook himself. He needed to focus on Deanna, not
himself, but he had to ask. "Why didn't you come to me
first?"

"Because I didn't think you believed in me or my innocence. You certainly never asked me if I killed Agatha." He winced, but Deanna didn't know how to tell him
anything but the truth, so she continued.

"You made it clear you didn't think I was well enough
or capable enough to stand on my own, make my own
decisions. Like so many others, you judged me by the
fact that I'd been in an institution for ten years and
therefore couldn't have an intelligent thought in my head.
But what hurt most is that you ignored me, Clay. You too
easily discarded my feelings as not important."

She was partly right. "I'm sorry," he said. "I never meant to make you feel inadequate, Deanna. Sometimes when a person is fighting his own demons, he takes his temper out on those he most wants to protect. It's crazy, but that's human nature. Let's get a couple of things straight. At first, I never asked you if you killed your grandmother because—" he decided at that moment to be totally honest "—I was afraid you might say yes, and I couldn't have stood that. Then, after talking to you, even before I read any of Grandfather's papers, I knew you were innocent."

He paused to collect his thoughts. His damn smart mouth wasn't going to trip him up this time. "Deanna, I didn't ignore you or your feelings. On the way here this morning I had a long conversation—let me rephrase that—listened to a long lecture from Mary about you and your life at Twelve Oaks. She made me feel like the lowest of dirty dogs for kissing you. Then she wrung a promise out of me that I wouldn't do it again."

Deanna wanted to strangle Mary. "For how long?" she asked.

"What?"

"How long is this promise supposed to last? Till I'm an old lady with gray hair and no teeth?"

A laugh escaped him, and he wanted desperately to wrap her in his arms. And intended to do just that, but not at the moment. To hell with Mary and Bob, he thought, and anyone else who tried to stop him. He was going to take things slow and easy, but that was the only promise he'd make. "I'm sorry as hell that I hurt you. Believe me, I wouldn't deliberately do it again for the world."

They'd veered so far away from the real purpose of their talk that it took a moment for Clay to remember what it was. "We've gotten offtrack, Deanna. I don't think we can afford to do that right now. What about the man who was following you? Tell me about him. What does he look like?"

"I'll show you." She stood up and glanced around. "Where's my suitcase?"

Clay left to retrieve her suitcase from the hallway. He was confused. Had she taken a picture of the man? When he returned to the den, she pounced on the case and opened it. He watched as she frantically pulled clothes out, then a sketch pad.

"Here." She handed the pad to him and joined him on the couch. He was obviously taking too much time studying each drawing, and when he came to the one she'd done of him, she snatched the pad away and pulled out the series of library sketches. "This man."

"Tell me about him." She was a talented artist with a gift for detail. Clay listened to her as he studied the drawings, then spread them out in front of him on the coffee table. When she finished, he continued to stare at the drawings. Something bothered him.

"What's wrong?" Deanna demanded.

"This man." He pointed to a tall thin figure.

"No, Clay. Not him. This one." She pointed out the older, bald-headed man. "He's the one I saw in the alley."

"Look at this, Deanna. You've drawn two men in minute detail. The others, Danny Hudson, the people in the library and outside, are vague, kind of blurry. But these two you were focused on. Maybe not consciously, but..."

Deanna propped her elbows on her knees, rested her chin on her fists and studied her drawings for long moments. "You're right, but I can't for the life of me tell you why I did that."

She was adorable, Clay thought, with her hair in wild disarray from her drive in the convertible. Her color was back and her eyes shone like sapphires "Let's forget these for a minute," he said. "Tell me about the man in the alley."

Deanna told him every detail of the encounter, as if she were replaying it like a movie in her head. "Are you sure this was the same man as at the library?"

"No doubt at all."

"What did Judge Harrison say?"

"Not much. Mostly he listened. God, he was nice. And you know what? He believed me. The funniest thing was, after I told him what I remembered, he smiled as if I'd said something that really pleased him. Then he told me to talk to you, tell you everything, too." She leaned back against the couch, suddenly very tired. "Would you go get that gardenia and throw it out?"

Clay recognized the signs. The combination of excitement and fear was finally taking its toll. "Deanna, I'm not going to lie to you and try to kid you. Like my grandfather, Bob and I feel someone worked very hard and spent a lot of money to keep you legally locked away. Now that you're free, we believe you could very well be in danger. With what you've told me about the man following you, I don't want you to stay here."

Deanna gazed off into the distance a long time before responding to his question. "Am I going to have to live the rest of my life hiding from whoever's out there?" she said at last. "If so, I might as well be locked up again. I won't do it. I'm tired of paying for a crime I didn't commit. It's time, Clay, to find out who killed my grandmother."

CHAPTER NINE

Washington, D.C.

FRANKLIN FITZPATRICK tugged and twisted angrily at his tie as he held open the front door of their town house for his wife. He yanked the silk material from around his neck, stuffed the tie into his jacket pocket, then fumbled to unbutton the first strangling button of his shirt, all the while watching with fury-filled eyes as Alice sauntered past him.

He let the heavy door deliberately slam shut, enjoying the sight of her stiffening back as he followed her into the living room. "What the bloody hell has gotten into you?" he yelled. "You were rude to the secretary of state and snubbed Senator Hargus's wife. The president noticed, for God's sake."

Alice Jefferson Fitzpatrick whipped around and shouted back at her husband. "You SOB, when were you going to tell *me?*"

The venom in her voice left Franklin speechless for a second, and his mind scurried to determine whether she'd found out about his latest affair. But he decided she wouldn't be in such a snit over his peccadilloes if she had. Anyway, as of tonight his affairs were over for good. The president had let him know it was time to clean up his act. Hell, his lifeline had been cut off by a few words from the man, and if Alice knew she was once again about to become the recipient of his lust, she'd probably divorce him.

"And don't give me that feigned look of innocence, Franklin Concord Fitzpatrick. You know damn well what I'm talking about."

He was only half listening as his gaze roamed over her. She was still a fine-looking woman, tall and willowy with high small breasts and long shapely legs. Hell, she was even sexy. He walked to the antique Chippendale cabinet, retrieved a bottle of Grand Marnier and two heavy crystal snifters.

There'd never really been anything wrong with their love life, he told himself as he poured them each a healthy amount, except her unwillingness to be adventurous. When he thought of his secretary, Betty, and her young, hard athletic body, he wanted to groan out loud. He was going to miss their little trysts.

Franklin took a large sip of his drink. Once he was sure his expression was neutral, he turned and handed Alice hers. "I truly don't know what you're so bent out of shape about."

"You put in for your retirement without even discussing it with me."

He eyed her over the rim of his glass then took another sip, trying to quash the fierce anger that welled up inside him. "Alice, you know very well—" the sarcasm in his voice grew as the volume rose "—God, I've told you enough times, I can't keep my commission if I'm going to run for president."

Alice glared at him and set her drink on the table with an emphatic thump. She turned to march from the room when the contempt in his next words stopped her cold.

"Don't walk away from me, damn you. I told you a month ago that I'd signed the papers. If you'd keep your butt home and stop museum-hopping all over the country with your son, you might remember. And speaking of Henry, where's he hiding?''

"Henry's at his studio, painting."

Franklin snorted and shifted his gaze to two of his son's so-called works of art hanging on the living room walls. Contemporary surrealistic impressionism, he was told. Like hideous gaping wounds, they were wedged between the Degas and Vermeer's *Woman Reading a Letter.* It was almost sacrilegious to see Henry's wild blots, grotesque swirls and garish colors beside those masterpieces.

"Alice, how, with your heritage and knowledge of art, can you look at that and not call it what it is—crap. Crap! Surely you see it."

"Actually, Franklin, two dealers are very interested in your son's work. They say his paintings are fresh, and typical of the times. They see the violence and anger in them."

"They're crap, Alice. And Henry doesn't have a violent or angry bone in his body. He's a wimp." Franklin's eyes narrowed. Usually any criticism of Henry would bring out the lioness in his wife, but tonight she seemed preoccupied and unwilling to argue. He was about to ask what was wrong when she held out her glass for a refill. Surprises seemed to be in the air tonight. She never drank more than one.

"Just because Henry has a medical problem and was unfit to join the service, like all Fitzpatrick men, and go to Vietnam, doesn't mean he's weak. Henry has very strong feelings. He loves beauty and nature."

"So do I, but I don't go around joining clubs to save owls and woodpeckers or spend half my life in museums. And let's get something straight. The only medical problem Henry has is a yellow streak down his back. My flower child, hippie, draft-dodging brother and your liberal, bleeding-heart father saw to it that your son got out of serving.''

Alice Fitzpatrick's whole demeanor changed. Her expression turned to stone, her green eyes almost glazed over with rage. She struggled hard to keep her feelings under control. ''Leave Darren out of this, Franklin.''

''Oh, sure. Don't blame anything on baby brother. He's as big a sissy as Henry. Hell, they've spent so much time together it's no wonder Henry takes after him.'' Years of resentment at watching his wife and brother tiptoe around their relationship boiled over. If he was going to have to give up his affairs, so was she. The problem was, she didn't know he was aware of her affair.

''If Henry spent time with Darren, it was because you weren't here, Franklin. There was Korea, then Vietnam, the war rooms, the meetings, the trips overseas. The service always came first. And don't tell me it was your duty. I've had it.'' She quickly drew her hand across her throat in a cutting motion. ''I'm up to here with duty. So don't say another word about Henry or how he was raised. You of all people have no right to criticize anyone.''

''What's that supposed to mean?''

''Really, Franklin, don't make me spell it out for you. We both know about your little vices.''

For a second he was speechless. She'd never thrown his affairs in his face, at least not openly. No, she'd been more subtle.

''You want to talk about vices, do you? Okay, let's discuss your vice. You realize I said that in the singular—vice. As in Darren. Do you think I'm stupid? Did you think I didn't know you crawled into his bed every chance you got?''

"And you gave me plenty of chances, didn't you?'' She'd always thought if he ever found out he'd kill her. But she could tell by his expression that he didn't care. The agony of years spent loving one brother and living with the other washed over her like a tidal wave. Her anger knew no boundaries and she lashed out. "Besides, sweetheart, your baby brother's better in the sack than you are."

Her words were like a punch to his gut, but he fought to control his temper and, when he finally had it in hand, said, "Well, honeybuns, your days of shacking up with baby brother are over. Do you hear me? The president is going to nominate me. I'll be running for president. You'll love being first lady and you know it. So from this moment on, we wipe the slate clean and become the happy couple once again."

The vision of being the first lady, a Jefferson in the White House, was appealing to Alice as she realized that all her husband's dreams were about to come true. Everything he went after he got, and she had no doubt that he'd be president. The idea that she was going to have to make more sacrifices for him stuck in her craw like a rock, but instead of overwhelming or defeating her, it set her mind racing with a thousand thoughts of revenge. She smiled.

Franklin watched the play of emotions on his wife's face. Power, social prominence and a place in history were as seductive to her as they were to him. She didn't fully realize it now, but she'd give up anything he asked to be first lady, and the closer he got to attaining his dream, the more willing she would be to overlook any of his bad habits. Alice was smiling at him strangely. He suddenly felt uneasy.

"A happy couple, Franklin? And just what do you plan to do with that overactive libido of yours? In other words, what are you going to do for sex, dear heart? You'll have to give up your women, because I won't be like some first ladies. I won't be cheated on and pretend I'm not only blind but dumb.

"That's a public humiliation I will never endure, Franklin. You'll have to give up your vices, or the press will get wind of your peculiarities and your women and they'll have a field day. Wouldn't they, sweetheart?" She took the last sip of her drink. "So, I give up Darren to be first lady, but if you think you can slip between my sheets whenever the urge hits, you're a very stupid man."

He'd never hit a woman in his life, but then he'd never wanted to as badly as he did at that moment. Blackmail, that was what it was. "You wouldn't dare," he blustered, but deep down he knew she was capable of doing exactly as she threatened.

With a sarcastic "Good night, Mr. President," Alice laughed almost hysterically and walked from the room. She'd truly loved Franklin when she'd married him, but it had taken only a short time before she realized he'd wooed her only to gain entrance into her family and money. Well, she'd shown him that a Jefferson was made of stronger stuff than an Irish Fitzpatrick, despite his royal lineage. Her grandmother would have been proud of her today.

Franklin realized he'd been hoisted on his own petard. He headed for his study, and once there, the door firmly shut, he poured himself a man's drink, a fine old Scotch he'd been saving for special occasions. After savoring a few mouthfuls he chuckled. Stupid bitch. Did she really think he was going to give up women? Hell, other presidents satisfied their needs. Keeping his affairs from the press, his wife and his enemies would fall on the shoulders of the Secret Service.

As far as he could see he had only one real problem. Deanna Deveraux. Thinking of her turned the smooth Scotch bitter in his mouth. Why in the hell hadn't Sid called him? It'd been days with no word and he was worried. He reclined in the big leather chair and propped his feet up on the corner of his desk. Leaning his head back and closing his eyes, he pictured himself in the Oval Office with Betty.

Franklin was so deep in his fantasy that when his private telephone rang it took a moment for him to realize what was happening. He dropped his feet to the floor and grabbed for the receiver, switching on the scrambler before he picked it up. The caller was Sid.

"What's going on down there?" Franklin snapped. "I heard a reporter was killed after interviewing that girl."

Sidney was tired, hot and mad as a wet hen. He hated Texas, especially this hellhole Houston. He was sick of following that crazy girl around, and he wanted to know why he was doing it.

"Sir, it was one thing to keep tabs on Miss Deveraux when she was locked away. I never objected to running your errands and taking care of your private business. But Deanna—" he listened with savage pleasure to the general's growl of distaste at hearing her name "—is out and about. I can't keep tabs on her day and night. I have to sleep sometime."

"I know, I know. You're my right-hand man and—"

Major Sidney Sawyer, for the first time in his career, cut the general off short. "This is not a one-man job, and if you want me to continue tailing her, then I need some backup."

Alarmed, Franklin said hurriedly, "No, no. That's not an option, Sid."

"Listen, Deanna is free and she's been digging into her grandmother's murder. She's smart, sir. Much smarter than anyone gives her credit for." For a moment he thought they'd been disconnected, the general was so quiet. "That's not all, sir. She has a high-profile lawyer. Actually the new man is the grandson of Taylor Lambert—a guy named Clayton Lambert. And it gets worse. There's a retired police detective, now a private dick named Bob Spencer, working with Lambert. Get this— he was on the Deveraux case ten years ago."

"They won't find out anything," Franklin mumbled, trying to reassure himself as much as his aide. He grabbed the bottle of Scotch by the neck, but instead of pouring a drink, he tipped the bottle up and chugged down a hardy amount.

"Oh, it gets better, sir," Sidney said sarcastically. "She's moved into her grandmother's house."

He almost choked. "She's *what?*"

"The lawyer and private detective are with her all the time. They don't let her out of their sight."

"Have they spotted you?" Franklin asked. He noticed that his hand was trembling, and he hated the fear eating at him. He wanted to end this torment once and for all.

"No, but you better know someone else is following her."

That bit of information almost undid Franklin. He couldn't speak, and he struggled to maintain his sanity. A thought struck him and he asked, "Is the man following her short, bowlegged and bald?"

"Yeah. You know him? For God's sake, who is he?"

"I know him and you don't need to have any worries from that quarter. He's just like you, Sid, someone's trusted right-hand man. No danger there." The tension in him eased. Franklin had thought for a moment that it might have been the police or the feds. He knew the FBI would have to investigate his past, but they'd never look in Texas unless someone tipped them off.

"Our only problem," Franklin told Sidney, "is that damn girl."

"I hope whatever reason you have for wanting her watched is a good one, because things are happening here."

"You're doing a fine job—"

"Bull, sir," Sid growled. "I've screwed up big time."

A silence settled between them with only the noise of the security scramble hissing and buzzing in their ears. Franklin ventured into the quiet. "The reporter?"

"Yes, sir." For a moment Sidney wondered how the general knew, then he remembered there was one other person in Houston on the general's payroll. "I tailed Deanna to the library where she was researching her grandmother's murder. There was a reporter there who got real chummy with her. After she left, I sidetracked the reporter for a little conversation. He was curious why I was interested in the Deveraux case. I made up some cock-and-bull story about being a reporter from Dallas, but the guy tripped me up. We were arguing when all of a sudden he goes strangely quiet. He recognized me, sir. Told me he'd seen the wire-service release about your speech on the evils of Russia's military buildup. You remember the speech, the one you made at Harvard a couple months ago? I was standing at your shoulder and the photographer caught me."

"Damn," Franklin muttered.

"He put us together, then my interest in the Deveraux case. I didn't think you'd want him asking questions, so I took care of the problem."

The way he always had, Franklin thought. "I understand, Sidney, and I don't know what I'd do without you." His aide had killed the reporter—killed the man for him—and if he was ever caught, Franklin had no doubt Sidney would save his own butt, protesting he'd been given orders.

"To be honest with you, General, I no longer feel I can continue here if I don't know what I'm watching for or up against. I can't help you if you continue to keep me in the dark. You're going to have to confide in me, sir. What hold does Deanna Deveraux have on you?"

Franklin had wanted to dump the ambitious major, but now he realized he was stuck with him, probably for life. And if that was the case, then Sidney Sawyer was going to get his hands a whole lot dirtier. "I understand, Sid. And I'll tell you this much—the girl could destroy me and anyone connected with me. You'd better come on home. We'll have a long talk before you return to Houston, and I'll fill you in. By the way, the president's given me the green light, and I've resigned my commission. You need to do the same if you're going to the White House with me."

Dallas, Texas

GILBERT FOLEY rubbed his face vigorously as the long list of figures became a blur. He was exhausted but refused to give up. Someone was raiding his corporations. Like a mangy lone wolf, whoever it was had been eating away at the perimeters, gobbling the smallest companies and working his way up to the real muscle.

Gilbert stood and stretched, then walked over to the wall of windows twenty floors above downtown Dallas. The city was mostly dark, which surprised him until he glanced down at his watch. No wonder—it was three o'clock in the morning.

The first sign of trouble had been in Louisiana, where his oil rigging outfit had had its supply of steel cut out from under it. The foreman had had to lay off almost all his employees. Gilbert had sent his oldest son, Barton, down to investigate, and on the boy's return was assured everything would be up and running in no time. But Gilbert was concerned. Without the material for refitting and repairing his oil-rig equipment, some of his wells had stopped pumping.

Then there'd been the strike at the oil refinery near Houston. Like a chain reaction, five other of his refineries, two in Texas and three in Louisiana, had shut down. Then out of the blue, air pollution had become a public issue and he'd had government people crawling all over his chemical-processing plants, slowing production. He'd had to send his youngest boy, Richard, to Washington to grease some palms so they'd call off their inspectors.

The bottom line? He was losing money hand over fist. It was flowing out fast, and the steady stream of incoming profits had dwindled to a trickle. The money drain had been going on for months without anyone noticing, and that was what angered Gilbert the most. He employed the best and smartest Ivy League accountants and they'd screwed up. He wanted to know why and how. No one tried to take what was his, and he was determined heads were going to roll.

There was a soft tap on his office door and he growled, "Come in." Then he watched beneath heavy-lidded bloodshot eyes as three of his vice presidents from the accounting department eased into his office. He waited until they'd settled down in the line of chairs before his desk. They looked as worn-out as he was, which gave him a grim satisfaction. "Well?"

Doyle Preston was the most senior and had obviously been elected by the others to break the bad news. He swallowed hard. "Gilbert, I hate like hell to tell you this..."

"How much have we lost?" Gilbert demanded.

"Moneywise, in the millions," Doyle quickly replied. "My department's still tallying. But it's the stock we're worried about, Gil. At first the buy-up was small stuff, spread out over all your companies. But lately large blocks of Foley stock have been snapped up."

"I never authorized any Foley stock to be released. How'd that happen, Doyle?"

Doyle cringed. "Gil, I hate like hell to tell you this..."

Gilbert was too tired and angry to play games. "You've said that before. Spit it out, Doyle."

"It's your boys, Gil. Barton and Richard."

"That's the most asinine load of crap I've ever heard, and if you want to keep your high-paying job, Doyle, I'd advise you to go back to the books and investigate." In his anger Gilbert had risen to his feet and was leaning across his desk, his tired eyes hot with fury. "Don't cover up your department's screwups by blaming this on my boys."

Doyle paled. "I swear, I'm not passing the buck."

"Let me tell you something, Doyle. Barton and Richard have been at each other's throats for the last two years. They're competitive, ruthless and ambitious. I taught them that, but my boys would never turn on their dad. Never." His head ached and he was feeling almost dizzy. He sat back down, then picked up the papers and reports Doyle had slid across his desk.

Gilbert read for almost half an hour. When he was through, he sat still for so long that the men in the office thought he might have fallen asleep.

He looked up at them with tears in his eyes. "I can't believe this, my own boys."

"You shouldn't be that surprised, Gil. You've been teaching them the business since they were old enough to talk. You were the very one who showed them how to take over a company, how to raid it from the inside."

"But Barton and Richard? They're not smart enough to take on something of this magnitude on their own. Who's helping them, Doyle?"

"There's no one else, Gil." Doyle was exhausted. "Look, I can imagine how tough it must be to accept this, but if we don't act quickly, you're going to lose over half the Foley empire. And all of your employees' jobs are at stake.

"You know very well, Gil, that both boys are very intelligent. Barton could talk the skin off a snake, and it's almost scary the way Richard can manipulate figures."

Gil glanced down at the stack of incriminating papers again. He sighed and nodded. "You gentlemen go home to your families. Get some sleep. We're going to have to work hard and fast to repair the damage."

The room was almost empty when Doyle paused at the door. "I'm sorry as hell, Gil."

"Me, too. Where are they?"

Doyle shook his head. "Hiding out somewhere, directing the shots by phone. We've tried to trace some calls to a couple of Barton's women, but no luck. I doubt you'll find them until the smoke settles one way or the other. Get some rest, Gil."

"Good night, Doyle." Gilbert stared at the two photos of his sons. They were handsome men, with experience beyond their years. He'd seen to that. Somewhere deep down, buried in the anger and hurt, he was proud of them. They were his boys, after all. But to turn on their old man, to bite the hand that had fed, clothed, educated them—hell, even given them their first woman when they turned thirteen . . . God, they were ungrateful bastards.

He'd just have to teach them that their old man wasn't about to roll over and play dead. But there was one thing he had to be careful about, and that was the Houston problem. If his sons or his stockholders got wind of that scandal he'd be ruined for good—for life.

The thought of Houston reminded him that he hadn't heard from Harry. He was just reaching for the telephone and one more try at his old friend's hotel room, when the phone rang. He knew it was Harry. He was the only man who would dare to track him down at five o'clock in the morning. "Hey, Harry, where've you been?"

Harry Dobbs immediately knew something was wrong. Gil was a morning man. He'd never used that subdued tone of voice before. "What's happened, Gil? Is it the boys? They're not hurt, are they?"

Gilbert laughed. "No, old friend, the boys are more than all right. I'd say they're riding high 'bout now."

Harry didn't like the sound of his boss's laugh. But before he could offer to come home if he was needed, Gil asked for a report.

"I heard there was some trouble down there with a reporter. You involved in that?"

"No." Harry was sick to death of Houston and almost too tired to crawl out of bed in the mornings. He took a sip of coffee and made up his mind. "I'm too old for this, boss. Since the Deveraux girl's been out of the sanitarium, I've done nothing but run my butt off. It was one thing to check up on her when she was locked up. I mean, we knew where she was at all times, even when she was in school.

"This is a whole new ball game. I can't be chasing around day and night. Why don't you let me call in a couple of men in my department to do this job?"

"That's out of the question, old friend. You're the only man I'd ever trust with this. I need you more than you'll ever know. Now, fill me in on what's happening down there."

Harry felt his resolve melting away. Gil needed him. "She's been researching her grandmother's murder. Tell you the truth, Gil, there's something about the girl that bothers me. I tailed her to the library thinking it was going to be a piece of cake. But let me tell you, she's a slick customer. She gets inside and takes a seat so she can see everyone that comes in, checking out everything like a pro."

Gilbert thought he couldn't feel any worse than when Doyle had left his office, but he was wrong. Anger and hurt were one thing, this consuming fear was another. But Harry was talking and he had to force the fear away and pay attention.

"Taylor Lambert's grandson, Clayton, has taken over her case. From what I've been able to find out about him, he's a ruthless, top-notch criminal lawyer who doesn't take cases he can't win. A good man to have in your corner if you're in trouble, but not one to go against. Then there's this Bob Spencer, a private detective. He was working for old Lambert, and now he's helping the grandson with the case. I don't like it, boss.''

Gilbert wedged the phone between his shoulder and cheek and rested his face in his hands. "I don't like it, either.''

"Get's worse, Gil. She went to visit that judge who released her, the one that took over Judge Jones's bench. Tell you something, Gil, I could've sworn I spotted some feds hanging around the judge's chambers.''

"Oh, God," Gil moaned.

"Worse is yet to come. There's someone else keeping close tabs on Deanna." Harry stopped and closed his eyes, visualizing the man he was referring to. "He's your typical military type. All spit and polish even when out of uniform. The guy's tall, ramrod straight, thick dirty brown hair, graying a little at the temples, and a nondescript face. Military intelligence, I say. You got any idea what that type would be doing eyeing our gal?''

For a second Gil's relief almost overwhelmed him. "He's not our problem, Harry. I've got a good idea where he's coming from.''

Harry didn't have the heart to tell his boss that he'd failed him, that the girl had spotted him, and any further attempt at tailing her was going to be much harder. He just didn't have the heart for the job anymore. After all, what could one young girl do to a man as rich and powerful as Gilbert Foley?

"Gil, I'm tired. My arthritis is acting up and I don't know what I'm supposed to be doing here. You're keeping me in the dark and I can't do my job—whatever that is. Now, this is the way I see it. I head on back to Dallas, and we send down a couple of our boys to relieve me, and you and I sit down and hash this business out.''

"Damn you," Gil lashed out. "What did I say earlier?"

His boss had never used that tone with him before, and it hurt. But Harry was no man's flunky. "I can't do my job if I don't know the whys and wherefores. You've always turned to me when you had problems that needed fixing. What is it about this girl that makes you so nervous? You're going to have to trust me totally, Gilbert. After all, what can one girl do to you, of all people?"

"She can destroy me, Harry. Annihilate the Foley empire and everyone connected with it. But not only me, Harry. She can destroy my family. And you're right, you can't go on in the dark."

Harry Dobbs was shocked. It was the first time he'd ever heard fear in his boss's voice.

"I need you, Harry," Gilbert repeated. "More now than ever before. Come on home for a few days, and I'll fill you in on everything before you return to Houston."

CHAPTER TEN

A SLEEPING HOUSE should be a quiet house, Deanna thought. Especially—she glanced at her bedside clock—at four o'clock in the morning. But a strange noise, not the squeaks and creaks of an old house she'd become accustomed to, had awakened her.

She lay in her bed listening, trying to put a name and location to the sound. It was familiar, yet its source eluded her. It seemed to be coming from directly below her bedroom, from the living room. She was a rational person and didn't believe in ghosts. Even so, she couldn't control the way her heart hammered against her chest or the deafening roar of blood pounding in her ears. And of course it wasn't ghosts that she had to fear.

After giving herself a quick pep talk for courage, she slowly folded the covers back and eased out of bed. The hardwood floor was cool beneath her bare feet, and she shivered.

The dark had been her enemy for years, and as she moved away from the bed, she silently congratulated herself on her strategically placed night-lights—one in her bedroom, one in the hall and another at the top of the stairs, where she stopped, cocked her head and listened. Beyond the light was a cavernous blackness, a dark hole filled with all her fears. Her hand was frantically searching the wall for the light switch when another noise stopped her. This time she recognized the sound; she'd

made it herself a number of times. It was the sound of
someone bumping into one of the metal folding chairs
she'd set up in the living room so Clay and Bob could
work.

Deanna whirled around, remembered how the floor
under her feet creaked and hugged the wall as she rushed
down the hall to what had been her grandmother's bedroom. Pushing open the door, she hesitated. The dim
light from the hall didn't penetrate the bedroom, and it
was pitch-black. "Clay," she called, her voice barely a
whisper, then waited. Nothing happened. She gritted her
teeth and ventured into the room, feeling her way,
touching the end of the bed and following its contours
around to the side.

God, she couldn't even hear him breathing. What if it
was him downstairs and she was up here making a fool of
herself? She was still feeling her way when something
reached out and grabbed her arm, pulling her deeper into
the darkness. She opened her mouth to scream but no
sound came out. The blackness had finally caught up
with her and was about to suffocate her.

"Deanna? Dammit to hell." Clay eased his grip.
"What're you doing? I could've hurt you." He released
her and was reaching for the lamp on the bedside table
when something she was trying to say penetrated his anger and relief. She was gripping his bare thigh and whispering, or at least he thought she was, because he had to
ask her to repeat what she was saying.

Her words were barely audible, coming out in hoarse
fits and starts. He would've answered her, said something, anything, but she had a death grip on his thigh, her
nails digging into his flesh like knives, and if he opened
his mouth it would be to emit a howl of anguished pain.

Deanna took a few shallow breaths and tried again. "Someone's in the living room."

She was only a black shape in the darkness before him, yet the room almost vibrated with her terror. Clay dislodged her fingers from his leg and clasped her hand in his, rubbing it as he whispered, "At the foot of the bed there's a robe. Give it to me."

"Call the police."

"Deanna, they're liable to take forever to get here. I'm going to go have a look." He kept his voice calm. "Now hand me my robe, please, and stay here."

"Forget the robe, and I'm going with you."

"Deanna, I'm naked. And you're staying here."

It was an intriguing picture, she thought, despite her fear as she searched behind her for the robe. Damn the darkness.

Clay slipped out of bed and into his robe, securing the belt. He heard the rustle of bed covers and reached in the direction of the sound. Almost immediately he yanked his arm back at the firm warm flesh he encountered beneath a soft fabric. "Dammit, stay put," he growled.

Deanna watched Clay's dark bulk as he slipped out of the room, allowed him just enough time to turn down the hall and was out of the room herself. No way was she going to stay there in the dark by herself. When she reached the top of the dimly lit stairs, her legs began to wobble dangerously, forcing her to sit down on the first step. She strained to hear over the pounding of her heart.

Why was it so quiet? Surely Clay was okay. Logically she knew he'd been gone only a few minutes. Still, what if he was hurt? A thousand what ifs ran through her head. She was debating whether or not to move from her safe position to the bottom of the stairs, when lights began to come on throughout the house. She waited until the stairwell was bright and Clay reappeared before asking, "Well?"

Clay wasn't sure whether to tell her the truth. His instinct was to protect her, which meant he'd have to lie. Then he remembered his promise to be straight with her. "The guy came in through the kitchen." He didn't tell her that whoever had entered the house had opened the new dead bolt, a sturdy mechanism that should have deterred the most persistent criminal. But the lock had been picked by a professional—he was sure of it—with only a few scratch marks to mar the shiny new brass. He'd have to wait for Bob to confirm his theory.

"Did you see anything?"

She was shaking and he wrapped his arms around her and hugged her close. "No, he must have heard me coming. We need to check and see if anything's been stolen."

"What?" She managed a laugh. "Some of Grandmother's old furniture? There's nothing here worth stealing. Besides, I only heard the noise in the living room."

"We still need to check. If he didn't take anything, then he was looking for something and a lot of your grandmother's papers are there in the boxes I brought from the office."

Deanna felt some of her tension lift. "At least you believe me this time."

"I've never doubted you, Deanna."

It seemed longer than just a week ago that she'd told Clay about the man in the alley and that she was being followed. Clay and Bob had kept a close watch on her, but neither had seen the bald-headed man, or for that matter anyone showing any undue interest in her. The last couple of days she thought she'd detected doubt in their voices whenever they questioned her about the men in the drawings.

"I don't know about you," Clay said, "but there's no way I could go back to sleep. How about some coffee?" She felt so right in his arms that he hated to let her go, but her nearness was arousing him and he knew he needed to put some distance between them before he lost his resolve to behave.

"If you'll make it," she said, feeling cold when he set her free.

"Of course." He eyed what she was wearing and smiled.

"What's so funny?" She glanced down at herself, at the extra-large men's T-shirt she was wearing as a nightgown.

The soft material clung to her, leaving little doubt as to what it was outlining, and even though the hem reached below her knees, it still managed to show off the exciting curves underneath. "Maybe we'd better get dressed first." He should have known she'd look as sexy and alluring in a T-shirt as an expensive silk negligee. He groaned inwardly.

While the coffee was perking and the fragrant aroma drifted through the house, Deanna and Clay searched the living room, trying to determine if anything was missing. Deanna looked around her. Two metal tables were positioned in the middle of the otherwise empty room, with five metal folding chairs scattered around at odd angles. Two half-empty cardboard file boxes were open next to the tables, and papers were scattered over the tabletops.

Clay studied the papers on one of the tables. It was a mess, his mess, and though everything looked topsy-turvy there was an order to it. "There's nothing missing." He walked over to the other table. "Tell me again what you heard. What was it that woke you?"

"I was already awake before I heard the noise." She glanced around the room. The curtains were pulled tightly across the windows to keep out prying eyes, the room was stark and depressing. The only adornments, if you could call them that, were her sketches, which now decorated one of the bare walls. Bob and Clay had thought they were important. Each time she drew a new one, Bob would have a photocopy made, which he would tack on the wall in what looked like a haphazard display. It took her a couple of days to realize that he was placing the drawings in the chronological order of her life.

She was absently studying her sketches and said, "I heard this sound...." She bumped her hip against the back of the folding chair, the rubber tips on the legs making a distinctive noise as they moved across the hardwood floor. But her attention was riveted to the wall. "Clay." She didn't even turn to look at him. "Clay, he took some of my drawings."

"What?" Clay was at her side instantly, studying the wall, too. "Which ones?"

"The sketches I did at the library are gone."

"I'll be damned."

"Why?" she asked. "Why just those?"

"Beats me." But he thought he knew, and he wanted to wait and run it by Bob first. He touched her arm to get her attention. "Coffee's got to be ready. I don't think straight without my first cup."

All through breakfast she watched him. The way he moved, searching for what he wanted or taking a cup and saucer down from the cabinet, the way he stood with the refrigerator door wide open while he decided what he needed. He was as lost in the kitchen as she was, but he looked good in the homey setting. She munched her half-burned toast, a new gourmet delicacy among the singles set, he'd teased her, and she was actually getting to like it.

She finished her toast, then announced, "I can't stand this house any longer. I'm going shopping today to buy some furniture."

Clay handed her the morning newspaper. "Fine, but not without—"

"I know—not alone." She snapped the folded paper open then smoothed it flat on the table. "Maybe Bob or William or one of William's sons can tag along behind me." She regretted her words the minute they were out of her mouth. "Sorry. But after being pretty much alone for so long, to suddenly have constant companionship makes me nervous."

Ever since she'd seen the man in the alley, Clay and Bob had decided that she wasn't to be left alone under any circumstances. Bob was there during the day. Clay stayed the evenings and nights. William, old Mr. Lambert's chauffeur and her friend, sent over his sons, who had a landscaping-and-maintenance company, and they'd become the yardmen. Even William, who was too old, she thought, to be masquerading as a handyman, was climbing ladders, working the flower beds and helping trim trees in his free time.

Her neighbors must have thought she was being taken advantage of because her lawn was mowed practically every day. Yet with all their watching and waiting, after more than a week, nothing had happened—until this morning. She was almost relieved. At least she knew, and so did everyone else, that her fears weren't a figment of her imagination.

Deanna glanced up from the newspaper and caught Clay smiling at her. "What?"

Clay loved to watch her in the morning. The way her freshly washed skin glowed; the way her blond curls, not yet tamed, framed her face; the way she nibbled at her food while she devoured the newspaper word for word, section by section. "I don't believe I've ever seen anyone take such an interest in the newspaper."

At first she was angered by his comment, then realized that even though he thought he knew what her life was like in the sanitarium, he really didn't. She propped her elbows on the tabletop and rested her chin on her fists. "I read the paper because for ten years it was the only dependable source of information and news I could get on a daily basis."

"But you went to school, even college. Surely you covered current events, politics, and then discussed them with your friends."

Deanna chuckled. "Clay, our educational system only cares about teaching dates and events, not cause and effect. As for friends, I didn't have any at school. Remember where I lived. Every day when my classmates got together I had to go back to Twelve Oaks."

"What about television? You said earlier that you got to watch TV."

"Yes, I did. But I didn't have one in my cottage and what I watched was closely monitored by Dr. Gresham." She could see that what she was telling him still wasn't sinking in. "You're free to watch anything you want. If something doesn't appeal to you, you simply change the channel. I wasn't allowed to watch the news because for so long the Vietnam War was the main topic. The doctor thought it was too graphic and the coverage of the war protesters and draft dodgers went against his beliefs. Dr. Gresham had been in the service and thought the protesters and draft dodgers should all be shot. When Martin Luther King and Bobby Kennedy were killed, I wasn't allowed to watch their funerals because it might have upset me. The real reason was Dr. Gresham is a bigot and had no use for either man."

The more Clay heard about Dr. Gresham, the more he despised him. He couldn't believe one man could have so much control over anyone's life.

"I missed the live coverage of Woodstock, the Kent State shootings, the war protester's march on Washington and President Nixon's impeachment. I had to read about the deaths of Jimi Hendrix and Janis Joplin. I missed seeing the Watergate hearings and the end of the war. There are a thousand more events I missed seeing on television and only learned about by reading newspapers, magazines and books."

"The doctor didn't restrict what you read?" Clay asked.

Deanna laughed. "You must be kidding. If it hadn't been for Raul, Mary and a couple of others, I wouldn't have had anything to read."

Clay reached across the table and grasped Deanna's hand. "I'd like to strangle that man."

"Now do you see why I can't stand Dr. Gresham and how scared I was when I thought I might have to go back? He ruled my life, Clay. From the very beginning he liked to play these little mind games with me, trying to get me to remember what I couldn't. I learned early on how to play his game, too. Speaking of newspapers, how is it they reported Danny Hudson's murder and my name was never mentioned?"

Clay chuckled. "Like Bob, I have a few friends in high places, too. I simply made some calls, threw out a few threats about lawsuits and defamation of character."

He realized then that in a different way, her way, she'd gone through as much hell as he had in Vietnam. Like him, she was a survivor. The more he was around her, the more he admired her strength, her intelligence and her humor. He looked forward to the mornings and their quiet time together. He savored seeing her across the breakfast table. Actually, he suspected, he was falling in love, but there was nothing he could do about his feelings, and he certainly wasn't going to let her know how he felt.

"You're in a thoughtful mood all of a sudden," Deanna said as she gathered up her dirty dishes. "Anything you want to talk about?"

"No."

She leaned against the cabinet and studied him through narrowed eyes. "You're not keeping anything from me—for my own good of course—are you?"

"Just a little, but only until I figure it out, then I'll tell you." He laughed. Everything about her made him feel good inside—the tilt of her head when she was listening intently, the way the corner of her mouth twitched when she was trying to be serious but wanted to laugh, the way her blue eyes took on a certain gleam, a wicked sparkle, when she was up to something. He found himself smiling all the time he was with her.

Clay carried his dishes to the sink, then glanced at the clock on the kitchen wall. "I think I'll go take a shower and get dressed. I need to go to the office and take care of some business. Bob said he'd be here early, but I think I'll give him a call and see if he can make it even sooner."

"Clay, it's five-thirty in the morning." But he didn't hear—or deliberately ignored her—and was already dialing.

"That's strange," Clay muttered. "Bob's not home." He scowled fiercely at the telephone as if he could intimidate it into making Bob answer, then shrugged. "I'm going to take a shower." He was halfway out of the kitchen when he stopped and said, "A young man by the name of Herbert Snow is going to pick up all my grandfather's Deveraux files at the warehouse and bring them by here. I forgot to tell William or his boys, or Bob. You do it for me, okay?"

"Fine," she agreed. "And I'll do the dishes," she called after his retreating form, "even if it is your turn."

Clay popped back into the kitchen doorway. "You're a peach. I'll do double KP duty."

"Yeah, yeah. You're full of promises, but you don't follow through, do you?" She knew very well she was egging him on and for the life of her couldn't imagine why she was doing it. Nor could she drag her gaze from his. It was magic, she thought, the way she was feeling.

It was the sultry tone of her voice, the double entendre, the unspoken sexual challenge Clay heard, that stopped him dead in his tracks. Somewhere in the back of his mind a voice warned him not to take that first step, but he was being pulled toward her as if he'd lost all control. It was those long nights lying awake, picturing Deanna in her bed, then imagining her in his bed, that were drawing him like a magnet, making him take those few steps.

Gently Clay grasped her shoulders and pulled her to him slowly. Then he lowered his mouth to hers, telling himself not to be a beast this time and scare the hell out of her. Her mouth was soft, sweet, and opened immediately at the touch of his lips. He hesitated only a moment before his tongue slipped inside and he kissed her deeply, gathering her closer, feeling the way her body molded itself to his.

Deanna was floating. Every muscle in her body felt weak and wobbly. Her hands glided up his arms, feeling the softness of the knit shirt and the warmth and firmness of the muscles underneath. She slid her hands around his neck, then up the back of his head, savoring the sensation of the thick and silky blond hair running through her fingers.

When the kiss changed, deepened, she relaxed, snuggled closer, wanting to melt into his body. And when the kiss stopped and he pulled away, the disappointment was gut-wrenching. It took a second for her to open her eyes, and when she did he was staring at her with the strangest expression.

"Wow," she finally managed to say, and smiled.

"Yes. Wow." Clay set her aside, ashamed of himself. He wanted to apologize but couldn't find the words to make her understand what had happened to him or how he'd let himself react to her challenge. Something inside him had made him deliberately set out to not just kiss her, but to test his ability to excite her to the point of distraction. Now he was going to have to gracefully back away, when all he wanted to do was carry her up to his bed and make love to her. "I think I'll go take a cold shower."

"That could be an awful shock to the system," she said, a little puzzled by the barely controlled tension radiating from him.

"That's the idea. Try it and you'll see what I mean." She put on a great front, but she didn't understand what was happening, and the confusion in her eyes stabbed at Clay's heart. He couldn't let her think it was something she'd done to turn him away. Still keeping his distance, he leaned forward and kissed her tenderly on the forehead. "I could stay here and kiss you all morning, Deanna, but I need to get ready for work."

Clay made himself walk out of the kitchen, all the while praying that his resolve wouldn't fail him. Guilt was a great emotion deflater, and he felt as limp as a pricked balloon. If it were humanly possible, he'd have kicked himself in the butt all the way up the stairs for taking advantage of her inexperience.

Left frustrated, exhilarated and sadly empty, Deanna watched Clay leave, wondering how one man could make her feel such a bewildering array of emotions. She needed to have a long talk with Mary.

DEANNA STOOD at the living room door watching Clay as he placed a stack of papers in his briefcase. He was dressed in a three-piece suit, his professional attire, she thought. It amazed her how a man's personality changed along with his clothes. She'd seen him in many guises—casually dressed, in shorts and bare chest, jeans and cotton shirt. He'd helped her work the flower beds, fooling around and acting silly. They'd stood side by side in the kitchen trying to figure out directions in a recipe because neither could cook.

Then put him in a suit and his whole demeanor changed, even the timbre of his voice. It was all very amusing and she'd told him so. He'd just laughed, then said that a man needed to have his disguises to hide behind. Deanna had found that profoundly sad.

She coughed now to get his attention and smiled when he paused and glanced at her. "I know what you mean now about the cold shower," she said. "It does tend to totally clear the mind and calm the...nerves."

Clay had had a long talk with himself and felt he had the situation under control. "Good. Have you heard from Bob?"

She ignored his question. "Maybe we could take a cold shower *together* and see what happens."

His breath was cut off so fast he felt momentarily paralyzed. Then a picture popped into his head, and it was as if someone had turned up his body heat fifty degrees. He managed to look at her, saw that wicked little sparkle in her eyes and laughed, shaking his head. He'd made up his mind that what Deanna needed was to flex her feminine wiles, to try her wings where men were concerned, so to speak. And he didn't intend for her to experiment on anyone but himself. He'd just have to endure the frustration and the body heat. "One of these days you're going to get in real trouble teasing me like that."

"Promises . . ."

Clay yanked up his briefcase and headed for the front door. He was starting to sweat. "No, you don't. We played that game in the kitchen. I think I'll wait on the porch for Bob to arrive." The morning air was a cool balm on his hot face. Maybe he'd bitten off more than he could chew.

Deanna grinned, deciding enough was enough, and followed him outside. She sat on the porch railing and let her bare feet dangle over the edge. "Are you going to be at work all day?"

Her jeans were too tight and her blouse too thin, he thought, and glanced down the street. "No. What're you going to do today?" Lord, they were talking like an old married couple.

"I'm going shopping, remember?"

"Not by yourself . . ."

"I know, I know. I'll take Bob or William. I have to buy some furniture. I can't stand this place the way it is." His question reminded her of their intruder, and all of Clay's and Bob's warnings surfaced in her mind. She was no dummy and didn't intend to make herself an easy target for anyone.

"Buy a new cookbook," he said. "Something easy, maybe one written for children so we'll understand it. Or you might ask someone what sifting is or how you beat and fold egg whites."

Deanna nodded. The recipes were perplexing to her, too. They fell silent, enjoying the serenity of the morning. Clay rocked in the porch swing, and from her perch on the railing she swung her feet in rhythm with him. Both were so lost in their own thoughts that Bob had parked his car and was climbing out before they realized he was there.

"I didn't think you were such an early riser," Clay called out. Bob had turned his back to them as if getting something out of the front seat. "I tried calling you around five-thirty, but you didn't..." His voice trailed away in disbelief when he saw that Bob was helping Mary out of the car. Then he glanced at Deanna to see if she had caught the significance of the unanswered phone and the couple's appearance together at seven in the morning.

Deanna was trying to hide her smile. She glanced at Clay and winked, then hopped off the railing and joined him at the top of the porch steps. Mary and Bob were having a little trouble looking them directly in the eye, and she jabbed Clay with her elbow and whispered, "Don't embarrass them."

Clay nodded. "Bob, you need to call one of your friends and have him come check the lock on the kitchen door. We had an uninvited guest about four this morning.''

''Damn!'' Bob grasped Mary's arm to help her up the porch steps.

Mary yanked her arm free. ''I'm not an invalid, Bob, and I'm not helpless, so stop babying me. The doctor said I'm almost one hundred percent.'' She headed directly for Deanna. ''Are you all right?''

''Fine. Clay scared the intruder off.'' Deanna wanted badly to tease Mary and had to force herself to behave. ''Whoever it was stole a couple of my sketches. Come on—I'll show you.''

The four of them headed into the living room and studied the copies of the sketches Bob had hung on the wall.

''Seems funny that the guy only took the drawings you made at the library,'' Bob observed. He glanced at Clay. ''Aren't they the same ones I gave Judge Harrison copies of?''

''Yes, they are. And the only thing those drawings had in common was the inclusion of the bald-headed man. But look down there.'' Clay pointed to a couple of sketches along the bottom of the wall. ''Those are the ones Deanna did of the same man in the alley. Why didn't he take those, too?''

Deanna had been following the conversation with interest as she studied the wall. Suddenly the answer hit her. ''Because it wasn't the bald-headed man he was interested in. It was the other man, Clay. The one I'd drawn in such detail and you couldn't figure out why.''

''Right. I think we've just established that there are two men following Deanna.''

''More like a whole football team,'' Bob said, then wished he hadn't. ''I meant to tell you, when I took the copies of Deanna's sketches to Judge Harrison, there were a couple of federal boys helping him with the Judge Jones investigation. When they saw the sketches they got all excited. Wouldn't admit they knew who one or maybe both of the men were, but I think they know something. Anyway, yesterday that house across the street, you know, the one for sale..." He waited until everyone nodded, then went on, "Suddenly a couple takes the sign down and moves in. I had William and his boys watching off and on all day yesterday. Lights and water are on, but get this—the only furniture they've got is two chairs."

Deanna watched Clay and Bob, wondering if she'd missed something. Maybe they had some telepathic system and knew what each other was talking about, but she didn't, and hated being left in the dark. She glanced at Mary to see if her friend, who was older and wiser about men, understood what was happening here. Mary looked as confused as she was. "What's going on?" she demanded.

Clay absently threw his arm around Deanna's shoulders, caught Mary's disapproving gaze and immediately dropped it to his side. "The couple are federal agents. They're watching the house, and most likely if you leave they'll be following you."

"Oh, great." Then she began to laugh. "Do you mean to tell me that everywhere I go I could have two men I don't even know, then maybe Clay, Bob or William, maybe even William's two sons, plus two federal agents, all following me?"

Bob started laughing at the picture she was describing. "Oh, and let's add our esteemed police department to the parade. I've already seen my old partner a couple of times."

"Well," Deanna said, "I think I'm pretty safe, don't you?" The sound of three people shouting "No!" at the same time made her jump.

Clay picked up his briefcase, kissed Deanna on the forehead and glared at Mary, daring her to say anything. "Don't let your guard down for a minute. Remember what Bob taught you."

"Clay, would you wait a moment?" Mary asked. "I have something I have to tell you and Deanna." She looked at Deanna, her distress all too visible. "I quit my job yesterday."

"Oh, Mary." Deanna hugged her. "What are you going to do?" When Mary didn't respond, she drew back.

Clay was annoyed and looked at his watch, then caught something in Bob's expression and froze. He didn't know whether he wanted to hear this or not.

"Deanna," Mary began, ignoring the looks of concern directed at her, "please forgive me for not telling you about this sooner, but I wasn't sure who I could trust to help you until now." She grasped Deanna's hands and held them close to her before going on.

"Right before you were to leave Twelve Oaks I heard something. Actually, we got a new dictating machine for Dr. Gresham, and I wasn't familiar with it and accidentally left it on. After Dr. Gresham had dictated his daily reports and I was transcribing them, I realized what I'd done. I'd left the machine on and recorded a telephone conversation he'd had.

"Deanna, Dr. Gresham was reporting your release to someone, talking about you in a most unkind way. It was obvious that whoever he was speaking to wasn't a stranger. He'd spoken to this person about you before, and from the way Dr. Gresham was talking, answered questions, this person knew a lot about you, too."

She felt Deanna's hands go limp in hers and squeezed tightly to keep her from pulling away. "I took the tape home with me and hid it. Please believe me, I was going to turn it over if anyone tried to send you back to the sanitarium." There were tears in Mary's eyes. "I should have told you about it earlier, though."

Deanna was shocked by the fact that Dr. Gresham was discussing her case with a stranger, and she stood silently, trying to figure out who it might be and why, when she realized that everyone was staring at her expectantly. She hugged her friend. "I know you'd never hurt me, Mary. I just wonder who Dr. Gresham was talking to."

"More like reporting to, from his tone of voice," Bob said. "Mary played the tape for me yesterday, and I told her to get away from Dr. Gresham because I was going after him. He's dangerous and shouldn't be called a doctor."

Clay sat down on one of the folding chairs. "Why would a doctor of Gresham's intelligence and reputation report Deanna's condition and impending release to someone?"

"Money?" Bob growled. "Listen, by this afternoon I'm going to have a history of the man's bank account. I got a friend works for his bank. I'll also get hold of Twelve Oaks' phone records for the past ten years."

"Don't tell me," Deanna said. "You have a friend at the telephone company."

"You bet your life I do, kid, and we're about to start playing hardball. So you better run your errands today and get back here, because after tomorrow you're confined to the house." He sensed an argument and held up his hand. "That's the way it's gonna be."

Clay picked up his briefcase. "I've got to get to work." He kissed Deanna on the cheek and whispered, "Be careful." Then, as he passed Bob, he said in a low voice, "You've got everything under control?"

"Hell, no," Bob whispered back. "But it's nice to think so for a few minutes."

"Yeah, well, keep her safe, Bob."

Deanna watched Clay drive away then grabbed Mary by the hand and pulled her up the stairs into her bedroom and shut the door. "I have to ask you—what's it like when you fall in love?"

Mary blushed and sat down on the end of the bed. "Deanna, I know you've guessed about Bob and me. But I'm older and—"

"Not you, Mary. Me. I think I'm in love. Do you get all warm and soft inside when Bob kisses you?"

"Leave me out of this. And you're not talking about love, you're talking sex. Has Clay been pestering you? I knew his staying here with you at night was wrong. If I'd felt better—"

"Pestering! No. He kissed me again. And, oh, Mary, I didn't just tingle all over, I sizzled."

"That's not love!" Mary snapped. She thought she'd had an understanding with Clay Lambert. Obviously she was going to have to have another talk with him.

"I sizzled all the way down to my toes."

Mary bit her lip to keep from smiling. "That's not love."

"It was magic. That's the only way I can describe it. Pure magic. I was floating."

"I thought you were sizzling?"

"That, too."

"It's lust, Deanna."

"Mary!" Deanna opened her eyes and glared at Mary. "How can you say that? Every time I look at him I get the strangest feelings." She grabbed Mary's arm. "He sleeps in the nude."

"Oh, Lord." Mary groaned and shut her eyes. "I don't think I want to know how you know that."

"I lie awake thinking about him in the next room. I'm having all these fantasies. I tell you, it's love."

"It's lust, Deanna," Mary said, but with less force this time, her smile touched with secret memories and her eyes a little dreamy. "And isn't it the most wonderful thing?"

CHAPTER ELEVEN

BOB SPENCER was a strong man, big and full of energy. He'd endured the horrors of war, the physical and emotional grind of police work. But nothing in all his experience had prepared him for shopping with two women bent on spending money. He'd driven them across half of Houston to find exactly the right item. Then back to the same store they'd left earlier to compare fabric, patterns and colors. He'd tagged behind them for what seemed like miles and miles, weaving in and out of all types and styles of furniture until he was dizzy. And it wasn't even noon yet. His back was killing him, he was dying of thirst, and his poor feet—they'd gone numb about an hour ago.

He glanced ahead at Mary, trotting along in her spike heels beside Deanna, and sighed—she had great legs. But he didn't understand how a woman who was recovering from pneumonia, who found dusting and running the vacuum exhausting and talked him into doing it for her, had the stamina for this marathon. At least Deanna had the good sense to wear shoes that looked comfortable. The thought that whoever was tailing Deanna was probably just as tired as he was brought him sharply back to the reality of the situation.

The possibility of danger and the fact that he'd let his fatigue slow him down gave him a spurt of energy, and he readjusted the bags he'd been burdened with. The women were way ahead of him and he jogged to their side. They were chatting nonstop and he forced himself to pay attention. Half the time they treated him as if he wasn't there and he'd learned a lot about the two just by listening.

Deanna looped her arm through Mary's and picked up her pace, eager to get to Neiman Marcus. "Clay tried to cook us some steaks out on the grill like Bob did the other evening. The problem was we didn't remember how long Bob cooked them. After a while Clay brought them in and we tasted them, but they were raw inside so he put them back on the grill. We did that a couple of times until they were ready. They were okay, a little overdone and tough and only half as much meat as we started out with, but Clay said he could do it right the next time by figuring out how long the meat was on the grill and subtracting the times we took it off to taste.

"Of course I had my own problems—one of the potatoes I put on to bake exploded. I guess if a direction says to bake at 350 degrees, 500 won't make it cook faster."

Bob watched, horrified, as Mary stopped in the middle of the Galleria, laughing so hard she was crying. They were making such a spectacle of themselves that he knew if he didn't get away from them fast, people would think he was as crazy as they were. He gave them a disgusted look, walked about ten feet away and leaned on the railing overlooking the ice rink below. Pretending to watch the skaters, he began searching the crowds for their tails.

He'd caught sight of the two federal agents in the Galleria earlier but couldn't remember which store they'd been in. Somewhere along the way he'd spotted the bald-headed man, and it had taken all his strength not to confront the guy, but he couldn't leave Deanna and Mary unprotected. Besides, the old fellow didn't look as if he would last much longer, anyway. The one man he wanted more than anything to catch sight of eluded him, but he was out there—watching, Bob was sure of it. At least the police weren't in today's parade, he thought, then realized the women were on the move again. With a groan of pain he pushed away from the railing and took off after them.

They had almost reached Neiman Marcus when Mary sensed a sudden change in Deanna. She followed the girl's gaze, and when Deanna would have moved on faster, Mary dug in her high heels, forcing her to stop. "You can't avoid it forever."

"I've done a pretty good job of it so far." Deanna tugged at Mary's arm. "Let's go."

"No. I think it's time you faced your devils."

Deanna stared at the store before her—Fleur's. The two display windows were artfully decorated with graceful mannequins dressed in fashions already hinting at the fall season. It was a select location, one her grandmother had started negotiating for through the wife of the developer long before the Galleria was even built. Agatha Deveraux wanted out of her Rice University Village shop and the small-time operation there. She planned, even designed, the layout of the new store and determined it would shine right up there with the best specialty shops. And she wanted to be as close as possible to Neiman Marcus, the exclusive Texas store.

Agatha was never to see her dream fulfilled, but her manager and assistant, Lamar Maxell, and old Mr. Lambert had made it happen, following Agatha's design specifications as if they were law. Deanna, despite what everyone thought, had kept up with the boutique's rise to fame. She'd never had any desire to see it personally, though.

"Agatha Deveraux," Deanna said, "was a witch. Even my mother, her own daughter, didn't like her very much. She was obsessed with her dress designing and the shop and didn't have room for anyone or anything else."

"But she taught you how to design and sew."

"Yes, but not with some noble plan in mind. She did it so I could work for her—child labor, Mary. I was her granddaughter and... Oh, hell, I don't want to talk about her."

They were directly in front of the store and Mary gave Deanna a little shove. "You're your own woman now. There's nothing to be scared of. And remember, Deanna, you own the majority of stock in that boutique. The people in there actually work for you."

"Don't push, Mary." Deanna hung back. She saw the look of disappointment on her friend's face and sighed. "Okay, you're right. I don't want to go in there because I'm scared. Not of them—" she motioned toward the shop "—but my memories. For the two years I lived with Grandmother, all she talked about when she wasn't screaming at me was her new shop—what it would look like, her plans to make it the most fashionable, talked-about boutique in Texas. I'm afraid even after all these years there'll still be too much of Grandmother in there for my peace of mind."

"How are you ever going to know unless you go in?"

Mary, always the voice of reason, Deanna thought with disgust. But of course she was right.

"Why don't we all go in there," Mary suggested.

"Oh, come on, Mary," Bob moaned. "Not me, please."

"Hush up, Bob Spencer. You're supposed to be Deanna's bodyguard, aren't you? How can you guard her if you don't stay beside her?"

"I could watch from the door." But already he was following them in, his frown fierce. "All this frilly crap makes me itch," he mumbled.

The first thing that struck Deanna was the lack of anything remotely connected with her grandmother except for the shining black boxes with the white silk gardenia and the black-and-white shopping bags she saw customers carrying out. Looking around at the carefully placed dress racks, feeling the material brush against her arms, was enough to send her deeper into the depths of the shop.

In her own talented way Lamar Maxell had turned her grandmother's dream into her own. The boutique was full of designs by Saint Laurent, Blass, Klein and Galanos. Deanna was in heaven, surrounded by Halston's skimpy dresses, a Dior camisole-top dress, a Givenchy voile halter dress with a shockingly low back. There was Valentino and Laug. Deanna reverently touched the silver-white beaded top over a narrow brown-and-cream-striped crepe skirt of a Galanos evening gown.

Evening gowns were Deanna's passion, the silks, chiffons, the stiff satins and brocades. She loved the glitter and shine of sequins and the rich luster of pearls. She rubbed the luxurious turquoise silk of a Valentino skirt between her fingers. *If I was a designer,* she thought, *this is what I'd spend my time doing—evening gowns.*

She was so lost in her fantasy that it took a moment for the whispering voices to reach her. She parted the tall rack of Adolfo knitted wool and silk suits and glanced at the two women standing to one side of a Queen Anne desk.

The ten years since she'd seen Lamar Maxell had been kind to the woman. She was tall and striking, with a graceful elegance and strong presence. It was the other woman that snagged her attention, though. Deanna knew she'd seen her before, but at the moment couldn't place her. The woman was as tall as Lamar, but where Lamar was handsome, the other woman had a more classic beauty—perfect bone structure, pale skin, big brown eyes and thick straight hair that would do anything asked of it with great style.

Then Deanna realized who she was, Lynn something-or-other—Clay's friend. In the same instant she recognized the shock on the faces of the two women.

"Deanna? Deanna Deveraux?" Lamar asked as she moved toward her. Lynn, meanwhile, watched silently, forcing a polite smile. Though she didn't want to admit it, ever since Clay had taken on the Deveraux case, he'd distanced himself from her. According to the latest gossip, he'd been seen with a petite blonde at a car dealership.

There was even a rumor circulating that he was having a full-blown affair with a client, the same blonde. And Lynn knew, as surely as if Clay had told her, that he was seeing Deanna Deveraux. She couldn't understand it, though. The girl was a murderer and should be locked up, not allowed to run around free, seducing the man she was in love with.

Maybe there was something she could do to help the situation along. A couple of words in the right ear, a hint here and there. After all, she hadn't lost Clay yet. He'd told her yesterday when he finally returned her calls that he wanted to meet her at the country club about three for a drink.

Lynn moved quickly beside Lamar and said, "Hello, Miss Deveraux. Do you remember me?" Her voice was overly loud in the quiet store, the question spoken slowly as if her target was either hard of hearing or dim-witted.

Deanna flinched. "Yes, of course, but I don't believe I remember your name." She watched the other woman register surprise. Obviously she was used to instant recognition.

Lamar made introductions and offered to show Deanna around the shop.

"No! I mean, thanks, but no. I can see you've done a wonderful job." Deanna sensed Mary moving closer to her side and Bob behind her. "I have other shopping to finish." She turned to leave, but Lamar touched her arm.

"Deanna, please, we need to talk about Fleur's. I've repeatedly asked Mr. Lambert to talk to you about selling out to me, but he wouldn't hear of it. Can't we discuss it soon?"

"I'd be happy to tell Clay when we have dinner this evening that you need to talk with him," Lynn said.

Deanna was feeling trapped, as if both women were moving in on her. "Sure." She backed away. "I'll have to talk to Clay—my attorney—first."

"I understand," Lamar said. "Where can I reach you?"

Deanna wanted nothing more than to get away, and without thinking said, "I've moved into Grandmother's house." She heard Bob make a strangling sound and knew she'd made a mistake.

"Wait, just one more thing." Lamar looked pointedly at Mary's outfit, a loose pink silk shirt with wide cuffs and a short flaring skirt. "Chloë?" she asked.

Mary looked down her small nose and in her most haughty voice said, "Of course not. A Deveraux."

Well, Deanna thought as they walked out of the store, that'd left them with their mouths hanging open in shock.

Once out in the Galleria, Deanna said, "All of a sudden I'm tired. Let's skip Neiman's and go home."

At first Bob sighed with relief, then said ominously, "You shouldn't have told the bitch where you were living." But the women weren't listening to him, so he shrugged and shook his head, hoping nothing would come of Deanna's slipup.

"Who was that woman Lynn?" Mary asked. "You didn't see the way she was looking at you. For Pete's sake, she hates you, Deanna."

"She's Clay's girlfriend." Deanna felt sick. "And he's having dinner with her this evening."

"No, he's not," Bob said, and both women swung around and stared at him. "She's a liar. He's not having dinner with her. He'll be with you. I know that for a fact."

"You're sure, Bob?" Mary asked. She could see the hurt and disappointment in Deanna's eyes and felt for her. The very thing was happening that she'd warned Clay Lambert about—he was going to cause Deanna heartbreak. She could just kill the man.

"Sure? Of course I'm sure, Mary. I told him I wanted to take you to dinner tonight and he said no problem, he'd be home by four-thirty. Said it plain as day."

They'd reached Bob's car and were getting in when Deanna asked, "Why would she lie like that?"

Bob and Mary exchanged knowing glances and Bob stuffed the bags in the already jammed trunk.

"Ask Clay to explain," Mary offered with a smile. She knew Deanna would do just that—ask an honest, straightforward question and expect the truth. Let him get out of that one, Mary thought.

WILLIAM AND HIS SONS met them in the driveway and helped Bob carry all the bags, boxes and packages into the house.

"The only thing happening around here is that Herbert from the office delivered the boxes Mr. Clay sent for. We stacked them in the living room."

Deanna thanked William and told him he and his sons could leave for the day. Bob and Mary were going to stay with her until Clay showed up. It didn't take long for Mary to cajole her out of her blue mood. Bob stretched out on the couch in the den, telling them to whistle if they needed him. But they were already rummaging through their purchases and he might just as well have saved his breath.

Once the new towels and facecloths were stored in the linen closet and the designer sheets and bedspreads put on the beds, the women were pulling curtains down from the windows and hanging up new ones. Mary tried not to notice how often Deanna glanced at her watch. When five o'clock rolled around she shook Bob awake for no other reason than he was a man and didn't deserve to sleep while she was so upset.

The sound of a car in the driveway sent Deanna flying to the dining room window. "It's Clay," she said as she raced back into the kitchen and up the ladder positioned next to the sink. She ignored Mary and Bob's amused looks. "If you're through putting the valance on the rod, Mary, hand it to me."

Deanna's timing was perfect. She'd just finished hanging the French country curtains when Clay strolled in. Her look of genuine surprise at his arrival almost made Mary laugh out loud. With interest she watched them closely. For the first time she caught Clay's unguarded expression and wondered if she'd been wrong.

When Deanna smiled at him the man looked as if he'd been given the moon and stars.

"Sorry I'm late." Clay held up two large paper bags. "I stopped and picked up Chinese food for dinner." He glanced at Bob. "I hope you're still planning to take Mary out for dinner because I only got enough for two here." He set the bags down on the kitchen table. "I understand you went to Fleur's today."

"How'd you know?"

"I met Lynn for a drink at the country club."

"I see," Deanna said.

Mary pinched a fascinated Bob on the arm. "Let's go."

"What? And miss this?" Bob whispered, looking from Clay to Deanna. "Okay, okay." He quickly stood up with Mary pushing and poking him all the way. "I don't understand," he hissed fiercely. "You're the one who said you wouldn't trust Clay as far as you could throw him. Now you're leaving them alone?"

"I've changed my mind." She picked up her purse. "Bye, Deanna. I'll call you tomorrow. Clay, those boxes you had delivered are stacked in the living room."

Clay waved absently as they left. He'd had a tough afternoon, and by the looks of it, his evening wasn't going to be much better. "How'd it go at Fleur's?"

"Not as bad as I thought it would be—at first. Lamar wants to buy me out."

They were skating around the issue and both knew it. "And how do you feel about that?" he asked. "After all, it's a lucrative business and your grandmother did start it."

"I told Lamar I'd think about it. To be honest, for years I dreamed of taking Fleur's over and making a success of it on my own. But after seeing the shop today, I realized that my dream was just a way to get back at

Grandmother. Actually I think I'd like to destroy Fleur's. I hate the thought of anything my grandmother had a hand in. You must think I'm awful, feeling like that about a dead woman.''

"I think you're human, just like the rest of us. And from what I've heard, your grandmother wasn't a very lovable person.'' Clay began moving around the kitchen, gathering plates and silverware. He shrugged out of his jacket, pulled off his tie and discarded his vest, then he unbuttoned his shirt and rolled up his sleeves. "Did Lynn say something to upset you today?''

Something inside told her to lie. "Why would you think that?'' But the joy of seeing him walk through the door and knowing Lynn was a liar made her want to tell the truth. "She told us she was meeting you for dinner. I was confused, I guess, because you didn't mention it to me.''

"Confused?''

"Miffed, then.''

Clay smiled. "I'll accept miffed.'' He set the table and held out a chair for Deanna. "Lynn lied to you. I told her I'd meet her for a drink at three and I don't believe that constitutes dinner.''

"Why would she lie to me? I don't even know her.''

"But I do, and I'm sorry if she said or did anything to upset or hurt you because of me.'' He opened the bags and began pulling out the cartons. "Lynn had some mistaken ideas about me, but I straightened her out today.''

Deanna wanted to ask what mistaken ideas and how he'd straightened her out, but his statement was like a door slamming shut in her face. She didn't have the courage to open it again.

"Now, can we get back to normal?'' Clay asked. "Tell me about your day.''

After a long leisurely dinner, Clay opened another beer and wandered into the living room while Deanna cleaned up the kitchen. He spotted the eight stacked boxes and, setting down his drink, carried one to a table.

Deanna found Clay leaning back in his chair, his bare feet propped up on the table, a stack of papers in his lap and a couple in his hand. He was so engrossed in what he was reading he didn't hear her. When she spoke his name for the third time he jumped, and she saw him immediately slip whatever he was reading under another stack of papers on the table. He was trying to hide something from her. She walked over to the table, pushed his hand away and, when he tried to stop her, yanked the paper out from under the rest.

"I didn't want to upset you," he said.

Deanna read the paper and smiled sadly. "Did you think that I didn't know?" She waved her birth certificate at him. "My grandmother seemed to take delight in reminding me that I was illegitimate—a bastard, she'd call me when she was really mad."

What else, Clay wondered, had Deanna endured at the hands of that bitch? He wanted to take her in his arms and comfort her. But she'd already dismissed the issue as if it meant nothing to her. Yet he could see it hurt her. "Did your mother know you knew?"

"Yes." Deanna picked up another paper. "What's this?"

"Your grandmother's will. Did you ask her about your father? What did your mother tell you about him?"

Deanna flipped through the document, reading random paragraphs. "Mom said she'd tell me when I was old enough." She reread a sentence, then pointed it out to Clay. "Is this polite legal jargon or what Grandmother said?"

Clay read out loud. " 'To my beloved granddaughter, Deanna, I leave my entire estate.' It's probably her words. Why?"

Deanna pitched the document on the table and started walking out of the room. Clay called her name and she stopped.

"My beloved granddaughter," she said sarcastically. "Why would she say that? She hated me."

Clay couldn't tell her why and watched as she left the room. She'd made the dining room directly across from him her sanctuary, surrounded herself with her sewing machine, the two half-clothed dress dummies, easel, paints and drawing material. He'd learned over the past week or so that when she was troubled she'd head for the converted dining room and sketch or sew.

He moved his chair so he could surreptitiously keep an eye on her. Sometimes he'd hear her there in the middle of the night or the wee hours of the morning. He left her alone to work out her problems, but leaving Deanna to herself was one of the hardest things he'd ever done.

Deanna picked up her sketch pad. She knew he spied on her, and if it had been anyone else she would have resented it, but somehow she thought he was watching over her. "Clay. . ." She raised her voice so he could hear her.

"What?" he called back, his deep voice vibrating across the space between them.

"Do you know the two things I miss?"

"No. But you're going to tell me, aren't you?"

"Of course." There was laughter in his voice and she smiled. "Music and television. Tomorrow I'm going to buy me a stereo system and the biggest TV they make. Will you watch old movies and dance with me?"

"Anyplace, anytime." Clay saw her nod her head and return to her drawing, and he relaxed. Whatever was eating at her, she'd worked through it.

The house was quiet with only the occasional sound of paper being shuffled or Deanna's soft mumbling as she talked to herself while she drew. But that tranquillity was suddenly shattered by a loud crash. Deanna screamed.

Clay shot out of the living room and slammed his fist against the light switch, plunging them into darkness. Then without thinking, he tackled Deanna to the floor and covered her body with his as a second missile crashed through the broken window. There was a solid thud as something hard hit the floor. The first thing that flashed through Clay's mind was, *Grenade*.

He pressed down harder on Deanna's shaking body, trying to cover every inch of her as he mentally counted off seconds. When nothing happened, he raised his head, saw the shards of glass glinting in the dim light and two round objects. His mind was crazy with fear, seeing the pinless pineapple shape, the dull glow of military green. He couldn't move, thinking he'd miscounted and any second the last thing he'd see was a bright flash.

His senses began to calm as reason returned and he saw that the objects were merely rocks. He moaned, then quickly turned Deanna over. "Are you all right?" She was shaking and crying, and he rolled off her and onto his side, gathering her in his arms. "Hush. It's okay. Some kid threw a couple of rocks through the window."

"I'm braver in the light," she whispered against his chest. "And don't lie." She sniffed. "No kid did that."

"Are you cut? Did any glass hit you?"

"No, I'm fine. Scared out of my wits. But I can't breathe."

"God, what's the matter? Tell me where it hurts."

"You're squeezing me to death."

"Sorry." But he only loosened his grip a fraction. "Listen, I'm going to crawl across the floor to the front door and see if I can spot anything. You stay put."

When he let her go she took a couple of deep breaths and did exactly what he told her not to. She wasn't about to stay in the dark room alone and scooted across the bare hardwood floor as fast as an ant after sugar. When she reached the entry hall she stopped. The small lamp from the table in the living room was a poor excuse for a light. Clay was nowhere to be seen, and she remembered how fast he'd moved earlier.

She could see the half-opened front door, but she couldn't hear anything. An eternity slipped by. She tried to talk herself into following Clay. What if someone had knocked him in the head and he was hurt or dying? What if he needed her? Forcing her legs to move, she put her back to the wall, then worked herself to an upright position. She was concentrating so hard, trying to overcome her fear and make her stiff body cooperate, that she missed the sound of feet on the porch steps.

What caught her attention was Clay's loud cursing. Most of the words she'd only read in books and some were completely foreign. Deanna grabbed the door and swung it open, then immediately jumped back in fright when Clay yelled at her to "shut the damn door!" But she was so stunned she could only stand there, scarcely breathing.

The porch light was out, but the moonlight and the faint illumination from the living room was enough that she could see clearly. The word "murderer" had been scrawled across the front door in black paint, so fresh and thick that it dripped down the bright red door like something out of a horror movie.

Clay stomped up the porch stairs and into the house, grabbing Deanna roughly by the arm while slamming the door shut with his other hand.

"Don't try and tell me that a kid or a neighbor did that," she said. "They don't know who I am."

"It's a psychological game to scare you."

"Well, it's doing a pretty good job."

"And it's a warning," Clay said.

"How many more of these warnings do I get?"

"Not many, I'd say. I'm afraid whoever's after you knows or has a good idea you've regained your memory. What he or they don't know is what you remember. After a while whoever it is, is going to get weary of the guessing game and weigh his options. He's not going to jeopardize the time, money and effort he's spent over ten years. He'll opt to protect his own interests."

"How?"

"I'm not going to sugarcoat this, Deanna. As much as I wish I could lock you away forever to keep you safe, I can't. You have to take some of the responsibility of safeguarding yourself."

"What will he try to do, Clay?"

"I think his next move is to silence you before you can point a finger his way."

She'd stopped listening as her mind grappled with what he'd just said.

"That means we have to find out who was responsible for keeping you in the sanitarium, who paid off the judge and was getting reports from your doctor. We need to—"

"He's coming after me, isn't he?"

"Look at me and listen." He waited until she was staring directly at him. "It's ugly, I know, but, Deanna, I think it's going to get worse."

"Why?"

"He's killed twice."

"Clay. What do I have to do to make him—or them—stop?"

"Tell us who killed your grandmother and why."

"But I don't know."

Clay tapped her forehead. "Somewhere in there I think you do know."

Deanna shook her head. "He's going to kill me, too, isn't he, Clay?"

"I can almost guarantee he's going to try."

CHAPTER TWELVE

SLEEP THAT NIGHT was elusive.

Deanna tossed and turned, her mind racing, reliving the terror of what had happened earlier and creating a few horrifying scenarios of her own. The bed covers were a tangled mess around her legs.

She was cold and pulled the covers up to her neck.

She was hot and kicked them to the foot of the bed.

She flipped over on her back and stared at the ceiling, wondering if Clay was lying awake, too. She gave up the wrestling match with the sheets and blanket, declaring them the winner, and rolled out of bed, catching a glimpse at the clock as she did. Four o'clock in the morning, she thought, was a reasonable enough time to slip downstairs and do some sketching, she decided. The idea for an evening dress had been teasing her ever since she'd been in Fleur's.

Deanna quietly eased down the hall and was just passing Clay's room when he called her name. She paused at the doorway, trying to see him, but the darkness was unfathomable and his voice as disembodied as if he were a ghost. She shivered.

"Can't sleep?" Clay asked. What little light there was in the hall illuminated the gentle curves beneath the cotton T-shirt, and desire stirred his blood like a hot poker. "Want to talk?" His heart leapt when he saw her move toward him, but when she stopped only a foot over the threshold, he felt the sinking sensation of acute disappointment.

"Would you turn on the light, please?"

He remembered how much she hated the dark and reached over to flick on the bedside lamp. The low-wattage bulb afforded only a tiny circle of light, but it was enough. He patted the bed as he pushed himself to a sitting position, his back against the headboard.

Deanna tried to ignore his bare chest and the knowledge that he slept naked. She could feel the heat of his thigh against her and swallowed. "I couldn't sleep," she said, feeling tongue-tied and awkward. She could have kicked herself. Of course he knew that. Why else would she be wandering around the house this time of the morning? Her heart was beating so fast and loud she wondered if he could hear it.

"I couldn't sleep, either." Clay caught her hand, and without thinking what he was doing brought it to his lips and kissed her palm, lingering over the softness there. When she closed her eyes he moved his mouth to the inside of her wrist, then pulled her forward a little so he could kiss the crook of her arm.

Slipping his hands beneath her arms, he half lifted her closer to his side. When she didn't resist he caught her face between his hands and ran his fingertips down the soft skin of her cheeks, over the curved line of her lips, around her ears, then up to her temples. Still holding her, he gently kissed each closed eyelid, and then his mouth captured hers. His tongue eased between her lips, urging them apart, and when she complied he kissed her deeply, knowing he would never drink his fill of this woman.

She seemed to melt against him, and he could feel her heat, feel the firmness of her breasts against his chest, the way her arms tightened around his neck. As the kiss intensified, he slid his hands beneath her buttocks, drawing her closer, wanting to crush her soft pliant body into his.

When Deanna suddenly stiffened, Clay released her at once. Though his body pulsated with desire, he knew she was an innocent and he needed to go slow. Maybe he should do the right thing, the mature thing, and stop altogether before he lost control completely. Let Deanna decide when and where she wanted to make love. But, dear God, she tasted so good and felt even better.

Deanna tilted her head back and gazed into Clay's eyes. His expression was serious and his hazel eyes were dark pools of raw emotion. She shivered slightly and whispered, "Why did you stop?"

"Do you know what's likely to happen if we go on?"

"I have a good idea."

"Do you?" He tried to smile but didn't quite succeed. "Do you really?"

Deanna grasped his hand and placed it on her left breast. "Feel my heart beating."

His hand was suddenly on fire.

"I'm twenty-three, Clay. I know all there is to know about making love—in theory. It's the practical application that's sorely lacking in my education. I guess you think I'm too forward—no finesse?"

Clay couldn't help it. He started to laugh, then hugged her tight.

She braced her arms on his chest and studied him intently for a moment. "This man-woman stuff is very confusing. I want you more than anything, but today when I thought you were with Lynn, I felt hurt. I kept wondering if you'd been with her, made love with her...."

Clay barely heard what she was saying. All he was aware of was his physical response to her lush body half-sprawled across his.

"Come here," he whispered, and closing his eyes, he eased himself down onto the bed and positioned her along the length of his body. It took a moment for his breathing to return to normal.

Deanna lay in his arms, and when his hands drifted down her sides, past her waist to her hips and the hem of her T-shirt, she held her breath. When she felt the shirt being pulled upward, she lifted her hips and then helped ease it over her head and shoulders. She lay naked, and then suddenly the sheet, the only barrier between them, was gone and her flesh was touching his.

Her hands seemed to have a will of their own as they began to explore new territory. Clay's skin was hot to her touch, the hair on his chest coarse and prickly. She rubbed her cheek against it and felt the ferocious pounding of his heart. "I'd have thought our bodies would feel the same, but they don't."

"I should hope not." He tried to laugh, but only a strangled sound came out, so he closed his eyes, reveling in the touch of her artless fingers. She seemed to gain courage with each of his moans, and when she accidentally brushed against his rigid arousal, she paused and timidly caressed him. He thought if she continued he might lose control.

Clay opened his eyes, heavy with desire, and watched as she examined his body, touching him with her fingertips and her lips, exploring and tasting him until he couldn't stand it any longer. Grasping her shoulders, he pulled her up and kissed her long and deep.

"You know something?" she said against his mouth.

"What?"

"You were right. We're not at all alike."

He chuckled and rolled her over onto her back, scattering light kisses down the side of her neck until he reached her breast.

Deanna gasped and threw her head back. She'd never felt anything so wonderful in her life and wanted it to go on forever. When Clay's hand traveled lower, cupping the soft mound of curls between her thighs, she tensed for a moment, but at his gentle caress she relaxed and prayed he would never stop touching her. And as a subtle tension grew within her she squirmed beneath him, drawing him closer. She knew she wanted something to happen, but wasn't sure what.

Clay hovered over her a moment, fighting for control as he saw the flush of passion on her cheeks. He watched as he eased his way slowly into her, holding her tightly against him. With each gentle thrust she gasped, but when he would have stopped, she lifted her hips to his, moving rhythmically with him.

Deanna felt as if she would shatter into a million wonderful pieces. She felt the tension in her build and moaned with the half-pain, half-pleasure of it. Instinctively she wrapped her arms and legs tightly around him. Suddenly the tension seemed to peak, and a feeling of total release surged through her. Dimly she was aware of the muscles beneath her hands tightening to rigid cords, and then with a groan Clay collapsed on top of her.

After a moment Clay shifted onto his side, struggling to slow his rapid breathing. His hands stroked Deanna's back in a soothing motion, then, leaning on his elbow, he raised himself and gazed at her. He'd expected—what? Regret? Pain? Anger? But instead, she was smiling at him, her blue eyes sparkling with laughter.

"If you say you're sorry," she said, "I swear I'll do something truly evil to you. You're not sorry, are you?"

"Absolutely not. But you—how do you feel?"

"Wonderful."

Clay laughed and kissed her breast. "No. I mean—"

Deanna placed her fingers across his lips. "Please. Don't ask me to analyze what happened, I don't want to talk it to death. I just want to remember it as the greatest feeling in the world. Could we do it again, soon?"

Clay laughed again and gathered her in his arms. "Just as soon as I regain my strength." He reached down and drew the sheet over them. It felt so good to have her next to him, so right, that he wanted nothing more than to wake up in the morning and watch her sleep. The thought that someone might take Deanna away from him struck deep. He had to find out who was after her, who wanted to hurt her.

"It wasn't at all like what I've read about," she said sleepily.

"I should hope not." He brushed the hair away from her cheek and kissed her lightly.

"What's happening between us?" she whispered against his lips.

"I wish I knew," he mumbled in reply.

When he stopped kissing her she asked, "But you're the experienced one. Shouldn't you know these things?"

"Under normal conditions I'd say yes, but this is all new to me."

"Mary says it's just lust, but I don't agree. Do you think it could be love?"

Clay chuckled almost self-mockingly. "Well, let's put it this way—it's a healthy mixture of the two."

Deanna yawned and snuggled closer, pleased by his answer. "I think I can get some sleep now."

DEANNA SERVED COFFEE and buttered toast to Clay, Bob and Mary in the living room, then stood back, yawning hugely. She'd awakened alone in Clay's bed around seven and staggered sleepily downstairs to find him with the telephone stuck to his ear as he sipped coffee. When she'd moved toward the coffeepot, picking up the newspaper off the counter, Clay had quickly hung up, snatched the paper from her, then rushed her back upstairs, telling her that he'd talked to Bob at Mary's house and told him what had happened.

Deanna knew something was going on behind her back. Clay had found a hundred things for her to do. When Bob and Mary arrived she'd left the room on one of Clay's cooked-up errands, and when she'd returned the atmosphere had become tense. She knew they'd been talking about her. She tested her theory a couple of times by excusing herself, waiting a few minutes, then slipping back in the room. As soon as she reappeared, all conversation ceased.

"Okay, that's it," she said. "Something's going on and I want to know what it is." She looked at each one, but her gaze lingered on Clay. "You promised no more secrets. That you wouldn't hide things from me."

Clay nodded and reached behind him.

"Clay, don't," Mary ordered.

"As much as we'd all like to, we can't protect Deanna from this sort of thing. We can't keep her in the dark, Mary. Surely you know that." Clay watched Mary's shoulders slump as he handed over the morning paper.

With a puzzled expression, Deanna took the paper and slowly unfolded it. The front-page article jumped out at her, and she immediately sat down. "Oh, God," she said softly. "It's all about my release from Twelve Oaks and Grandmother's murder."

"It gets worse," Clay said as he held out his hand to keep Mary from rushing to Deanna's side.

"They make it sound like the law has released a butcher, a monster, on the innocent public. That I'll probably kill again." She turned the page to the continuing story, and after a moment she glanced up, a dazed look in her eyes. "Clay, they've all but accused me of killing that reporter, Danny Hudson. How can they do that?"

"The paper has been very careful, Deanna. They've intimated all those things, never come right out and accused you. As for the reporter, they only say he was doing a story on your release and his body was found behind the library after he met you there for an interview."

"But it makes it sound like I killed him, and I didn't. Why would he do something like that?"

Clay frowned, then saw that Bob and Mary were as confused as he was by her question. "Who are you talking about?"

"Why, the man following me, of course. This is his doing, isn't it? Like the rocks thrown through the windows and the paint on the front door?" She stood and waved the newspaper. "Is this supposed to be another warning?" She'd said something important because they all tried to avoid her eyes at once. "What's going on?"

Clay reached out to put his arm around her shoulders, but she shrugged him away. "It wasn't the man following you. He prefers to work in the dark and wouldn't want so much public attention. Deanna, the owner of the paper is an old friend of Grandfather's. I gave him a call this morning, and after I explained a few facts pertaining to this case he told me his editor was given the story, the initial story, by Lynn and the rest the editor filled in on his own. I knew we couldn't hold the press off forever, but Lynn..."

Clay ran his fingers through his hair. He'd already endured thunderous looks from Mary and Bob. "I can't tell you how sorry I am. I never thought Lynn could be so vindictive."

Mary gave an unladylike snort. "Men! Haven't you ever heard the old saying that hell hath no fury like a woman scorned?"

Clay ignored Mary's comment. "Deanna, I told Lynn yesterday that she and I were through, but I didn't tell her I was involved with you. I thought she understood. When I left she wasn't angry or upset."

"Of course not," Mary added sarcastically. "She was too busy planning her revenge."

Deanna sighed wearily. "I guess it was bound to happen." She smiled at Clay and wrapped her arms around him. "I don't blame you, really I don't."

Mary's mouth tightened into a grim line. Bob thought it was as obvious as the nose on his face that the young couple had been playing house in more ways than one. But he realized that Mary had just that minute recognized it. He had a feeling Clay was going to have some questions to answer. He also thought that a distraction was in order. "Listen, Clay. We're here to help, but you haven't explained what your plan is."

Clay was glad of the interruption. He turned to Deanna. "As much as I'd like to hold you all day, we've got a lot of work to do." He pointed to the stack of boxes. "But first I want you to know that William's sons are going to be stationed at the front and back doors." Clay had called both men earlier that morning and they'd readily agreed. At six foot four and about 250 pounds each, they would, he hoped, be a visible deterrent to anyone remotely interested in harming Deanna. And they would be armed.

He expected Deanna to protest, but to his surprise she was silent, so he continued, "Whoever killed Agatha Deveraux has worked behind the scenes for ten years. He's not going to be happy with all the sudden publicity and will be afraid that if Deanna contradicts the newspaper article, someone might believe her, that there might in fact be another killer." He held up his hand before anyone could question him.

"What we have to do is find out why Agatha Deveraux was killed. The first place to start is with all of these—Grandfather's files on the case. We're going to read ever scrap of paper, every note, bill, IRS return, financial statement and investment. Then we'll put them in chronological order and take a look at the whole picture and see what, if anything, we have."

Silently, and with dread, they all gazed at the boxes, each thinking what a monumental job was ahead of them. Clay and Bob thought a lead, a clue, was in the files and had been missed. Mary was sure if there was anything it would have been found long ago by old Mr. Lambert.

Deanna dreaded the job but for her own reasons. The boxes contained documents that related to her grandmother's life, and everything about her grandmother had only spelled misery for her.

The morning had gotten off to a bad start, Deanna thought, and went progressively downhill. By noon everyone was tired and suffering eyestrain. The legal mumbo jumbo was hard for everyone but Clay to wade through, and they were in need of an accountant to decipher the financial statements. But Clay kept them at it like a dictator with a heavy whip. And to add to the tension, he'd arranged for the broken windows to be repaired that morning.

Deanna slipped out of the room and into the kitchen. She was digging through the refrigerator for something for lunch when Mary walked in. Glancing over the top of the fridge door, she saw the determined look on her friend's face. For the first time in ten years Deanna didn't want to share what had happened between her and Clay with the older woman. The experience was too personal and belonged to her and Clay exclusively. For some reason she felt if she told Mary that she and Clay had been intimate, she'd be betraying something precious.

Mary recognized the sudden maturity and sighed. "I'm not going to pry. Nor am I going to tell you what to do. You're a grown woman, but remember, if you need me for any reason, I'll always be there."

Deanna hugged Mary. "Thanks. I'm pretty sure I love him, Mary."

"I know. That worries me. You don't have anything to judge your emotions by. No experience." She shrugged and smiled apologetically. "Sorry. I said I wasn't going to interfere."

"Are you and Bob serious?" Deanna wanted desperately to change the subject.

"Yes—no. Oh, Deanna, I just don't know." She pulled out a chair at the kitchen table and sat down. "That old saying 'Once burned, twice shy,' is true. I had a disastrous first marriage. He was a beautiful, charming, sexy man, much like your Clay. But he turned into a mean drunk who liked to use me as his personal punching bag. When he wrapped his car and his new girlfriend around a tree and died, I was glad. That was fifteen years ago and I've never really trusted men since—except Bob Spencer. There's just something so gentle and loving about that big guy." She smiled a little self-mockingly. "He told me the second time he visited me in the hospital that he was going to marry me. I laughed then, but you know what? He was right. I think I am going to marry him. That's why I can't tell you not to follow your heart about Clay. For the second time in my life I'm going to follow mine."

Tears filled Mary's eyes, and Deanna quickly rose and hugged her. "Oh, Mary, that's wonderful. I'll admit I don't know a lot about men, but I like Bob and I think he's a good man. Are you going to let me make your wedding gown? Have you decided when—and where?"

Mary laughed, wiped her eyes and looked up guiltily. "I haven't told Bob yet."

"You have now, angel face," Bob said from the kitchen doorway.

Deanna thought it was a good time to leave, and she was on her way to tell Clay the news when William opened the front door.

"Morning, Miss Deanna. There's something here for you." He moved so she couldn't see around him and grinned. "Mr. Clay," he called out, raising his voice, "it's here."

Deanna watched Clay hurry out of the living room and exchange a conspiratorial grin with William.

In a blaze of color and whirl of expensive perfume, a young woman, a total stranger, grabbed Deanna's shoulders and kissed her cheek. Then she laughed, a happy tinkling sound that made Deanna want to laugh, too.

Deanna blinked in confusion. The woman was tall, with dark blond hair and deep green eyes. She was wearing a dress in the most shocking, outrageous shade of purple.

"I've scared her, Clay."

"Well, look at you, Liz. You resemble a walking, talking eggplant." He grabbed the young woman's arm to keep her still and they both turned toward Deanna. "This bundle of nervous energy, this loudmouth, this busybody, nosy, very pregnant girl is my sister, Elizabeth Lambert."

Liz patted her stomach. "Elizabeth Lambert Chapman. My brother forgets that his baby sister's a married woman." She stood back and studied Deanna from head to toe.

Deanna chafed at the inspection, wishing she'd dressed in something other than jeans and a simple white cotton shirt. She glanced down at her bare feet and grimaced.

"You don't look like a murderer."

"Liz!" Clay roared. "For God's sake!"

"Well, she doesn't. She looks exactly what she is, a beautiful woman who, I might add, my big brother is absolutely crazy about. And I can see why." She kicked off her high heels, then put her hands on her hips and frowned at William. "What's keeping them, William? Why haven't they brought it in?"

"Because, Miss Lizzy, you won't stop talkin' long enough for a person to tell you to move out of the way."

Suddenly the entry was crowded with people, everyone laughing, talking and being introduced. But Deanna couldn't figure out why, and was reluctant to let go of Clay's arm, which she'd grabbed onto like a lifeline. He pulled her directly in front of him and covered her eyes with his hands.

"Don't peek," he said.

Peek? she thought. She couldn't move or seem to find her voice. Then she took a deep breath, telling herself that nothing bad was going to happen, not with Clay so close. She could make out strange noises—thumping and scraping sounds, and male voices grunting with exertion, then whispers and muffled laughter. When Clay dropped his hands she was too excited to open her eyes.

"Deanna," he said. "Look."

She squinted, barely lifting her lids. All at once her eyes widened and her mouth fell open. A huge color television and stereo system sat in her entry. She knew everyone was waiting for her to say something, but she couldn't find her voice. No one had given her a present in such a long time, except for Mary and Mr. Lambert at Christmas or on her birthday.

Deanna lightly ran her fingers over the smooth screen. Then she lifted the top of the stereo and stared at the turntable. She took a deep shaky breath and looked around at everyone: William, his face shining with a wide smile; his two sons, Homer and William Junior each mirroring their father's grin; Mary and Bob and Clay's sister. Then she turned around and looked at Clay. A lone tear spilled over and rolled down her cheek. "I've never had such a surprise before. I love you," she said softly.

The tear tore at his heart. He didn't care what anyone thought, and gathered her in his arms and kissed her long and hard. When he pulled away he whispered, "I said I'd watch old movies with you, didn't I?"

"And dance with me," she whispered back.

"Yes, and dance."

"Anytime, anyplace, you said." She was smiling through her tears.

"But not right now."

"Hey, you two," Liz said, "stop the lovey-dovey stuff. You're embarrassing everyone." She forcibly pried her brother's arms from around Deanna. "Do you see those two boxes?" Deanna nodded. "My husband and I had the most marvelous time this morning buying record albums. Clay said since we were the same age our tastes were probably the same, too." With a groan, she leaned over and picked up her shoes. "Well, I have to be off. Deanna, you'll get used to us. By the way, just so you know, Clay's the only sane one in our family." She waved and exited in a whirl of color, leaving a well of silence behind.

Deanna began thumbing through the albums. "There must be hundreds here. Oh, Clay." She held one up and said with awe, "Johnny Mathis."

Clay motioned for Homer and Junior to pick up the heavy television. "Put it in the den, will you? Homer, you're sure you can hook up the antenna?" When he nodded Clay stepped out of their way, pulling Deanna with him. "Break's over. I hate to be the one to put a damper on the fun, but we've still got lots of work to do." Everyone groaned.

Bob was reluctant to let go of Mary's hand. He was just about ready to tell Clay his good news when the telephone rang. It was for him. After a few minutes, with everyone trying to listen to his conversation, he hung up. When he turned around he was grinning like a man who'd just won a lottery. "Grab your purse, Mary," he said, then continued quickly to head off Clay's protest, "My friend at the telephone company has all the Twelve Oaks bills. He said he's got some very interesting information, too. We'll pick them up, then stop for a bite of lunch."

Clay watched them leave, feeling like a captain whose crew had jumped ship. He looked at Deanna and said in his best imitation of Bogart, "I guess it's just you and me, sweetheart."

Deanna laughed and said, "I'm hungry."

Clay shook his head, threw down the stack of papers he'd just picked up and smiled. "Me, too."

"We could play a couple of records while we fix lunch."

"No, we can't."

"How about we watch TV while we eat?" He shook his head again and she gave him a crestfallen look. "Come on, Clay."

"A quick bite, then back to the living room." He threw his arm around her shoulders. "Deanna, we can't slow down now. We have to find out what's going on."

They ate in the living room, surrounded by the scattered bits of her grandmother's life. Clay pitched a couple of papers into one box. "Another useless piece of information."

Deanna set aside her half-eaten sandwich and glanced up from what she was reading. She had four stacks of papers in front on her, each categorized. One pertained to Fleur's business matters, two were for her grandmother's personal and financial papers, and the last was for bank statements. "Here are just a couple of my grandmother's later bank statements. You know, I'm a little confused. Grandmother always complained about money. I always thought—"

"Excuse me, Miss Deanna." William stepped into the room. "The furniture people are here."

"What people?" Clay asked.

"My God, I forgot they were going to deliver everything today." She leapt up and was on her way out of the room when she remembered Clay. "It skipped my mind. But all the furniture I bought—it's here." She slapped her head as if to knock some sense into it. "William, Homer and Junior said they knew a needy family who could use Grandmother's old furniture. Can they get it out now?"

"Sure thing. Where do we start?"

"Deanna..." Clay said.

"Not now, Clay. All the furniture in both bedrooms, William. Then the den."

"Deanna..."

"Clay, can you help? If you, William, Homer and Junior can get the upstairs cleared out, then the movers can bring in the new stuff while you're clearing out the den. Then they can bring in the new den furniture."

He'd learned a couple of things he hadn't known about Deanna before, Clay thought with amusement as he struggled with his end of a heavy headboard. When she set her mind to something she got her way, and she was as good at giving orders as he was. Amazed, he'd watched the way she charmed the delivery men. Deanna Deveraux had a way of making men jump through her hoops with just a smile and her sweet voice.

She leaned against the wall in the den as Clay and Junior hauled the old couch out the kitchen door and into the backyard. The loud thump over her head made her flinch. One of the movers had dropped something. She had no idea men could get so testy simply because she couldn't make up her mind exactly where she wanted every little piece of furniture placed.

When she tried to use the back staircase, she found it blocked by an old mattress and box spring that hadn't been taken out yet. "You'd think," she mumbled as she headed toward the front of the house, "that those four professional movers would be more careful." Stopping abruptly in the entry, she realized that to reach the stairs she'd have to squeeze around and half climb over her new bureau and headboard. Organization was the key, she thought as she wedged herself between the closed double doors of the living room and the heavy bureau.

Immediately she became stuck. Reaching behind her
with both hands, she pried the pocket doors apart so that
she could step backward into the living room. She was
beginning to turn around when she sensed she was not
alone. Whirling around, she saw one of the movers, the
back of his uniform clearly marked with the store logo,
turning to face her.

"You're not supposed to be in here," she said. Then
she realized two things at once. The first was that one of
the boxes containing her grandmother's papers had
flames leaping out of it. The second was that the man
standing over the box was tall, with dull brown hair
graying at the temples. At that moment she recognized
him and attempted to back out the doors.

Deanna didn't think she'd ever seen anyone move as
fast, except maybe Clay. But before she could open her
mouth to call for help, he had his hands around her
throat, cutting off her voice and air supply. He was muttering at her as she struggled weakly.

She was going to die. She could see her fate clearly in
the eyes of her killer. But she didn't want to die, dammit. Deanna raised her hands and raked the sides of his
face with her nails, making deep gouges that drew blood.
When that did nothing to deter him, she panicked, kicking and clawing frantically until she felt her strength ebb
away and she crumpled to the floor.

The next thing she knew she was coughing and struggling for air while someone held her shoulders and called
her name. She opened her eyes and saw Clay's worried
face. Reaching out to him, she wrapped her arms around
his neck and held on for dear life. "It was the man at the
library," she said, her voice tremulous and hoarse with
pain. "Not the bald one, but the other."

"Don't talk. Don't move." She was trembling all over. He lifted her in his arms and carried her past the bureau, which had been shoved aside, and out into the entry. There he carefully lowered her onto the new couch. The protective paper wrapping crinkled under her weight. "Homer and Junior were bringing in the new couch when they spotted the open door. They saw him just in time. He let you go and they took off after him. William's calling the police."

"The fire?" she managed to say.

"Out. And don't worry, it was the box with the useless papers."

Her hair was a wild mane, and Clay gently brushed it away from her face. Rage, hot and murderous, bubbled up as he spotted the red marks on her neck, but he forced himself to stay calm. What the hell was he going to do? He'd thought he could keep her safe, but a killer had walked in right under their noses. One thing was crystal clear, though. Whatever it took, he was going to find the man who had done this to her. And when he did he would take care of him in his own way.

Deanna flinched at Clay's expression. She'd seen it before—on the face of the man who'd just tried to kill her. "Will he keep trying until he gets it right?" she wanted to know.

"No. I promise you that's the last time he'll get within fifty feet of you." Clay cradled her head in his hand. "I promise you, Deanna, he'll never touch you again, not while I draw breath."

CHAPTER THIRTEEN

DEANNA STOOD at the window in the dining room, the window that had been smashed by rocks, and watched the two police cars pull away from the curb.

She ignored the loud angry voices behind her. When the police had arrived, the two federal agents from the house across the street had sprinted over. Now Mary and Bob had returned, and all four of them were shouting, asking questions, demanding information. Deanna had walked away from them, seeking a quiet place to think.

Her mind kept replaying the attack, going over and over it, trying to figure out what it was her assailant had been muttering as he attempted to choke the life out of her. Something about the end, or it had to end, and he wasn't going to let her beat them. What she kept seeing was his face, the total absence of emotion there as he attempted to end her life. For whatever reason, she was totally expendable, a means to an end.

Deanna shuddered.

The arrival of a strange car at the front curb, the sound of doors slamming, brought her back to the present. She recognized the two men who got out of the car and she groaned. The thought of answering more questions made her feel ill, and she was about to call Clay when she saw Bob striding down the driveway to meet his old partner, Houston homicide detective Howard Haskel, who was approaching the house. She relaxed, but only for a moment.

Bob had obviously lost his temper at something Haskel had said. He started pushing his former partner, shoving the man back down the driveway. When the police officer was pressed against his car, Bob turned and walked up the driveway.

Deanna felt a presence beside her, a quiet friend standing guard, and turned to Mary. "I think our softspoken, easygoing Bob has just lost his temper."

"Yes, and it must be something to see. Did you notice that Detective Haskel didn't so much as make a move or open his mouth?"

"He was scared," Deanna said.

Mary nodded. "For his life," she added.

They grinned at each other.

"Where's Clay?" Suddenly aware of the quiet house, Deanna glanced around.

"He's escorting the FBI agents out the back. Doesn't want to alert the neighborhood."

Deanna laughed, her voice cracking with the emotional strain of the past few hours. "You mean you don't think they've noticed all the men hanging around, the broken windows, the word 'murderer' painted on the front door, movers in and out, smoke, screams, police cars and shouting? Then, of course, we have the newspaper to tell them that a murderer is living among them. No, I don't think they've noticed anything."

"They'll probably get up a petition to make you sell your house. Oh, my, yes. They'll even force you to leave town—no, the state. If that doesn't work, they'll force you to wear a sign around your neck so everyone will know what you are."

"Stop it, Mary," Deanna said, but she was smiling. "You just might be right."

"In any case, we have more important things to discuss. Bob's friend, the one at the phone company, really came through, but I'll let Bob tell you and Clay about it. Now, where'd that man get to? I know I heard Tinkerbell's light-footed tread echoing through the back of the house."

Deanna stared at Mary as if she'd lost her mind, then she burst out laughing. "Tinkerbell? You call Bob Tinkerbell?"

"Among other things," Mary said haughtily, and she grinned. "He's like a bull in a china shop, Deanna. In just a couple of days I've lost some of my grandmother's fine china, a crystal goblet and a lamp. But he's my Tinkerbell, so I guess I'll just have to endure it."

Bob and Clay came into the room at that moment, and when she saw Bob's fierce frown Deanna felt her spirits plummet. But as soon as he spotted Mary, the deep lines in his face melted away and he smiled.

"Good old Howie heard the emergency radio call and recognized the address. He had some mistaken idea that it might be a good time to question Deanna a little more." Bob chuckled. "I referred him to the house across the street. Told him a couple of federal agents would be happy to answer any of his questions."

"You said that," Deanna asked, "while you were pushing him down the driveway and off my property?"

Bob gave her a huge grin. "Howie's a bully. I just called his bluff."

"If you're quite through with the pleasantries," Clay growled, "can we get back to work?" He started toward the living room. "Deanna, why don't you go lie down."

He dismissed her as though she were a child. As if she meant nothing to him. About to tell Clay where he could go, she suddenly realized he was only worried and just as eager to discover her attacker as she was.

She followed everyone into the living room. "First of all," she said, "I'm not in the least tired and I'd much rather be working, doing something constructive, than staring at the ceiling, wondering when that man might strike again."

Bob nodded. "Besides, I need you." He opened the large manila envelope he'd carried into the room, pulled out a thick stack of papers and placed them on the table. He picked up a couple of sheets from the top and handed them to Deanna. "Do you know or recognize these two men?"

Deanna studied the first photograph carefully. It was of an older man dressed in an expensively cut suit. But it was the man's eyes that drew her attention, and though the black-and-white picture couldn't reveal their color, they were light and piercing. In the photo his hair appeared streaked, making her think it might be salt-and-pepper gray. His face was deeply lined around the straight nose and rather thin lips, and crow's feet fanned out from the corners of his eyes. Deanna thought the face had character, but for some reason the word "ruthless" popped into her head.

The second black-and-white photograph was altogether different. This man stood arrow straight in a military uniform. He had a thick head of very light hair, possibly gray, and his expression was serious. His eyes squinted against the sun, and the well-shaped mouth was set in a stern line. He was handsome, though, and probably a real charmer when he wanted to be. And yet he looked as if he could make men of greater stature cower.

He was positioned behind a podium, surrounded by other men in uniform, and was apparently making a speech.

Deanna studied both photographs again carefully, shaking her head as she did. "I've never— My God, look at the man standing behind the one in uniform—that's the man who tried to strangle me today."

Bob and Clay exchanged a smug glance. But instead of being upset by her revelation, they were only mildly interested. It wasn't the response she wanted and Deanna demanded, "Who are these men?"

But Bob, rather than answering, handed Deanna another photograph, one, like the others, that had obviously been copied from a newspaper. It didn't take her but a second to recognize this man. "He's the older man—the one in the car in the alley. Who are the other men, Clay?"

Clay had taken the photographs and lined them on the table in front of Deanna. "Think hard, Deanna. Are you sure you've never seen these two men before?"

"I'm positive."

"This man—" he pointed to the photo of the man with salt-and-pepper hair "—is Gilbert Foley of Foley Incorporated International in Dallas. He's one of the richest men in Texas. Hell, probably the United States, if the truth be known." Clay then indicated the photo of the man from the alley. "That's Harry Dobbs. He's head of security for Foley's, and he and Gilbert Foley go way back, even before Foley started his empire. This man—" Clay pointed to the photo of the man in uniform "—is General Franklin Concord Fitzpatrick, chairman of the Joint Chiefs of Staff, personal friend and confidant of the president of the United States. The man standing behind him on the podium, the one who tried to kill you today, is Major Sidney Sawyer, a career officer with naval intelligence until he became the general's aide and right-hand man.''

Deanna didn't say anything. She was shocked and confused.

Clay realized she hadn't made the connection. ''Deanna, the men following you work for two very rich and powerful men. Can you think of any reason they'd want to harm you?''

''I haven't a clue.''

''That isn't all,'' Bob interjected before Clay could go on. ''I got the telephone records of the sanitarium for the past ten years, ever since you were locked away there. Dr. Gresham called once a month to two Washington phone numbers. One was to the Pentagon. We can only assume it was to the general's office, because the other number was the general's residence. Fitzpatrick's been getting reports on your welfare from the good doctor, and the doctor has deposited monthly checks from a Jackson Corporation in Virginia. I don't think it'll take much checking to find the general's behind that company.''

Bob was on a roll and wasn't about to let anyone, especially Clay, steal his thunder. ''Now, here's an interesting fact that you ladies might be able to answer. There's a pay phone on the third floor of Twelve Oaks, and each month someone would call Foley Incorporated in Dallas. That someone was more than likely reporting to Harry Dobbs. Can either of you think who it could be? A nurse or orderly? Maybe a person on staff or a patient?''

''Pat,'' Mary said without thinking. The name just slipped out.

''Oh, Mary, no,'' Deanna murmured.

Mary had shocked even herself, but after a moment she shrugged and nodded. ''Patricia Nelson, she's the only nurse who deliberately became close friends with you. And, Deanna, think of all the new clothes she was always buying and the vacations. Why, right now she's in France. I made out the payroll and I know how much she makes. It's not enough to support her life-style. I just never thought about it before or had reason to."

Deanna found a chair and sat down. "Why?" It was all she could say as the three of them stared at her, waiting for her to solve the mystery. "I don't understand any of this."

"Neither does Judge Harrison," Bob said. "We took him copies of all these papers before coming back. I'll tell you something. The federal boys working with the judge paled when they saw the evidence on the general. Acted like they were in shock and said something about the general being the next president. If that's the case, from the way things have been going in government lately, I don't expect a lot of assistance from the FBI. They'll be scared and pull in their horns." Bob chuckled. "But I'll tell you something, the judge was mad as a hornet, and I'll bet he won't let the federal boys make him cool his heels."

Clay groaned, and Bob fell silent. "For God's sake, Bob, what have we done?"

"Huh?" Bob said, echoing everyone's thoughts.

"Doesn't matter if it's the general or Foley, by making the connection we've just put Deanna's life in greater jeopardy. Someone in the upper echelon wants this hushed up quickly and quietly."

"How can my life be in any more danger than it already is?" Deanna wanted to know. "He or they or whoever can only kill me once. But I'm not going to stand still and let that happen. I'm tired of being a victim. What do we have to do to stop this person?"

"Find out the motive," Clay said. "And the only way is to start here." He waved his hand over the stacks of papers. "I think the answer is here if we just dig in and look."

Four hours later, they stood back and studied the individual stacks. Each had taken a category and thoroughly inspected the papers one by one. Clay rubbed his eyes tiredly. "The court records, including all the trial transcripts, don't tell us anything that Bob and I didn't already know." He looked questioningly at Bob.

Bob shook his head. "Investments, tax returns, accounting reports are blank as far as a clue goes." He glanced at Mary.

"Nothing," she said. "I've gone over all the financial statements and records, including Fleur's monthly and annual reports. There's just nothing there that stands out."

Everyone turned toward Deanna, but she shook her head. "I didn't find anything in Grandmother's personal papers, either."

Clay stood up and stretched. He knew what he was about to suggest wasn't going to win him a popularity contest. "I say we all switch categories and dig in again." He grinned when everyone began to protest.

"There's one thing I can't understand," Deanna said after she'd changed places with Bob and flipped through a couple of investment records. "Where did Grandmother get all her money?" Everyone stared at her. "She was always complaining about being broke, or near it."

"Your grandmother was a wealthy woman, Deanna," Clay said.

"No, she wasn't."

"Maybe she just didn't want you to know," Mary suggested.

"No. We weren't rich, and from the number of investments she made, the initial amount of money she had to invest must have been substantial."

Clay felt a chill slither up his spine. He almost fell over backward in his hurry to get up from his chair. "Let me have a look at those." There was a note of excitement in his voice. Mary and Bob felt it and dropped what they were doing to join Clay at Deanna's side. "You're sure your grandmother wasn't rich?"

"I'd bet my life on it. Clay, her shop was doing okay, but I remember seeing her sitting at the kitchen table with a stack of bills before her, trying to decide which ones to pay first and which ones she could let go for another thirty days. You see, some of her customers were late paying *their* bills. One time I asked her why she just didn't call the customers who were indebted to her. I got a slap across the face, along with a lecture about how wealthy people thought it was their right to keep others waiting—something to that effect. But I definitely know she worried over the bills every month."

All the while Deanna was talking, Clay was frantically rummaging through the stacks of papers. "I know I saw it somewhere," he murmured, then held up a sheet of paper. "When your grandmother came to the law firm and my grandfather for the first time, she had 250 thousand dollars she wanted to invest. That was when Grandfather made her draw up a will."

Clay shuffled through another stack of papers. "About two months before your grandmother was murdered, she brought another 250 thousand dollars to Grandfather to invest, as well as handle the IRS reports for her."

"You're telling me that my grandmother had five hundred thousand dollars. That's not possible. It's just not possible, I tell you."

"But true," Bob said as he glanced over the statements Clay had handed him. "I saw this but never questioned it because I assumed it was profits from Fleur's."

"Where did the money come from?" Mary asked.

"A better question," Clay said, "is *who* did the money come from? When a person suddenly comes into that kind of cash, I'd say someone died and left her a fortune." He glanced at Deanna.

"Mother was the only family Grandmother had left. And Mother had quit nursing to go to medical school."

"What about life insurance? Did your mother have any?" Bob asked.

"None," Deanna said. "Grandmother grumbled about that, too."

"Or," Clay continued as if he hadn't been interrupted, "someone paid her a lot of money for something." He looked at Bob. "Like blackmail maybe?"

"What better way to get herself killed if she got greedy or someone felt threatened and could no longer pay? I'm here to tell you, five hundred thousand dollars is a lot of money now. Think what it was ten years ago. A damn fortune."

"And," Clay went on, picking up Bob's train of thought, "who has access to that kind of money?"

Deanna was following them as if they'd written the names on the wall in big bold letters. "Gilbert Foley or General Franklin Fitzpatrick. But why?"

A pricked balloon couldn't have deflated as quickly as the excitement in the room. For a long time they worried over the question. Reason after reason was offered up and rejected. But one thing had become clear—Agatha Fleur Deveraux was blackmailing one or both men.

Mary had been quiet for a long while, deep in thought, when all of a sudden she jumped up and shouted Deanna's name. "Something's been bugging me. You said your mother quit work and went back to school. She was a nurse, wasn't she? Where did she get her education and training?"

"She was an army nurse. I guess they trained her. After I was born she left the service, and we moved back to Houston. She started working at Memorial Baptist Hospital. About six months before she died, she quit work. Said she wanted to be a doctor and was going to medical school."

"Where did a working mother with a young child get the money to quit her job and enroll in medical school?" Clay asked, his excitement overcoming his fatigue.

Deanna shrugged. "We didn't have any money to speak of. Mom worked the night shift so we could spend time together, and she made more that way. There were times she had to borrow money from Grandmother until payday. I clearly remember that."

"Deanna," Clay said, "medical school is very expensive. Think. Was your mother going out with a rich man at the time?"

"No, she didn't date much. She didn't have time, what with working nights and taking care of me."

Bob cleared his throat a couple of times, and they looked at him expectantly. Then he scratched his head. "Could your mother have known Foley or Fitzpatrick? Oh, hell, Clay. I just thought of something. They're all about the same age—Deanna's mother, Foley and the general. There has to be a connection."

"But what does that have to do with my grandmother's sudden wealth and her murder?" Deanna asked.

"Damned if I know." Clay said, and everyone felt their brief glimmer of hope fade away.

It was getting dark outside, and they were hungry and exhausted. Deanna rested her head on her folded arms, staring at the paper under her nose but not really seeing it—until something jolted her memory like an electrical shock. She picked up the bill for the storage of her grandmother's belongings, which contained an itemized list. "Clay, my mother kept a diary. She did for as long as I can remember." She held up the bill. "It says here that among the items my grandmother stored were two cedar chests. They're not at the house. Clay, one of those chests is Mother's. She kept her diaries there. Maybe they'll offer some clue as to what's going on. Maybe she knew what Grandmother was up to."

Clay grasped at the possibility, slim as it was. He glanced at his watch. "The storage company is closed, but I suggest we get there when they open first thing in the morning. For now I think it's time to call it a night. We're all too tired to think straight."

But Bob had one more question. "Deanna, how old were you when your mother died, and how did she die?"

Ever since she'd regained her memory, Deanna had deliberately shied from confronting her mother's death. But she couldn't escape the dreams that haunted her, dreams filled with pictures from the past. "I was eleven." She stood and began tidying up the papers on the table. "Mother was killed in a car accident. It took her hours to die before someone found us."

"Us?" Clay said, feeling his heart sink to his toes.

"Yes." She looked up from what she was doing and stared off into the distance, her hands still busy as she tried to detach herself from the dark memories that threatened to engulf her.

"It was night and we were coming back from a day in Galveston. I was asleep when it happened, but they said she lost control of the car and we rolled down an embankment." Deanna took a shaky breath. "We were trapped." The memories were coming too fast, the pain and horror too vivid, and she sat down heavily in the metal chair. "I was pinned in the back seat and couldn't move or reach her. But I could hear Mom in the dark, moaning. After a long time there was nothing but quiet until some men came and got us out."

"Dear God," Clay said, and pulled her to a standing position, cradling her in his arms. "No wonder you're scared of the dark."

"It's strange. For ten years I've insisted on a light being on at night. I didn't know until I regained my memory why I was so scared."

Clay held her tight. "Deanna, remember the other day when I tried to hide your birth certificate from you?"

"Yes." She loved the rumble of his voice in his chest and the steady beat of his heart against her ear.

Bob and Mary were straightening up their work areas but stopped what they were doing immediately. Mary thought poor Deanna had had enough for one day, but Bob motioned her to be silent. He wanted to hear what Clay was going to ask.

"You said your mother never told you who your father was, right?"

"That's right. Why?"

Clay glanced at Mary and Bob. "What do you think, Bob? Could Foley or Fitzpatrick be Deanna's father?"

"Could be," Bob said.

Mary shook her head. "If one of them is Deanna's father, it could mean he was Agatha Deveraux's murderer. But why?"

Deanna slipped out of Clay's arms. "What could Mother or Grandmother blackmail them with? Granted, it would've been an embarrassment for a married man of their wealth and position, especially one with political ambitions, like the general, to have it made public that he had an illegitimate child. But it wouldn't be reason enough to pay five hundred thousand dollars in blackmail and risk killing an old woman, would it?"

"No," Clay said. "I don't think either man would gamble on getting away with murder simply over the threat of public censure. Besides, it would be the woman who would have to bear the brunt of the criticism. After all, public opinion would just chalk it up to 'Men will be men.'"

"He's right," Bob said. "And I'm too tired to think anymore."

Clay saw Bob and Mary to the door, leaving Deanna in the living room deep in thought. But no matter how she approached the problem she couldn't find a solution and was beginning to think they'd have to accept the fact that they might never find one. She might have to live the rest of her life looking over her shoulder....

"Stop worrying it to death," Clay said. "We'll find out who's doing this and why."

"We may be dreaming, too, Clay."

"Why don't we put it all behind us for a while? Forget everything that's happened. Tonight let's just be a couple on a date and we'll go out to dinner. A nice restaurant where we can actually have some vegetables."

THE HOUSE LIGHTS were on when they returned. Junior was sitting on the front porch with a double-barreled shotgun resting across his knees, and Homer was stationed at the back door in the same fashion. Deanna felt sorry for them. They'd worked all day and were planning to stay the night. But Clay told Junior that he would take over, then winked at the grinning man and suggested he and his brother go home and get some sleep.

Deanna dropped her purse on the hall table and headed for the den. As she walked past the dining room, she paused as she caught her reflection in the full-length mirror. She stopped and stared at herself. Was that really her? The midnight blue chiffon dress with the white satin collar and cuffs was a copy of a Bill Blass original she'd seen in a magazine last year. The dress was nipped in tightly at the waist with a full skirt that swayed like a lazy sea around her knees. This was the first time she'd worn it, and it made her look sophisticated, sexy, not at all like the young girl she'd been only weeks ago.

She took a longer, harder look at herself. Why, she thought, it wasn't the dress that gave her this new maturity. She was a woman in love, and that love radiated from every part of her, affecting even the way she carried herself.

Clay found her in the den sitting on the floor, her full skirt like a soft cloud around her. Her high heels had been kicked off, one under the coffee table, the other beside the new floral couch. She was digging through one of the boxes of record albums like a child trying to find her favorite kind of candy in a candy dish.

"Oh, Clay," she said in awe as she held up a handful of LPs. "Johnny Mathis, Barbra Streisand, Neil Diamond, and this one's the Righteous Brothers." She started singing a few bars of "Soul Inspiration," then shifted to "Papa Was a Rolling Stone," by the Temptations, as she held that album up. "Put this one on, Clay, hurry." She handed him the Roberta Flack album. "I want to hear 'The First Time Ever I Saw Your Face.' Wait, wait. Put these on, too. Dianna Ross, Marvin Gaye, Al Green." She started humming again. "Wait! Here's a Rod Stewart—play 'Maggie May.' Oh, and Simon and Garfunkel and David Bowie. Play them all, Clay."

He was laughing, juggling the LPs like plates as she handed them to him. "Deanna, the turntable only plays one at a time." But he doubted if she heard him.

"Your sister and brother-in-law have excellent taste. Here's Gladys Knight and the Pips." She sang a few bars of "Midnight Train to Georgia," then held out another LP.

"No. I draw the line there. I will not listen to John Denver. Hey, hand me that Jim Croce album. It's great." Clay put Jim on the turntable and stacked the other LPs beside it. Then he pulled off his jacket and tie, unbuttoned his shirt and rolled up his sleeves. When "Time in a Bottle" came on, he held out his hand. "May I have this dance please, Miss Deveraux?"

Deanna let him help her to her feet, then stood uncertainly for a moment. "I've only danced with girls."

"Then you're in for a new experience and a real treat."

"You're teasing me, aren't you?" She was suddenly a little shy, and for a second she tried to take the lead, then remembered she was supposed to let the man do that. "Sorry."

"Maybe later it might be fun to try it your way. But for now..." He took her in his arms and drew her close.

She was a bit stiff at first, but Clay was a good dancer and she soon relaxed in his embrace. A small smile touched her lips. She'd been on her very first date to-night to a fancy restaurant. No one recognized her or gave her a second glance. She drank her first glass of wine, ate Caesar salad and lobster, and had a delicious chocolate mousse for dessert. She'd enjoyed everything. But most of all she'd enjoyed being with Clay. So many wonderful things had happened that day she could al-most forget the bad.

She smiled up at him as another slow Croce ballad be-gan. "Is this what's known as seduction?"

"Who knows where it might lead. Now hush and en-joy the music." It was amazing, Clay thought, but he was actually good at this. He'd never really enjoyed dancing before. But with Deanna, it was just right. He rested his chin on the top of her head, inhaled the sweet scent of her perfume and wondered if he should attempt to make love to her again so soon. He'd promised himself he wouldn't push her, but his good intentions seemed to be slipping away as she snuggled closer.

"Clay, is this ever going to end?"

"I hope not," he said.

She chuckled. "Not this, but the mess my life's in. I'm tired and I don't want to be scared anymore. I want a normal life, or at least something resembling a normal life."

Her eyes were mesmerizing pools, darkened by emo-tion to a deep violet blue. Clay felt as if he were drown-ing in their depths, and he welcomed the breathless sensation. The shadowy light in the room turned her hair to dark gold, and her skin was pale and petal soft.

"We promised tonight would be ours. No problems. No talk about what's happened." Though Clay found it difficult not to think about it when he saw the bruises still marring her neck. He couldn't ever remember wanting a woman so much, but it went beyond that. He wanted her not just for a day or a week or even a couple of months. He wanted her forever. But once again he reminded himself of his promise to take it slow, and he held her slightly away from him, fighting the overpowering desire that rose within him.

Deanna wondered if she was doing something wrong as he eased away from her. She'd seen enough movies to know that dancing was sometimes considered a form of foreplay, but that didn't seem to be happening here. Maybe she'd disappointed him. Maybe he was sorry they'd made love. Maybe... "Clay, are we ever going to make love again?"

He stopped, froze actually, and held her at arm's length. Then he threw back his head and roared with laughter. When he sobered, he gazed deep into her eyes and whispered, "Anytime."

"Anyplace?" she whispered back.

"Want to christen the new couch?" Clay's hands slid down to her waist and he lifted her up.

Deanna wrapped her arms around his neck and her legs around his middle. She tangled his thick hair in her hands and pulled his head toward hers. "The bed might be more comfortable."

"But not as naughty or as much fun." He kissed her deeply, and when he pulled away he said, "We can try the new bed later, too."

"Too? You mean two times? That won't wear you out?"

"And three, if you want to try your bed. I'm a big healthy man with a voracious appetite."

"Show me how big," she said, laughing as she tightened her legs and arms around him.

CHAPTER FOURTEEN

THE WARM BUTTERFLY KISSES up her spine forced Deanna to open one heavy-lidded eye. Through the tousled mass of her hair, she glanced over her shoulder and moaned, "Uncle! I give up. No more."

Clay worked his way up to the nape of her neck. He brushed aside her hair and began kissing behind her ear, grinning as she squirmed. "Wake up, sleepyhead. It's late."

"How late?" she mumbled, and tried to bury her face in the pillow, giggling as his breath tickled her ear.

"So late that I've already had my coffee."

"You didn't wait for me?" She rolled over and frowned at him. Clay was dressed in his suit. "Where are you going? You told me you were taking some time off."

"There's a snag with a case I had postponed. I have to make a show in the courtroom, then I'll be right back." Her frown deepened. "Junior and Homer are on duty. Now go back to sleep for an hour or two, and by then I'll be back."

She sat up, dragging the sheet with her to cover her naked body. "We're still going to the place where Grandmother's things are stored, aren't we?"

"Just as soon as I get home." He kissed her lightly on the lips, turned to leave, then stopped. "Deanna, do you know about . . . birth control?"

Her eyes widened. She hadn't given it a thought, and from the way Clay acted, neither had he. But it wasn't the question that put the mischievous sparkle in her eye; it was the hesitant tone in his voice.

"Well—" she bit her lip to keep from smiling "—one of the nurses told me that if a man French-kisses you, you'll have a baby. Mary told me to keep my knees together and I'd be okay, and Dr. Gresham told me the stork brought babies." She couldn't have asked for a better reaction. Clay looked stricken first with panic and then horror.

Deanna couldn't hold back the bubble of laughter and tried to bury her face in the pillow. She felt his weight on the side of the bed, then raised her head and started laughing again. He still didn't seem to be able to find his voice. "Of course I know about birth control, but I'm not on the pill." She shrugged a bare shoulder. "And you didn't offer..."

Clay took a deep breath. "Well, I am now. I'll take care of it." He stood up. "I have to get going." He caught the worried look in her eyes and realized that despite her teasing she was concerned about his reaction. He lied to reassure her. "Don't worry, I don't think anything will come of it." He leaned down and kissed her, long and lingeringly. "I'll miss you. Don't do anything foolish, Deanna." Then with a wave he was gone.

Deanna was left feeling bereft at first. Then she remembered something Clay had said and she shivered with delight. He said he'd be home. He'd called the house *home*. She flopped back and smiled at the ceiling. Old Agatha would roll over in her grave if she knew what was going on in her house. And sex had nothing to do with it. The house was alive with something that had never crossed its threshold before—happiness and love. The love she shared with Clay. Mary and Bob's happiness. Even Clay's sister had brought warmth with her. And William and his two sons came from a close-knit loving family. Her heart filled with a greater joy than she had ever imagined, Deanna snuggled under the covers.

SHE HATED to admit it, but Clay either knew her very well or was an expert on women in general. She'd done exactly what he'd said and immediately gone back to sleep for two hours. Frantic she wouldn't be ready by the time he returned, she bathed and dressed quickly and was waiting for him nonchalantly and a little breathlessly in the den when he walked in the door.

Clay eyed her as he loosened his tie and pulled it free. "You're ready to go?"

She looked at him haughtily down her narrow nose, then started to laugh. "Barely." She watched him slip out of his jacket, unbutton his vest and fling it across the back of a chair. The memory of last night came to mind and she felt herself blushing.

Clay noted Deanna's high color with amusement. He ducked his head to hide a grin, knowing full well what she was thinking. His mind had been distracted all morning with thoughts of the night they had shared. The urge to tease her was almost overwhelming, but he decided to wait until she was a bit more comfortable with her own sexuality. Clay glanced at the television. "Homer did a good job putting up the antenna. The reception and color's great." He put his jacket back on. "I gave Bob a call from the office. He should be here any minute."

"What if we don't find Mother's diaries or they don't tell us anything?" she asked. "What then?"

Clay could tell she'd been worrying the problem to death and sat down beside her on the couch. Picking up her hand, he held it firmly. "We keep looking. But we're not as bad off as you think, Deanna. We know the two men following you work for two powerful and wealthy men. We have proof that Foley and Fitzpatrick paid off Dr. Gresham, a nurse and Judge Jones. There were probably more payoffs to local officials at that time, including the police. But don't forget, we have Judge Harrison firmly in our corner. He's a tough old bird who's not intimidated by power, money or anyone in Washington, and he's angry at what's happened to you and determined that the justice system will eventually work to exonerate you. Bob talked to the judge this morning. The feds didn't back off the way everyone thought they would when they realized who was involved in this mess. I believe the slow wheels of the system are beginning to pick up speed."

Clay turned Deanna's hand over and kissed her palm. "So don't worry if we don't find any proof at the warehouse. It's just a long shot we have to follow at this point." He rose to his feet and pulled Deanna with him. "Come on, I hear Bob's car."

The drive to the warehouse turned into an adventure for Deanna, even though Clay and Bob seemed determined to argue and ruin her fun. They were lost in a part of Houston neither man was familiar with, yet neither would admit they were lost. Deanna was fascinated by their behavior. Several times when she'd suggested they stop and ask for directions, both men had politely told her to keep quiet, that they knew where they were. She made the mistake of voicing her opinion that if they knew where they were, why hadn't they found the place? The scornful looks she received silenced her.

It was past noon when Bob pulled up to the warehouse complex. They found the guard at the small security building asleep with the gates wide open. As Bob and Clay exited the car to have a talk with the man, Deanna glanced around. This was an old part of Houston, and she figured they must be close to the water. Sea gulls soared overhead, diving and circling, and there was a salty dampness in the air. She turned her attention to the three warehouses, each two or three stories high, their brick walls stained and pitted from age and weather.

After what seemed an eternity, she saw Clay and Bob coming back. Observing their thunderous expressions, she debated whether to ask what was wrong. Curiosity won over caution. "What took you so long?"

Bob just shook his head and started the car.

"The guy was drunk," Clay explained, "and wasn't sure what building your grandmother's belongings were in. He finally remembered to check the ledger, but it was almost impossible to decipher. Since the room number is on the key, he was able to narrow the buildings down to two." Clay angrily slammed the door. "I guess we just have to make our own search." He shook his head. "Can't imagine Grandfather using this place."

"Maybe that's why he picked it," Bob said. "He wanted to make sure if there was something there, nobody ever found it."

Clay smiled. "Sounds like something Grandfather would do, and I bet he could find the room blind-folded."

They stood outside the first warehouse, one with three stories, lost in their own thoughts. Then Clay opened the door and they all backed away at the odor that assailed them.

Deanna wrinkled her nose. "Smells like an old sock," she said. "Laced with mildew and dust."

"And other things," Bob grumbled ominously under his breath.

"Well, we'll never find anything standing out here," Clay said, and they followed him inside.

Deanna waited a moment, letting her eyes adjust to the dim light. "Did anyone think to bring a flashlight?"

Just then, Clay found a light switch. A row of low-wattage bulbs hanging above them dimly illuminated the surrounding gloom. They were in what seemed to be a long wide hallway with storage units located on either side. The units were defined by a thick steel fencing material, and each had a heavy door at the front, secured with a strong padlock and thick chain. Through the fencelike walls she could see furniture and boxes packed tightly into each compartment.

Bob cursed. "You're not going to believe this, but there aren't any numbers on the doors."

"Oh, hell. There has to be," Clay growled.

Deanna had been carefully inspecting the door nearest her and sighed with relief. "The numbers are on the padlocks."

"Wonderful," Bob grumbled. "You mean we have to look at every padlock in the place?"

"Seems that way."

And it got worse, Deanna thought, after an hour of walking and searching, for the numbering was not consecutive. The only good thing was that they'd managed to find the huge freight elevator.

Hot, dusty and frustrated beyond endurance, Bob called a halt. "It's already three o'clock. We're going to be here all night at this rate. And believe me, that's not something I'm looking forward to. Why don't we split up? Clay, you and Deanna go on up to the third floor, I'll take the stairs up to the second. If we don't find it here, then we'll head over to the other building."

The elevator shook and rattled as it started upward. Deanna grabbed hold of Clay's arm for support and comfort. "This is an awful place, Clay. I don't like it at all."

When the elevator came to a teeth-jarring stop, Clay grabbed hold of the release arm and strained to pull it open. When the metal door finally slid wide, they were met with the same layout as the first floor. Deanna waited just outside the elevator doors for Clay to find the light switch. She wasn't about to take one step into that pit of darkness. A scurrying noise made her shudder. "Clay," she called.

"Stay there. I think I've found it."

The lights were about as dim as those on the first floor, but at least they dispelled some of the gloom and sent any small creatures fleeing into the far corners. Deanna imagined squinty red eyes watching them from the shadows.

Clay touched her shoulder and she jumped. "Relax. We have a lot of ground to cover."

Deanna glanced down the long hallway. "I feel funny," she said.

"Funny ha-ha? Or funny strange?"

"Strange. Weird."

Clay grabbed her hand and led her down the hall. "That could be a sign that your mother and grandmother's room is up here."

"I'm not psychic."

"Maybe you're a witch. You certainly cast a spell on me."

"Clay, that's ridiculous." Then she stopped, realizing he was just trying to distract her.

He'd led her to the end of the hall closest to the elevator. "Okay. You start on that side, I'll look on this side, and we'll move down the hall together. Don't get ahead of me."

After about an hour they were both hot and tired and ready to call it quits. "I thought I saw another hallway back there."

"Clay, this place is like a rabbit warren." Her feet were hot and her new shoes pinched her toes. She wanted nothing more than to sit down, kick her shoes off and drink a gallon of ice-cold water. Afterward, she wanted to take a shower and get the dust and grime and God only knew what else out of her hair. "Let's go find it," she said.

There were only two storage units down the short hallway, and as Clay checked one, Deanna checked the other. Clay's whoop of success sent her racing to his side. He held the brass padlock out so she could see the number sixteen stamped on it. "This is the place," he said as he fitted the key in the lock. "Now, let's just hope the key works."

Deanna held her breath, then let it out in a whoosh of delight as the lock snapped open. She waited outside while Clay pushed opened the wire-mesh door and went inside. Abruptly a light came one and she blinked, shading her eyes at its brightness.

"That's probably Grandfather's doing. He wasn't fond of the dark, either, did you know that?"

"Yes. We used to talk about it, wondering why everyone else found it so irrational."

Clay pulled Deanna to his side and placed his arm around her shoulders. Neither was inclined to break the spell of a wise, gentle old man who had loved them both.

"I had no idea your grandmother had so much furniture," he said as he looked around with some trepidation. They could be there another couple of hours just moving the heavy furniture around to see where everything was.

"Most of it's junk," Deanna said. She spotted the Napoleon-era sideboard and a dry sink. "Though there are a few pieces she and my grandfather brought over from France I'd like to keep."

"Well, we're not getting anything done standing here. Tell me again what we are looking for?" he asked as he started to move a heavy ornate headboard out of the way.

"Two cedar chests." She was quiet for a moment, then said, "I remember, after Mother died, Grandmother packed away her things. The good things, items she thought I'd want, she packed in Mother's cedar chest. The others...I believe she marked those boxes with Mother's name and stored them in the attic. I wonder if they're here, too?"

It didn't take them as long as Clay had predicted to move some of the heavier pieces out of the way, making a path toward the back wall and the haphazardly stacked boxes. Deanna was squeezing her way between some tables when she stopped. "Did you hear that?"

"What?" Clay was hot and sweating and didn't hear anything but his own muttered cursing.

"Listen. There it is again."

"I didn't hear anything. What'd it sound like?"

"I don't know—a popping sound or a loud crack."

Clay stared down at his feet. "God, I hope it's not the floor giving way."

"Gee, thanks, Clay." She laughed nervously and glanced down. If she shifted her weight to one foot, the floorboards creaked, and through the cracks she could see a faint light from the floor below. "You make me feel so safe and secure."

"I saw a rat hole almost big enough for my foot to fall through."

"Clay!"

"No wonder you're hearing things. This place isn't exactly soundproof. I bet someone on the first floor could probably hear our voices."

Clay and Deanna labored over the antique sideboard, moving it enough so they could get around it. When Clay dropped his end, she was about to scold him, but stiffened abruptly. "Did you hear that?"

"You mean the scurrying and shuffling of roaches in the wall? Yeah, but you don't have to remind me." He saw her shudder with revulsion and had to bite his lip to keep from laughing out loud. She had a couple of dark smudges across her cheeks and one wide one across her forehead that looked like war paint.

Deanna caught his amused glance and knew he must think she was spineless. "I think it was Bob calling us."

They'd reached a stack of boxes and Clay moved them out of the way. Yelling as loud as he could, he called out to Bob, telling him they were still on the third floor. When he did it a second time, Deanna covered her ears. His voice seemed to vibrate through the building and bounce hollowly off the walls and ceiling. They waited, and when there was no answer, Clay shrugged and picked up another box. "He'll probably be up here in a few minutes."

"Clay, look." He had moved enough boxes out of the way that she could see the two cedar chests, one resting on top of the other.

Like two treasure hunters, they felt the excitement of the end of the hunt. Fatigue dissipated and they worked hard, struggling to remove the boxes that still covered the top of the chests. When they were finally cleared away, Clay and Deanna lifted one chest off the other and set them side by side. They stood, breathless, staring at the cedar trunks with dread and exhilaration. It took a minute for them to realize that each chest had a lock.

Deanna's shoulders slumped. "I forgot about those."

"Not to worry." Clay dug deep in his pocket and removed a Swiss Army knife. "I'm always prepared." He worked diligently on one lock for what seemed like ages until it finally opened, then he moved to the other and opened it. "Which one do you want to go through first?"

"You take one, I'll take the other," Deanna said.

"I don't think so, Deanna. These are yours, part of your past, your family. As much as I want to find a clue to what's happening to you, I think you should be the one to open them."

She thought he was being silly, and to prove her point she flipped up the tops of both chests. They gasped as the pungent odor of mothballs and cedar assaulted them. Clay sneezed and Deanna wiped her eyes. When she finally caught her breath, she said, "There, I opened them. You look through one and I'll take the other."

She knelt beside the chest closest to her, then hesitated, recognizing it as her grandmother's. With a hand that trembled, she brushed away some of the mothball crystals, removed the layer of tissue and reached for the antique lace that Agatha Deveraux had brought from France. At the last moment she caught sight of her dirty hands and wiped them on her slacks before she lifted the lace shawl to one side.

Clay sat down in front of the other chest. The first thing he picked up was a large thick envelope. He read the writing on the outside and said, "These are your mother's things." He opened the envelope and began shuffling through the papers, trying to read them as quickly as he could. "It's all Department of Defense and military papers." He read on. "Did you know your mother was a surgical nurse with a MASH unit during the Korean War?" He made a mental note of the dates as he scanned Nancy Deveraux's discharge papers. Deanna must have been born about eight months after her mother's release from the army.

"I didn't know that." Deanna paused in her search, then started digging through the contents of the chest again, moving delicate lace and fabrics from one side to the other. If her grandmother had done only one thing for her, something of value, it was to instill in her a knowledge and appreciation of quality. Her fingers touched something familiar and she pulled it out a bit further. It was a cotton garment bag. Her heart began to beat faster. She remembered seeing two exquisite old-fashioned gowns that her grandmother had later told her were Worth originals she'd brought from France. When her hand slipped beneath the bag and ran over the covers of two small leather books, she knew immediately what they were, but only had a second to wonder why her grandmother would have them before Clay's shout caught her attention.

"Deanna! Here are the diaries!" He pulled out one after another of the small leather-bound books, stacking them to one side.

She moved next to Clay and peeked into the chest. Her breath caught painfully in her throat as she picked up a small, faded and torn stuffed bear with one black button eye missing and hugged it to her chest. She squeezed her eyes tightly shut, wanting to cry, but the lump in her throat wouldn't budge.

Her mother had given the bear to her when she was a baby, and it had become her security symbol. The bear went everywhere with her. After her mother's death, her grandmother had taken away the stuffed toy, telling her she was too old for such nonsense. What surprised Deanna was that her grandmother had saved the bear and packed it away with the rest of her mother's belongings.

"There seems to be a couple missing," Clay said as he flipped through each diary. "Looks like the ones for the years before you were born."

Deanna was about to tell him where she'd seen the missing diaries when she heard a noise. "Clay. There it is again."

"You must have supersensitive ears," he said absently as he picked up some papers and started leafing through them. "I don't hear a thing. Deanna, these are some of your mother's bank statements. Did you know she made two deposits within days of each other totaling twenty-five thousand dollars?"

She didn't answer Clay immediately, but waited a moment more to see if the sound would come again. When nothing happened, she said, "Where'd my mother get that kind of money, Clay?"

"Listen to this..."

But she wasn't listening to him. Her hearing was attuned to a noise behind her. She felt a chill, a slight shiver, and slowly turned her head. Then she clutched Clay's arm. "Clay," she whispered.

Clay glanced around and froze. Immediately he recognized the bald-headed man from Deanna's drawings. He also spotted the revolver in the man's hand and the way it was pointed at Deanna's head. "What do you want?"

Harry Dobbs had had a bad day and wasn't up to answering questions. He simply motioned for Deanna and Clay to stand up. He stood aside and signaled them to leave the storage room.

"You know who he is, don't you?" Deanna whispered.

"Yes—Harry Dobbs. Remember the photo?"

"What's going to happen, Clay?"

"Shut up." They both stared at the old man when he spoke. His voice was deep, like the hollow sound of someone talking into a barrel, and rough, as if he'd smoked too many cigarettes. "Let's get a couple things straight, Mr. Lambert. You make a move toward me, I shoot the girl. You give me any grief, I shoot the girl. You think because I'm an old man, half-crippled, you can take me. Try, I shoot the girl. Then I'll shoot you. You got that?" He waited until Clay nodded, then motioned them down the hall.

He didn't speak again until they reached the freight elevator. "Get in and remember what I said."

Deanna closed her eyes as the elevator jumped and jerked its way downward. Clay squeezed her hand hard. When the doors opened and they followed the man out, she almost stumbled. She glanced down as Clay steadied her. "Oh, my God." Her toe had caught on an empty shoe, and as Clay tightened his hold on her, she caught sight of the sock-covered foot it had fallen off. She gasped and felt her knees go weak as she stared at the supine body.

Clay, too, spotted the man sprawled on the warehouse floor, clenched his teeth and quickly turned Deanna around so she wouldn't have to look at the dead man. "That's the man who tried to strangle you, Deanna."

"Is he . . . dead?"

Clay had seen death many times and there was no mistaking the glazed stare. "Yes."

"Come on, you two," Dobbs grumbled. Then, because the girl's expression touched him, he added, "It was him or me. Besides, he killed that reporter, and believe me, he was planning to do the same to you two."

"That makes us feel better," Clay said sarcastically, but immediately regretted his words when Dobbs shook the gun at them.

"Get moving," Dobbs growled.

It was time for their miraculous rescue, Clay thought. Way past time. He only hoped Bob was careful. The old man might be slow on his feet, but Clay had a feeling he was a crack shot, and from the look he'd given them, Clay was sure the old guy would suffer no remorse if he had to kill them both.

Like Clay, Deanna was wondering where Bob was. Did he know what was happening and was he waiting for his chance? Her question was soon answered as they approached the door. She moaned and leaned against Clay. Bob Spencer was slumped against one of the storage-room doors, the upper portion of his shirt soaked with blood. Tears filled Deanna's eyes. "Oh, Clay!"

Clay gave her an quick shake, then firmly wrapped his arm around her shoulder and squeezed hard. When Deanna glanced at him, she thought he looked at her with a strange expression and shook his head a fraction.

The sky was beginning to darken when they stepped outside, but the heat hadn't dissipated and it was like walking into an oven. Deanna tried to think, but her mind was blank with fear. When they stopped at the rear of a large dark car, she stiffened. And when the old man, keeping a close watch on them, pulled out a set of keys and inserted one in the trunk, she froze.

"Get in," Dobbs ordered.

"No." Deanna began to back away but didn't get very far with Clay's arm around her.

Dobbs pointed the gun at them, then at the trunk. "I said get in."

"Clay." The black hole of the trunk yawned deep and dangerous. "I can't."

"What's this?" Dobbs took a step toward them.

Clay held up his hand. "We'll suffocate in there."

The old man glanced at the trunk, then at the two of them. With the skill of a marksman, he quickly fired two shots into the open lid. "Now, get in."

"Man, can't you see she's scared to death of confined places?"

"Girlie," Dobbs's voice rumbled in the still night, "either you crawl in there now or I'll put a bullet into your lover's knee. Then, if you still ain't moved, I'll plug him in the shoulder. You'd be surprised how many bullets a man can take before he bleeds to death."

Deanna couldn't talk or move. All she could do was stare at the darkness of the trunk. Even with the threat to Clay, she couldn't make her muscles move, couldn't talk. Her mouth was parched and her heart was pounding so loud in her ears she thought her eardrums would burst.

Clay sensed her paralyzing horror, and before her knees gave way, he scooped her up in his arms, climbed into the trunk and lay down. The trunk seemed roomy with the lid up, but when it was shut the darkness closed in on them. For a minute he could see nothing, then as his eyes adjusted to what little light the two bullet holes afforded, he could just make out Deanna's face. She looked absolutely terror-stricken, and he drew her tightly against him.

"I can't breathe," she managed to say.

"Listen to me, Deanna." He held her face between his hands. "I'm here with you. You're not alone. Now, take a deep breath."

She tried, fighting to get control of her fears, but they threatened to overwhelm her and she started shaking all over. Little by little she made herself focus on Clay and what he was saying. When she thought she was calm enough to speak she asked, "What did you say?"

"Bob was alive. And I don't think he was that badly hurt. But he's smart. He didn't know how many of them there were, so he did the only thing he could—played dead." The car started to move. For a while the crunch of the gravel under the tires was almost deafening until they turned onto a paved road.

"But how do you know? Oh, Clay, what're we going to tell Mary if you're wrong?"

Her breathing was a little more controlled, Clay thought, but she was still trembling all over. "He opened his eyes, Deanna, and winked at me." He realized the best way to keep her sane was to keep her talking.

"You're sure?"

"I promise."

"You're not just saying that?"

"No. He's alive and I'll bet right this minute he's getting help. Remember the security guard's shack? There was a telephone." He didn't tell her there was a good possibility the guard was dead. And if that was the case, then more than likely the phone line was dead, too.

"Clay," she sobbed, "I can't stand the dark." She started gagging and covered her mouth. After a moment she said, "The smell of gasoline is making me sick. It brings back too many memories. I can hear my mother moaning...."

"Did you know I told my family I'd met the woman I was going to marry?"

Her lungs felt empty and she fought for air. Finally, what Clay had said penetrated her numb brain and she sobered. "You what?"

"I told them all about you."

"All?" If she closed her eyes she seemed to be able to control her panic.

"They wanted to meet you right away, but I told them to wait until you were a little more comfortable with the idea of getting married."

Her mouth turned up in a tremulous smile. "How can I get used to the idea when you haven't even asked me yet. And why haven't you asked?"

"Mary thinks I'm already moving too fast. Maybe she's right, but I don't care anymore. Can you imagine what she'd think if I told her I knew from the moment I saw you in my office that you were the woman I was going to marry? She'd find some way to have me committed or arrested." He could feel the car slowing to make a turn, then speeding up again. They must be on the freeway now.

"Where's he taking us, Clay? What's he going to do?"

He ignored her question. "I'm sure Liz, being the blabbermouth in the family, called everyone and told them what a sweet, wonderful, beautiful woman you are."

"Yes," Deanna said.

"Yes what?"

"I'll marry you."

His lips found hers and he kissed her lightly. God, he thought, if she'd only stop shaking. He admired her, though. She was trying so damn hard to be brave.

"Tell me about your family," she asked.

Clay thought he heard the sounds of an airplane for a second. "There are three of us. Dan's the oldest, two years older than me. He's a pediatrician and is married with two children. There's me, of course, the most intelligent and handsome one in the family, and Liz. Dad used to be with the firm, but the last five years he's been teaching law at the University of Houston. I think he typifies the absentminded professor. Mother's a housewife and social butterfly. She has a quirky sense of humor, but she's a very loving woman. She's really going to like you."

The car made a sharp turn and Deanna was thrown backward, knocking her head on the spare tire. She reached out, clawing air until she touched Clay's shoulder. Grabbing him, she held on for dear life as they bounced over a rough road.

He could feel her paralyzing fear returning and said, "So your grandparents were from France? Where in France?"

"Paris," she gasped, fighting to regain what little composure she had left. "I'm not sure when they left. Grandmother never liked to talk much about it, but Mother was born here soon after they arrived." The car slowed, then came to a dead stop. Deanna had watched enough television and read enough murder mysteries to know they were being taken to some far-off, deserted place where they were going to be shot and their bodies abandoned.

She wadded Clay's shirt in both fists. "Thank you, Clay. For helping me and loving me. I love you more than my life."

He caught the sound of goodbye in her voice and was touched. He tried to silence her, by placing his fingers across her lips so he could hear what was going on outside. But she knocked his hand away.

"I just wish..."

He did the only thing he knew to keep her quiet. He kissed her, holding her head firmly while he listened to the sounds from outside. He was positive about what he'd heard and finally released her, leaving her breathless.

The trunk suddenly opened and they both blinked, holding up their hands to shield their eyes from the blinding light.

"Get out," the old man ordered, and he dropped the beam of the flashlight to the ground so they could see what they were doing.

Clay climbed out slowly, all the while taking in every detail he could as he turned to help Deanna.

She looked around in surprise. "Where are we?" she whispered in his arms just before her feet touched the ground.

"The airport—I'd say the section where private planes are hangared."

"Move it," Dobbs growled, and pointed to an obviously private luxury plane. The engines were revving, the door was open and the steps lowered. "Move, I said."

Deanna took a firm hold on Clay's hand. "I've never flown before. Is he going to push us out over the ocean?" But Clay didn't have time to answer her question as they were prodded up the narrow steel steps.

Once they were securely belted in, Harry Dobbs produced a pair of handcuffs and cuffed their wrists together. "Just in case you get any ideas." He gave the pilot the go-ahead to take off, then made himself comfortable in the seat facing them.

When they were airborne and Clay felt a little more certain they weren't going to be killed outright, he tried his hand at a few questions but found the old man a real match for his skills. He glanced at Deanna's head on his shoulder and stared out the small window. Exhaustion had set in and he saw no reason to wake her. That time would come soon enough.

The bump and jar woke Deanna abruptly. Disoriented, she straightened in the seat, trying to figure out where she was. She glanced out the window and saw a blur of lights speeding by. "Where are we, Clay?"

"I'd say we just landed in Dallas."

CHAPTER FIFTEEN

CLAY WAS RIGHT, they were in Dallas—on a private airstrip. He noticed the name of the city on a sign over the large metal hangar. He tried to get Harry Dobbs to confirm the location, but the old man just ordered them out with a wave of his gun and pointed to the waiting limousine. He then climbed in behind Clay and Deanna, taking the jump seat so he could keep a close eye on them.

Clay held Deanna's hand in his as they rode through the night in silence. He was trying to figure out an avenue of escape, but so far none had presented itself. The chauffeur never even glanced in the mirror at them, and Clay knew he was one of Foley's trusted men. The windows of the limo were darkened so the passing traffic couldn't see inside. And when they reached downtown Dallas, the car swung like a lumbering beast around the corner and immediately descended a ramp to an underground parking area beneath a high rise. The limo slowed to a stop a few feet from an elevator door.

Once again they were herded into an elevator like animals being led to slaughter, Clay thought. They had no option but to follow.

Deanna moved closer to Clay's side, wanting his warmth to reassure her that she wasn't alone. She was frightened, yet there was a surprising undercurrent of excitement pounding through her veins. She sensed she was about to find out who had killed her grandmother and why, and why she'd been forced to take the blame. After ten years, just maybe the truth was going to come out. The problem was, she and Clay would probably be the only ones to know. She felt the heavy weight of responsibility on her shoulders and looked at Clay as the elevator stopped. "I'm sorry," she said.

"For what?"

"For getting you involved in my life—in this mess."

"Shut up, you two," Dobbs ordered, "and get out. The boss is expecting you." He pointed to a set of ornately carved doors.

For a second Deanna hung back, then she stepped out of the elevator, straightened her shoulders and walked ahead of Clay and Harry. When she reached the doors, instead of knocking, she grabbed a doorknob in each hand, turned them simultaneously and shoved the doors open. The man sitting behind the big desk looked up, startled, then quickly rose to his feet.

Gilbert Foley stared at Deanna Deveraux, his eyes wide with shock, and the years suddenly fell away. He was a young man again. Wild and reckless and hopelessly in love. He'd seen pictures of Deanna and knew of the resemblance, but he wasn't prepared for the exact same color of her eyes or that all too familiar spark of anger. Her hair was the same shade of blond, like spun sunshine. He wasn't ready for the graceful way she moved, her back straight, her shoulders squared. She was the spitting image of her mother, and it took a moment for him to remind himself that he was staring at Nancy's daughter. The years of guilt were an oppressive weight, and he sat down heavily.

Deanna and Clay both noticed the tears in Gilbert Foley's eyes and his shock at seeing Deanna. They didn't miss the way the blood drained from his face or the manner in which he sank down into his chair, the wind knocked out of his sails.

Deanna sat down in the chair facing Gilbert and studied him. He looked just like the photograph she'd seen, except instead of a clear sharp gaze, his eyes were sad. Suddenly she wasn't afraid anymore. She smiled at him and watched the way he swallowed. "You loved my mother, didn't you?"

Gilbert glanced away, then looked at Dobbs and pointed to the doors. "Close them, Harry, and have a seat on the couch in case Mr. Lambert decides to get brave." He shifted his gaze reluctantly back to Deanna. If she only knew how much it hurt to see the image of Nancy. "Yes, I loved her. More than I can begin to tell you."

Clay stood fuming. "If you loved Deanna's mother so goddamn much, how could you let her daughter be locked away for something she didn't do? You do know that she didn't kill Agatha Deveraux, don't you? You've always known."

Clay didn't wait for Gilbert to answer. "Was Nancy Deveraux, and later Agatha, blackmailing you? Is that why you murdered the old woman and let a thirteen-year-old child take the blame? Then you set about keeping tabs on Deanna, paying off Judge Jones to make sure she stayed confined, in case she regained her memory and could name you as her grandmother's killer. You did all that to the daughter of a woman you profess to have loved?" Clay ended in disgust.

Gilbert had heard every word, every accusation and question the young lawyer spoke, but he never took his eyes from Deanna. And her gaze never wavered from his. She was strong, like his Nancy. The turbulent memories could no longer be contained. He was going to bare his soul that night for the first time in a long time, and the mere thought seemed to ease the heavy hand around his heart. His vision blurred for a second, then he shook his head and took a deep breath.

"Nancy..." His voice cracked as he spoke her name out loud for the first time in years. "Nancy wasn't blackmailing me."

Deanna's head was swimming with questions. But there was one that she had to fight down, knowing it wasn't the right time to ask just yet.

Instead, she cleared her throat and began elsewhere. "How was my mother able to quit work and start medical school? Where did she get twenty-five thousand dollars?"

"I gave her the money—in two equal payments."

"Why?"

"Why would I give her the money? Because she asked." Gilbert held up his hand to stop Deanna's question. "Not as a gift. Oh, I wanted to give her the money. Free and clear—no strings attached. But Nancy was too proud for that and only wanted a loan."

Clay snorted his disbelief, but there was something in the older man's voice and a look in his eyes that made him pause.

Deanna and Gilbert ignored Clay.

"Your mother was intelligent, Deanna. Far smarter than I was or am. After years of nursing, she wanted more than anything to be a doctor. Old Agatha wouldn't help her get a loan, wouldn't even cosign for one. If it hadn't been for you, she would have sacrificed everything. I loved her, and when she came to me and told me what she wanted to do, I didn't hesitate. But she made it clear the money was strictly a loan, and when she became a doctor, she'd pay me back."

Deanna believed him. For some crazy reason she knew in her heart he was telling the truth. She glanced at Clay and saw his puzzled expression and knew that, though he didn't want to, he believed Gilbert, also.

Clay was confused by Foley's honesty. Deanna had been doing a fair job of asking questions, but he thought she'd missed one important detail. "If you were handing out money to the Deveraux women, did you just happen to give Agatha Deveraux five hundred thousand dollars?"

The time for truth had come, Gilbert thought. "I gave the bitch money, but only 250 thousand dollars."

"Who'd she get the rest from?"

"Fitzpatrick."

Deanna held on to her chair and waited. She sensed Clay was about to ask another question and quickly reached over and gripped his arm. But he was too angry and she couldn't silence him.

Clay didn't know if he was right or not, but he had to ask. "So you killed her to stop her from blackmailing you and let Deanna take the blame?"

Gilbert's mind had wandered back to the past, and he shook himself as he realized what Clay Lambert had just accused him of. "I didn't kill Agatha."

Clay gave him a scornful look. "You expect us to believe you when you had your lackey there kill two men for you today? Maybe three, if you count the reporter."

"What's he talking about, Harry?" Gilbert demanded.

"I ain't a lackey," Harry growled softly as he glared at Clay, then he turned to his boss. "The major was trying to cut their friend the ex-cop's throat. When I ordered him to back off, he came at me. I shot him in self-defense. And the ex-cop ain't dead, he's just cut up a little." His eyes drilled holes in the back of Clay's head. "As for the reporter, the major killed him—said I was going to end up the same way. Man was crazy, Gil, plumb crazy."

Clay wasn't about to let Gilbert off that easily. "You paid off Judge Jones and the nurse at Twelve Oaks to keep tabs on Deanna and to make sure she never got out."

"No, no," Gilbert protested. "I was protecting her."

"From what? From whom?"

"If Deanna ever regained her memory, I had to know immediately so I could help her. As long as she didn't remember and was in the sanitarium, she was safe."

"You were willing to ruin her life to supposedly keep her safe?"

Gilbert turned to Deanna, his expression pleading. "To save her life, yes. It was the only way. There was too much involved."

"The truth was the only way!" Clay shouted. "My grandfather was trying to get at the truth, and you and Fitzpatrick stymied him at every turn."

"I tell you," Gilbert whispered, "I was protecting her."

"If you and Fitzpatrick were being blackmailed by Agatha, and you say *you* didn't kill her, then it must have been Fitzpatrick. But why? What could an old woman have on you and the general to make you that desperate?"

Gilbert stared down at his desk for a long time. Then he looked up and said, "Murder. Agatha found out that Fitzpatrick and I killed a man during the war and that Nancy was involved. I guess the old gal figured since her daughter was dead she had nothing to lose and we had everything to lose if the truth came out."

Deanna was stunned. Her mother was a dedicated nurse; she saved lives. To think that she'd been involved in a killing... It was ridiculous and completely unbelievable.

"What war?" Clay demanded. "Who did you kill, Foley, and how and why was Deanna's mother involved?"

There was a sound outside the closed doors. Gilbert's gaze, dim with memories, cleared. His mouth tightened into a thin line and he gave a hand signal to Harry Dobbs. The older man rose painfully from his chair and moved to one side of the door. "I called the bastard and told him I was bringing you here, Deanna. I told him it was time to face what we'd done. He wasn't very receptive to the idea and made his usual—"

He didn't have time to finish. General Franklin Concord Fitzpatrick walked in, and in his right hand was a small-caliber gun.

Gilbert Foley laughed at his old friend. "For God's sake, Frank, put the popgun away. You think you can kill all of us with that thing and get away with it?"

The general slowly lowered his arm, but not in response to anything Gilbert said. Unlike Gilbert, he hadn't seen any pictures of Deanna, hadn't wanted to, but now as she stood before him, he was transported back to the only time in his life when he had been truly happy. His Nancy was alive and standing in front of him. Then reality grabbed hold of him again, and he realized he wasn't staring at the woman he'd loved but her daughter.

WHEN THE GENERAL lowered his arm Deanna had risen to her feet to face him. Too much had happened for her to be intimidated by two, no, three, old men. They held all the answers to her questions, to the past. She'd been dragged here against her will, and she wasn't going to leave until she had the truth.

As she fixed her unwavering stare on the general, something inside him seemed to snap, and he stumbled toward the third chair in front of Gilbert's desk. "It's over, Frank," Gilbert said.

Fitzpatrick shook his head, still reluctant to accept the fact. "The president called me a few hours ago. The Secret Service has been asking all sorts of questions. The FBI wants a meeting concerning money funneled from my accounts to a judge in Texas." He raised his head and looked desperately at his old friend.

Gilbert's mouth set in a grim line. "I listened to your lies ten years ago, Frank. Oh, I knew they were lies. But back then I had as much to lose as you did if the truth had come out." He took a deep breath. For a moment he stared at Deanna, and his eyes seemed to lose their focus.

"Gil, don't," Franklin warned. "We'll lose everything."

Gilbert smiled sadly. "We already have, Frank. We already have."

The mood in the room grew tense, expectant, as everyone waited for Gilbert Foley to start his story. Clay thought he heard a faint sound behind him and turned his head. One of the doors stood half-open and he could see Harry with his hands crossed behind his back, his wrists clamped in a pair of gleaming steel handcuffs. Puzzled, he started to move in that direction but spotted Judge Harrison outside the door. The judge placed his finger to his lips and shook his head.

"It was in 'fifty-one,'' Gilbert began. "I was a major in the Marine Corps and stationed in Seoul. Franklin was with army intelligence and we met in a bar. Who'd have thought we'd become friends, drinking buddies. But it was a bitch of a war, and stranger things have happened, I guess.

"We were both wounded at the same time, different locations, but we ended up at the same Mobile Army Surgical Hospital—MASH—where Nancy Deveraux was a nurse. The kindest, most beautiful and caring woman we'd ever met. Frank and I fell head over heels in love with her. We vied for her attention. We joked and made fools of ourselves as only young men can. We lied, cheated, connived and disobeyed orders to be with her. I used all my connections to find out when and where she was going to take her R and R, and I'd be at the hotel in Seoul waiting, only to run into Frank. He had his connections, too.''

Gilbert and the general shared a knowing smile. "The problem was, we were both trying so hard to be charming and irresistible that our plans backfired. Nancy fell in love all right, but with both of us. She was honest and fair and told us she loved us equally and couldn't pick one over the other.''

"And don't think badly of her, either,'' Franklin broke in. "She was upset about the way she felt, and wanted, even tried, to break up with us both.''

"But we couldn't stand the thought of never seeing her again,'' Gilbert went on, "and so we decided that we could share our love. At first Nancy resisted, but you know what? She was as in love with the two of us as we were with her and couldn't bear to give either of us up. It didn't make any difference that Frank and I were both married or that we all might die the next day. So we became a threesome for dinner, drinks and dancing, and later, well one night it was me, the next it was Frank.

"I know it all sounds sordid now, but in the middle of a war, with death everywhere, it just never seemed wrong. In late 'fifty-three, we all knew the war was ending. Nancy got a pass to Seoul and we were there waiting. Man, did we celebrate that night. No one had any business walking, much less driving the jeep Frank managed to requisition."

Gilbert rubbed his face and stared at the desktop for a time. "We were barhopping that night—drunk on our asses—when we made a wrong turn."

"It wasn't my fault," Franklin whispered. "The boy stepped out in front of the jeep. I never saw..."

"The kid was an enlisted man with the U.S. Eighth Cavalry," Gilbert continued, "and once Nancy told us he was definitely dead, we all sort of sobered up. That's when Franklin came up with the idea to take the body out of town and bury him. Nancy was appalled. But it didn't take Frank and I long to figure out what we had to lose if we were caught. We convinced Nancy. After we'd buried the young man, we all swore we'd never speak of the incident again. Never!

"Our relationship soured after that. We tried to meet, but we suddenly had nothing to talk about. It was as if our conspiracy had destroyed the love we shared."

"What about the boy's family?" Clay ventured to ask.

"He was reported missing in action," Franklin said. "Later he was pronounced dead."

"And his family?" Clay persisted.

Franklin cleared his throat. "He was newly married, and later I checked to make sure his widow was receiving her benefits."

"That was big of you, General." Clay sucked in a deep breath and began speaking again. "So, somehow Agatha Deveraux found out what had happened and blackmailed both of you—but which one of you murdered her?"

Gilbert looked at Franklin. "Agatha came to me about a year after Nancy's death and repeated the whole story. I know Nancy never would have told her."

"Mother kept a diary all her life," Deanna said.

Gilbert nodded. "I figured it had to be something like that. Anyway, Agatha wanted money and I gave it to her. But I made it clear she'd better not come back for more."

"How clear?" Clay asked.

"I didn't kill her, if that's what you're implying. She never contacted me again."

"She did me," Franklin said. "I paid her, too. And it wasn't even a year later that she was calling again, demanding more. She'd been closely following my career. Agatha was a smart old bird and knew what I had to lose. I told her no more—I wasn't about to pay her another penny. But she sent a copy of a page from Nancy's diary to me and I flew straight to Houston."

Franklin glanced at Deanna and felt a stab of regret. How much she reminded him of Nancy. "I didn't know you were home. When I called earlier, Agatha told me what time to come so you'd be in school."

Deanna was surprised at how much the general seemed to have aged in the short time since he'd walked into the room. His face appeared drawn and his eyes were dull. He even appeared to have shrunk as he sat hunched in his chair, his shoulders slumped.

She thought about the shock and horror she'd experienced at her grandmother's death, and the ten years she'd been locked away without a past. As much as she wanted to pity him, in her heart she felt nothing but contempt. Deanna suddenly realized that more than anything she wanted him to admit what he'd done. She wanted him to say it out loud so there could never be any doubt. "You killed my grandmother?"

"Yes. But it was an accident."

Deanna shook her head. "You forget I was on the landing, General." Let him think she'd seen everything. It was the only way she had to ensure he would not lie.

Franklin had lived in fear of this moment for the past ten years. "The old bitch deserved to die. She kept telling me what the press would make of the story—what my wife and her family would do. I warned her, told her to shut up, but she just laughed. I saw everything I had worked for slipping away and she was to blame." A desperate spark of hope flickered in his eyes as he glanced at Gilbert. "We can still keep a lid on this fiasco, Gil," he began, his voice hoarse. "We—"

"You don't get it, do you, Frank?" Gilbert said. "It's finally over. For my own selfish reasons, I admit I didn't handle this very well. I'd convinced myself I was protecting Nancy's daughter when in fact I was just saving my own backside. Over the years it just got easier. But you've gone too far this time, Frank. You were too ambitious—wanting to be president, for God's sake. And you were even willing to kill again for it. But this time I won't stand by and let it happen. Dammit, man," he cried, "she's your own daughter!"

Franklin was speechless and for a moment stared at Gilbert as if he'd lost his mind. "You're crazy, Gil. And if Nancy told you that, she was crazy, too."

Deanna gasped. This was the final answer to all her questions.

"Nancy didn't have to tell me anything. But when I asked, she told me she honestly didn't know which one of us was the father, that it didn't matter. She loved Deanna. But I always knew the child was yours, Frank. You and Nancy were together more those last few weeks before we shipped out."

"Well, your logic is flawed. She's not my daughter. I can't have children. Never was able to because of the mumps I had as a kid. Rendered me sterile. I didn't even know it until I had a complete physical when I got home from Korea."

"What's this crap?" Gilbert stood up and leaned over his desk, his face bright red with anger. "What's your son, Henry? A figment of your imagination?"

"Oh, hell, Gil. Henry's not mine. He's my brother's son. Alice and Darren had been having an affair before I ever went to Korea. They're still having one. And I never said or did anything because it would have made me look foolish if the truth about Henry was made public. I'd have been a laughingstock. But I swear—" he glanced at Deanna "—she's not my daughter. And if she's not mine, she's yours."

Gilbert sank heavily into his chair. "Mine? My daughter?" He stared at Deanna blankly, his eyes glazed. The past came crashing over him like a tidal wave, almost drowning him with memories of Nancy. Things should have been different, he thought. He should have questioned her further, but everything in his life had just begun to come together at the time, and he couldn't risk anything that might have screwed it up. There were a thousand questions running through his mind, and he shook his head as if to clear it.

"Gentlemen." The voice from the doorway shocked them all. Judge Harrison walked casually in, followed by six unidentified men. The judge stepped aside and the other men moved quickly to positions beside Gilbert and Franklin. "Mr. Foley, General, these men are federal agents, and they're going to read you your rights and the charges against you."

Suddenly the room was in chaos. Everyone was standing and talking at once until the judge, with the authority he used in court, called for silence. The general started to protest loudly.

"Please don't say another word," Judge Harrison snapped. "Remember, you have the right to an attorney, General."

The judge walked within a few inches of the general, and because Franklin was taller, he was forced to throw his head back to look up at him. But this in no way minimized his power. "Before you scream your innocence to anyone who'll listen, let me tell you two bastards something." His razor-sharp gaze fixed on Gilbert for a second, then returned to the general. "We recorded everything said in this room. With the proof from Judge Jones's records, confessions from Ernest Gresham and Patricia Nelson, retired Houston district attorney Warren and a couple of police officials, we should have enough to put both of you behind bars for a long time." He backed away and motioned to the men standing guard. "Get them out of my sight."

Deanna felt dazed. Up till the moment the judge walked in, everything had seemed slightly surreal, as if she was being told a story about strangers that had nothing to do with her life. She watched in silence as the general and Gilbert Foley—her father—were handcuffed and taken away.

As Gilbert was about to pass Deanna, he stopped, shaking off the agents' hold on him, and stared for a long moment. Tears filled his eyes and he whispered, "My daughter—Nancy's child." He cleared his throat. "I'm sorry."

Clay stepped between Deanna and Foley. He grasped her by the shoulders and said, "Are you all right?"

"I don't know, Clay." She pressed her forehead to his chest. "It's all over, isn't it?"

"Yes. Mostly."

"I don't know what to feel." She glanced up. "He's my father, isn't he?"

"He seems to think so."

"My mother..." She couldn't finish.

Clay seemed to know instinctively what she was thinking. "Don't think less of her, Deanna." He grasped her face between his hands. One cheek was smeared with grime and her hair fell softly around her shoulders, framing her sad face in a golden glow. "Don't let anything they told you diminish your love or memories of her. War is a hellish place, Deanna. It's brutal and unmerciful and human life is insignificant. It does strange things to people, makes them see life in different ways. Your mother was a surgical nurse. Can you imagine what she was forced to deal with on a daily basis? You can't blame her for falling in love—even if it was with two men." He lightly kissed her lips. "Only remember one thing—she loved you."

Deanna wrapped her arms around his waist and hung on for dear life. He was right of course. She had no reason to think anything but good thoughts about her mother. She had loved two men, and those two men had loved her beyond the grave. Nancy Deveraux, Deanna thought, must have been someone very special.

A slight cough made them pull apart, and they turned together to face Judge Harrison. Clay held Deanna close to his side, his arm wrapped around her shoulders. "How did you find us, Judge?"

Judge Harrison chuckled. He wiped his bald head as if the habit of smoothing back the long-missing locks was a necessary part of his thought process. "We've had people on Deanna ever since she was released from Twelve Oaks."

"Bob!" Deanna gasped. "We forgot about him. Judge—"

"He's fine," the judge reassured her. "He's in the hospital with a knife wound in his shoulder and a pretty little lady standing guard like a bulldog."

"Mary," Deanna and Clay said in unison.

"Go on, Judge," Clay said. "How did you know to follow us here?"

"After the federal agents realized who was involved and the Secret Service briefed about the situation, it was fairly easy. Telephones were tapped—including yours, Deanna. We intercepted the call Major Sawyer made to the general and knew of the call Foley made to the general and his intention to fly to Dallas. We were only about twenty minutes behind you all the time. But we didn't want to make a move until we had a clear and concise confession."

Clay gave the judge a hard look. "You set us up?"

"In a manner of speaking. But we made sure you were in no real danger."

"Right," Clay snapped. He didn't like the idea that he'd been anyone's pawn.

Deanna was exhausted. She rested her head against Clay's shoulder and asked Judge Harrison, "What's going to happen now?"

"Oh, there'll be a trial. I'm going to see to that."

Deanna closed her eyes and shuddered. The thought that once again she was going to be the topic of headlines almost made her physically ill.

"I'm sorry, Deanna," the judge said. "But it's the only way to clear your name so there's never a doubt in anyone's mind that you were totally innocent."

"What do you think will happen to the general and Mr. Foley?" she asked.

"Deanna," Clay said. "They killed your grandmother. Well, the general did, but Foley knew or he wouldn't have had you watched all these years. And he was guilty of conspiracy in hiding the fact that they killed and buried a serviceman. What about the soldier's family? They have the right to know what happened to him."

"Yes, of course, you're right."

The judge made as if to leave, then stopped. "Do you two by any chance need a lift home?"

Deanna glanced at her grubby, wrinkled clothes, then at Clay. He was in the same condition. "Do you have any money with you?"

He shook his head and a smile twitched at one corner of his mouth. "Not enough to get us home."

"Then I think we ought to take the judge up on his offer."

It took a while for the judge to finalize arrangements to transport the two prisoners. The Dallas police were reluctant to let the federal agents and Secret Service leave town with one of their leading citizens. But when push came to shove, the government won out, and the government plane was refueled and cleared for takeoff.

It was the second time Deanna had ever been on an airplane, and she was determined to stay awake. She watched with wonder as they took off, the lights of the city fading quickly away, encasing them in darkness. Her heart pounded and her nails bit into Clay's palm. Then she noticed that the darkness was an illusion. Dawn was on the horizon, turning the clouds the color of ripe plums.

Like a shaft of morning sunlight bursting through the dark clouds, Deanna knew for the first time in her life that she was truly free. The shadows had been lifted from her dreams, the evil brought to light. She would probably always be uneasy with the dark, but she was no longer afraid. Clay would be there, holding her hand when she needed his strength, walking beside her if the fear returned. In her heart she felt sure she would always have him. And who knew, one day they might be blessed with a family.

Now that was a thought to build dreams on.

EPILOGUE

A THICK LAYER of snow covered the ground like a blanket. Soft glistening piles of the stuff weighted tree limbs, and deep drifts obscured small shrubs, turning them into puffy pillows.

Snow in Houston on Christmas Eve—it was nothing short of a fairy tale. Deanna inhaled the sweet scent of the pine tree that filled the room and suddenly felt at peace with the world.

She'd finished her story and glanced around, suddenly aware of her surroundings. For hours she'd been living in the past, but this was the present now. She was in her home with her husband, her children and her friends, and yes, even her father. She felt the familiar and loving weight of Clay's arm around her shoulders, and she reached up to grasp his hand. For a moment the silence from the children frightened her. Then she spotted Mary and Bob and smiled.

She vaguely remembered them coming in and quietly taking a seat to listen to her story. They were gray-haired now, but as much a part of the family as they'd always been. Deanna was pleased that her children called them Aunt and Uncle and loved them as much as she and Clay did.

She looked at her son, Taylor, and the twins, not sure what to expect. But they were smiling at her with those beautiful faces and still-innocent eyes. She realized by

Victoria's red nose, Samantha's sniffles and Taylor's bobbing Adam's apple that her story had touched them in a way she'd never expected. For the first time, she thought, they realized how much their parents loved each other, had from the very beginning.

"Well, Vicky!" Samantha stood up and looked down her nose at her twin sister. "Your great friend Jane's a liar. Mother wasn't crazy, after all."

"*My* friend!" Victoria squealed. "She's your best friend. You're always reminding me of that fact."

"Look, mouse, I never said that."

"Girls, girls," Clay said, bringing an end to their bickering.

But Samantha was not to be denied and directed her outrage elsewhere. "So, Mom, you mean poor old Gramps went to prison and his sons got all his money?" she demanded, jamming her hands on her narrow hips.

Deanna thought it was remarkable that her daughter had heard her story and felt only anger at the way her grandfather had been treated. Her children loved the old man, and Deanna had to admit he was good with them, always willing to listen to their endless chatter or their grievances whenever they thought they were being mistreated by their mother and father. He was also an easy touch and would slip them money from time to time, but Gilbert had learned his lesson and didn't spoil them.

"Gramps was found guilty of being an accessory and spent six years in prison. As for all the Foley money..."

Gilbert chuckled, then said slowly, his speech still affected by his stroke, "Those damn boys of mine got their hands on my empire, but they went bankrupt in those six years I was in jail. But this old fox wasn't down-and-out, my little princess. I'd socked away money in a Swiss bank account. When I was released, I invested in a couple of then unheard-of computer and software companies. Made a comfortable fortune again, and that all goes to your mother when I kick the bucket."

Victoria smiled her sweet innocent smile and asked, "What happened to Harry Dobbs, Gramps?"

"Old Harry was a good man," Foley mumbled, his mind wandering again back to the past for a moment. "Harry passed on sixteen months after I was in prison."

"And the general," Taylor asked, "what happened to him?"

Deanna smiled. Taylor was the considerate one, the just and fair child. "Since he was driving the jeep and it was his idea to hide the enlisted man's body, he was given ten years. There were arguments that he should have received life, but it was wartime. Alice Jefferson Fitzpatrick divorced him over the scandal. After serving five years of his sentence, he had a massive heart attack and died."

It would have ended there but for softhearted Victoria. "What became of poor Henry after his mother divorced the general?" she wanted to know.

"Well, that's a funny thing," Clay said. "He and the general actually became close. It was as if once Henry found out the reason his father—he always considered the general his father—disliked him so much, everything changed. Henry visited the general all the time, taking him copies of his reviews. I understand he's quite a successful artist. As for his mother, Alice, she caused a scandal of her own. The ink wasn't even dry on the divorce papers when she married the general's bother, Darren Fitzpatrick. I understand they're still very happy."

"Why would Jane Harmon be so mean?" Victoria asked. "Why would she want to embarrass us, Mom?"

Clay was the one who answered. "Because, darling, Jane Harmon's mother is Lynnett Overton Hamilton. She married Bob Harmon soon after I married your mother."

"She was in love with you, Daddy, wasn't she?" Sam asked with that bright devilish sparkle in her eye. "She was a woman scorned. And she used Jane to get back at you and Mother. I wonder what else she has in mind? Maybe something like that movie *Fatal Attraction*. You don't think after all these years she'll try to kill us?"

Taylor gave his sister a scornful look, then shook his head. "That's the stupidest thing I've ever heard come out of your mouth. One of these days that imagination of yours is going to get you in trouble."

"Dad," Samantha pouted. "Taylor called me stupid. Make him apologize this instant." Then, like a flighty bird, she changed the subject. "Come on, Vicky. Don't you think you've wasted enough of Mom's time with your silly prying?" She grabbed a stunned open-mouthed Victoria by the arm and pulled her to a standing position. "Just look at how wrinkled your new gown is. And after Mother went to all that trouble to make them." She grinned and winked at her father, then began pushing her sister out of the room. "And I don't care what you say, I think it's great that Mom's having a baby. Now let's get changed. We have a Christmas tree to finish and I want some more hot chocolate."

Taylor kissed his mother on the forehead and whispered, "You're the best, Mom. But, please, make sure this baby's a boy. I don't think I can take another female in the house." Then he followed his sisters out of the room.

Clay watched his children with pride, wonder and total confusion. He glanced at Deanna and shrugged. "They never fail to amaze me."

"Help me up, Clay. My butt's gone numb again."

Mary and Bob laughed and shared a knowing glance. "You had the same symptoms when you were pregnant with Taylor," Mary said. "So I predict you're going to have a boy." She tapped Bob on the arm. "Lift your old bones, darling. We've got to get the presents out of the car."

Deanna let Clay help her up and she held onto his hands for a moment, gazing into his eyes. "We've been blessed, haven't we?"

"That we have, love." Clay hugged her to him, feeling her warmth and the hardness of her rounded stomach against him. Her eyes were sparkling with love. Her untamable hair had come loose from its topknot, making a golden halo around her head. She looked as young and innocent as the first day she'd walked into his office, and he didn't think he could love her more than he did at that moment.

Deanna rested her head on his shoulder, thinking about the presents she still had to wrap for the children. The tree wasn't finished yet and the house was a mess. But she just couldn't seem to tear herself from Clay's arms. He'd been her rock, her friend, her lover and teacher through the years.

She sighed and opened her eyes, and her gaze alighted on her father. He was smiling at them with such a strange expression that it momentarily took her aback until she realized what it was—love and happiness. As he quietly wheeled himself out of the room, she knew she was, indeed, truly blessed.

![S] **HARLEQUIN SUPERROMANCE®**

WOMEN WHO DARE
They take chances, make changes
and follow their hearts!

Dangerous to Love
by Carol Duncan Perry

Vicki Winslow refuses to do the sensible thing—enter the
witness protection program. She's done nothing wrong and
she isn't going to cut herself off from her family. So now she's
hiding out, protected only by secrecy and her own wits—if
you don't count her eighty-seven-year-old great-aunt, her
poetry-quoting cousin, two large dogs, one rifle and a pet
skunk named Sweetpea.

Caine Alexander aims to change this situation. Not that
Caine's any knight in shining armor. *Hell, no.* A man could get
killed playing hero. Still, he's promised to protect Vicki, and if
any man can make good on such a promise, Caine's the man.
Too bad Vicki doesn't want his protection.... Because she's
stuck with it.

**Watch for *Dangerous to Love*
by Carol Duncan Perry.**

**Available in July 1995 wherever
Harlequin books are sold.**

Take 4 bestselling love stories FREE

Plus get a FREE surprise gift!

Special Limited-time Offer

Mail to Harlequin Reader Service®

> 3010 Walden Avenue
> P.O. Box 1867
> Buffalo, N.Y. 14269-1867

YES! Please send me 4 free Harlequin Superromance® novels and my free surprise gift. Then send me 4 brand-new novels every month, which I will receive before they appear in bookstores. Bill me at the low price of $2.89 each plus 25¢ delivery and applicable sales tax, if any.* That's the complete price and a savings of over 10% off the cover prices—quite a bargain! I understand that accepting the books and gift places me under no obligation ever to buy any books. I can always return a shipment and cancel at any time. Even if I never buy another book from Harlequin, the 4 free books and the surprise gift are mine to keep forever.

134 BPA ANRJ

Name	(PLEASE PRINT)
Address	Apt. No.
City	State	Zip

This offer is limited to one order per household and not valid to present Harlequin Superromance® subscribers. *Terms and prices are subject to change without notice. Sales tax applicable in N.Y.

USUP-295

©1990 Harlequin Enterprises Limited

Big Luke, Little Luke
by Dawn Stewardson

This July, meet the third of our Four Strong Men:

Mike Alexander was the best friend Navy pilot Luke Dakota
ever had. So when Luke received a letter from Mike's wife,
Caitlyn, he wasn't too concerned—until he opened it. In the
letter, Caitlyn told him about Mike's death and the birth of
their son, Luke. His namesake.

Drawn by a sense of responsibility to Mike, Luke arranged for
a leave of absence and set off for Arizona.

Once there, his life was sent into a tailspin. He learned that
Caitlyn's business was in the red, military intelligence
wouldn't leave her alone and, worst of all, she was convinced
that Mike's death was the result of foul play. Luke became
determined to help Caitlyn fight her unseen enemies. But
he soon found himself up against an enemy he couldn't
conquer—himself. Because Luke Dakota was falling in love
with his best friend's wife....

Look for *Big Luke, Little Luke* in July 1995
wherever Harlequin books are sold.

In June, get ready for thrilling romances
and FREE BOOKS—Western-style—
with...

WESTERN *Lovers*

You can receive the first 2 Western Lovers titles FREE!

June 1995 brings Harlequin and Silhouette's
WESTERN LOVERS series, which combines larger-than-
life love stories set in the American West! And WESTERN
LOVERS brings you stories with your favorite themes...
"Ranch Rogues," "Hitched In Haste," "Ranchin' Dads,"
"Reunited Hearts" the packaging on each book
highlights the popular theme found in each WESTERN
LOVERS story!

And in June, when you buy either of the Men Made In
America titles, you will receive a WESTERN LOVERS title
absolutely FREE! Look for these fabulous combinations:

♦ Buy ALL IN THE FAMILY
  by Heather Graham Pozzessere (Men Made In
  America) and receive a FREE copy of
  BETRAYED BY LOVE by Diana Palmer
  (Western Lovers)

♦ Buy THE WAITING GAME
  by Jayne Ann Krentz (Men Made In America)
  and receive a FREE copy of
  IN A CLASS BY HIMSELF by JoAnn Ross
  (Western Lovers)

**Look for the special, extra-value shrink-wrapped
packages at your favorite retail outlet!**

HARLEQUIN®   *Silhouette*®

WL-T

This June , for the first time in paperback

NEW YORK TIMES BESTSELLING AUTHORS:

SUE GRAFTON
TONY HILLERMAN

and many more…

Bring you

2ND CULPRIT

Newcomers, international names and old favorites offer up a varied itinerary for the adventurous traveler in crime! Join *New York Times* bestselling authors TONY HILLERMAN and SUE GRAFTON, plus an additional cast of 24 of the mystery genre's most popular authors, for 2ND CULPRIT, a choice collection of short stories.

Available in June wherever
Worldwide Mystery books are sold.

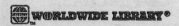 **WORLDWIDE LIBRARY®**

2CUL

Announcing
the New Pages & Privileges™ Program
from Harlequin® and Silhouette®

Get All This FREE
With Just One Proof-of-Purchase!

- **FREE Hotel Discounts** of up to 60% off at leading hotels in the U.S., Canada and Europe

- **FREE Travel Service** with the guaranteed lowest available airfares plus 5% cash back on every ticket

- **FREE $25 Travel Voucher** to use on any ticket on any airline booked through our Travel Service

- **FREE Petite Parfumerie** collection (a $50 Retail value)

- **FREE Insider Tips Letter** full of fascinating information and hot sneak previews of upcoming books

- **FREE Mystery Gift** (if you enroll before June 15/95)

And there are more great gifts and benefits to come!
Enroll today and become Privileged!

(see insert for details)

 PROOF-OF-PURCHASE

Offer expires October 31, 1996   HS-PP2